With her puny fists Joan battered a chest that felt like granite, trying to squirm away, but he suddenly shifted sideways on the seat and brought her down on her back beside him.

Drew braced an arm over her so she was trapped against the upholstery. Slowly his face descended and, mesmerised, Joan watched his mouth until it blurred out of focus. But he didn't kiss her; his lips skimmed her hot cheek, the faintest tickle of bristle scouring her skin.

'Do you know what I think, my lady?' he murmured against her small, sensitive earlobe. 'I think my conceit is making me believe your interest in me *is* personal. I think you're as eager to taste me as I am to have you.'

Author Note

This novel is the second of two books featuring characters linked by family and friendship. In *Tarnished, Tempted and Tamed* Lady Joan Morland's beloved stepsister Fiona finds happiness with dashing Luke Wolfson, following an adventure that plunges her into the midst of a smuggling gang.

In *Compromising the Duke's Daughter* Lady Joan is aware that impeccable behaviour is expected of a young woman of her privileged status. She is sure that a youthful peccadillo with one of her brother-in-law's rakish friends is firmly buried in her past. Then Drew Rockleigh bursts back into her life and Joan is astonished to see how low the handsome gentleman has fallen. She knows she owes him a debt of gratitude for having kept her secret…a secret that could ruin her and break her father's heart should it leak out.

Keen to prove that she trusts him, Joan probes the mystery behind Rockleigh's downfall. Infuriatingly, he seems not to need or want her assistance. But he does want *her*, and soon Joan realises that she wants him too, and will do her utmost to help him regain his rightful position in society.

The drama sweeps Lady Joan from the elegant drawing rooms of Mayfair, pitching her headlong into the squalid slums of the East End of London where, unbelievably, this duke's daughter finds she has fallen in love with a streetfighter and will do whatever it takes to capture Rockleigh's heart.

I hope you enjoy reading about Joan and Drew's passionate skirmishes, and the obstacles they must overcome on the road to winning their happy-ever-after.

COMPROMISING THE DUKE'S DAUGHTER

Mary Brendan

HarperCollins
P U B L I S H E R S
— Since 1817 —

First published in Great Britain 2016
By Mills & Boon, an imprint of HarperCollins*Publishers*
1 London Bridge Street, London, SE1 9GF

Large Print edition 2017

© 2016 Mary Brendan

ISBN: 978-0-263-06765-1

Our policy is to use papers that are natural, renewable
and recyclable products and made from wood grown
in sustainable forests. The logging and manufacturing
processes conform to the legal environmental regulations
of the country of origin.

Printed and bound in Great Britain
by CPI Antony Rowe, Chippenham, Wiltshire

Mary Brendan was born in North London, but now lives in rural Suffolk. She has always had a fascination with bygone days, and enjoys the research involved in writing historical fiction. When not at her word processor she can be found trying to bring order to a large overgrown garden, or browsing local fairs and junk shops for that elusive bargain.

Books by Mary Brendan

Mills & Boon Historical Romance

Linked by Character

Tarnished, Tempted and Tamed
Compromising the Duke's Daughter

Society Scandals

A Date with Dishonour
The Rake's Ruined Lady

Regency Rogues

Chivalrous Rake, Scandalous Lady
Dangerous Lord, Seductive Miss

The Hunter Brothers

A Practical Mistress
The Wanton Bride

The Meredith Sisters

Wedding Night Revenge
The Unknown Wife
A Scandalous Marriage
The Rake and the Rebel

Visit the Author Profile page
at millsandboon.co.uk for more titles.

For Sheila Hodgson, my editor,
with thanks for advice and support given
over many years.

Chapter One

'Get us from this infernal place at once, you stupid boy!'

'Calm yourself, Aunt, and please don't shout at Pip—it will only make matters worse. If he panics he might overset the coach, or trample somebody underfoot.'

'I wish the horses would trample the savages to death!' Dorothea warbled hysterically.

'Hush!' Joan slammed an unsteady finger to her soft mouth, hissing from behind it, 'If we infuriate these people, heaven only knows what will become of us all!'

Lady Joan Morland was attempting to combat her fright as well as pacify her companion. Joan knew she was to blame for their terrifying predicament, but her aunt's callous remark about running over their attackers had shocked and angered her. Just a short while ago Joan had been sitting in the same room as these folks' youngsters and she'd not willingly orphan any child.

Joan had wanted to visit a ragged school in the eastern quarter of the metropolis to assist her friend the Reverend Walters teaching at his vicarage. Thus, she accepted that it was her fault that their novice driver had taken a wrong turning and ended up in the heart of a slum. Pip was into his apprenticeship and was now allowed to drive the smaller carriages, but this calamity had proved that he hadn't the necessary experience to negotiate a detour about the London stews as his master would have done. The youth had plunged headlong into the midst of a crowd of spectators at a street fight. Their crested coach and team of fine chestnuts had drawn interest in the way bluebottles would swarm to a joint of prime beef.

'Get away…you vile creature!' Dorothea flapped her handkerchief at a bold urchin who'd clung to the side of the vehicle and was thrusting a grimy hand at her, palm up.

'Come on, lady, give us summat or I'll have them baubles off yer chest instead.' The boy bared a set of brown teeth in a grin while his filthy fingers mimicked an approaching spider.

Dorothea squeaked in alarm, jamming a hand over the pearl mourning brooch pinned to her cloak.

'Here…take this and please leave us be.' Joan slid forward on the seat to throw the boy some coppers dug from her reticule. He caught them deftly and leapt down.

Had Joan thought more carefully about it she would have realised that her action was inflammatory rather than calming. Within seconds of the boy whooping with glee, his hand aloft displaying his treasure, a horde had clambered on to the running boards. Youthful and aged faces began competing for space at the windows, all with the same wide, avaricious grins stretching their mouths. Dorothea clung to her niece, shivering, as the vehicle swayed precariously from side to side with the weight of unwashed bodies hanging off the coachwork.

'We are about to be murdered!' the hysterical widow screeched before rolling sideways on to the seat in a dead faint.

Joan pressed herself back against the luxurious

squabs of her father's coach, her heart hammering in consternation beneath her breastbone. Although her aunt had been raving moments ago, Joan had preferred Dorothea being conscious. At least they might have both alighted from the vehicle and attempted some sort of escape. Now Joan knew she was hampered by the need to stay with her aunt's comatose form because she couldn't in all conscience abandon her relative to save herself.

'Pip!' Joan yelled above the noise of the baying crowd. 'Can you hear me? Are you all right?'

'Can't move an inch forward or back, my lady. Hemmed in good and proper, we are,' the youth wailed, sounding on the point of tears.

Joan glanced fearfully at the prominent face at the window. A man who appeared to be middle aged, but might have been considerably younger beneath the caked dirt, was lasciviously licking his lips while looking her over.

'Reckon your daddy might pay more'n a handful of coins to get you back. You're a sight fer sore eyes and no mistake.' He dropped a crusty eyelid in a lewd wink.

'Miss High 'n' Mighty won't be worth a farthing if you tumble her first,' a rough female voice called out from behind and started off some raucous laughter.

Suddenly the lecher's face disappeared as he was yanked backwards and the door was flung open.

Joan shot to the furthest corner of the coach, her fists raised in readiness to beat off an assailant. Although she was quaking with fright, there was a piercing sadness in her breast that she'd chalked letters with children who had no better future than this brutishness to look forward to.

'What in damnation do you think you're doing here?' a cultured male voice barked. 'You stupid little fool!'

Joan blinked in astonishment and her jaw sagged. Heat streaked into her complexion at the sight of a man, stripped to the waist, his muscled chest and solid broad shoulders glistening with sweat. And so were his features, beneath a tumble of matted silvery hair that clung to his bronzed forehead and cheeks. It was a face that seemed familiar, yet she couldn't understand how that could be. Shock had rendered her speechless thus she was unable to demand he satisfy her curiosity by giving his name. And then he was gone.

But she could hear him shouting abusive commands at the mob and no more people leered in at her. A moment later the coach jerked one final time, then was set into motion. After a laboured start the vehicle picked up speed.

Stunned into inertia for some minutes by her ordeal, Joan shook herself into action and patted briskly at her aunt's dropped jaw to try to bring her round. When that didn't work she delved into Dorothea's reticule for some smelling salts. Having unstoppered it, she thrust the bottle beneath her aunt's nose, but the woman remained stubbornly unresponsive to her ministrations.

'Oh, well done, Pip. Oh, very well done, indeed.'

Joan felt light-headed with relief. She slid across the hide seat to peer out of the window at cottages and carts and people going about their business. Thankfully, it seemed they had taken a turning out of that awful place.

'I shall let my father know how excellently you are learning the ropes, Pip…'

But never must he know all the details of what has gone on today, Joan inwardly wailed. If the Duke of Thornley discovered what dangers his daughter had risked that afternoon, he'd have her under lock and key till Christmastide! Joan knew it would be hard to make her aunt button her lip. Dorothea was the world's worst blabber and reported to her brother every little slip her niece made.

'Pip…are we approaching safety yet? Where exactly are we?'

'Cheapside…now settle down and be quiet,' growled a rich baritone voice very unlike Pip's.

Joan dropped the bottle of smelling salts and craned out of the window, looking up. But she couldn't see any more of him than a long breeched leg and a single sinewy forearm terminating in grazed fingers entwined in the reins.

'Stop the coach at once. Whoever you are you may pull over immediately! I didn't give you permission to drive my father's coach!'

He obeyed her order with such alacrity that Joan tipped off the seat on to her knees on the floor and Aunt Dorothea almost landed on top of her.

Joan was scrambling upright just as the door opened and without a by your leave an athletic figure vaulted in and sat down at the same time she did.

She gawped at him in alarm while obliquely

aware of Dorothea stirring and muttering incoherently. Joan knew that once her aunt rejoined the land of the living, the woman was likely to swoon again at the sight of the dishevelled ruffian lounging opposite, even if he had now covered up his bare chest.

Yet he wasn't a ruffian; of that Joan was certain. Oh, he might be dressed in clothes that had seen better days, but they were of good quality. He sported a stylish, if stained, lawn shirt, and his brawny legs were encased in buckskin breeches that had once been fawn, she guessed, but were now the hue of mud.

Her protracted inspection seemed to amuse him and he raised an arm, wiping blood from his cheek with a sleeve. 'Well?' he sardonically asked for her verdict.

'Well what?' Joan breathed and with an inner jolt suddenly realised to whom she spoke. 'Well, am I disgusted by what you appear to have turned into, Mr Rockleigh? If that is what you require an answer to…then the answer is yes.'

'So you remember me, do you? I'm flattered.'

'There's no need to be,' Joan retorted hoarsely. 'Nothing about you pleases me. Now remove yourself from my carriage and let us proceed towards home.'

'No thanks from you, my lady? No offer to reward me for the service I have done you?' he taunted. 'At least on the last occasion that I saved you from yourself, you had the grace to apologise for the nuisance you'd been to me.'

'I didn't ask you to save me then or now!' Joan snapped.

'I'll take you back to Ratcliffe Highway then, shall I?' he suggested, lunging towards the door as though to again climb aboard the driver's perch and carry out his threat.

Joan snatched at his arm. 'You will not, you villain!' Her fingers sprang away from him as though he'd scalded her, although his moist skin warming her palm had not felt unpleasant. But the muscle she'd gripped had flexed to iron at her feeble restraint. She knew if he wanted to appropriate their vehicle, or do any of them harm, she'd not be able to stop him. Neither would young Pip.

'Remove yourself…please…before my aunt awakens and sees you,' Joan uttered coolly.

Rockleigh glanced at the woman sprawled on the seat, her eyelids fluttering. 'I'll go when you tell me what a duke's daughter is doing driving around the slums of Wapping.'

'I would have thought it quite obvious we were lost,' Joan returned.

'Is your father reduced to hiring such incompetents to steer his coaches?'

'No, he is not!' Joan spluttered indignantly. 'Pip has only recently been allowed to drive and I chose to employ his services today.'

'Ah...so you planned to keep your father in the dark about your trip, did you?' He idly assessed the coach's interior. 'Nice, but I imagine the Duke of Thornley has several better conveyances for his daughter's use. You might be older, my lady, but it seems you're no wiser,' he drawled, lazy amusement glinting in his hazel eyes.

'A remark that I could certainly return to you, sir, had I any wish for this conversation to continue.' Joan had blushed hotly at his astute interpretation of events. She had intentionally chosen to employ Pip and a plain carriage because their loss from service was unlikely to be noteworthy, should her father call for a vehicle to be brought round. The grooms would assume that the master's daughter and her chaperon had simply gone shopping locally. 'I recall you once had good connections and were friendly with my brother-in-law. But not any more, that's clear to see.'

'I've not fallen out with Luke Wolfson.'

'But I imagine he avoids your company!'

'I avoid his…'

'Ah, so you're ashamed of yourself, and I'm not surprised.'

'I'm not ashamed of myself. I do honest work for honest pay.'

'You were brawling in the street like a common criminal!' Joan choked out. She recalled Fiona mentioning that Drew Rockleigh had suffered a run of bad luck, but her stepsister had not made much of it. Joan imagined that Fiona was ignorant of just how low her husband's friend had sunk.

'Fighting for purses pays my way. What's your excuse for trawling through the squalor, my lady? Did you think it a novelty to come to see how poor wretches live and end up with more than you bargained for?'

'No, I did not! I was helping a friend teach those *poor wretches'* children to read…' Joan clammed up, furious that she'd allowed him to push her into explaining herself.

A shrill scream made Joan almost start from her skin; it announced the fact that her widowed aunt had come fully awake.

Without another word, but with a lingering stare that sent a shiver through her, Rockleigh jumped from the carriage. Joan could hear him talking in a low, fluid tone to Pip.

'Who was that?' Dorothea gasped out, a hand pressed to her heaving bosom.

'He...he did us a service and helped us find our way out of that slum,' Joan swiftly explained, rubbing energetically at her aunt's hand to soothe her.

Dorothea flopped back against the squabs. 'Your father will flay you alive when he discovers what you have done this afternoon.'

'There is no need for him to be apprised of it. All has ended well and no harm done to any of us.'

'Only by lucky chance!' Dorothea squeaked. 'What is our Good Samaritan's name? Your father will want to know it and reward him.'

'I...I...he didn't introduce himself,' Joan stuttered quite truthfully, glad her aunt had not recognised the boxer as a fellow who, not so long ago, had graced society with his elegant presence.

Once, Rockleigh had owned a house in Mayfair and a hunting lodge in the West Country, close to her father's ancestral seat. He had mingled with the cream of society although he'd rarely attend tame entertainments. Many a hostess keen to have such an eligible bachelor at her daughter's debut ball had been disappointed by Rockleigh's absence. But on one occasion when Joan had attended the opera with her father and stepmother she had spied Drew Rockleigh in a box opposite with a female companion. Her father had pretended not to know the identity of the pretty blonde when Joan enquired after her. She'd realised then that Rockleigh was out with his mistress. That sighting of him in Drury Lane had been about a year ago; Joan imagined that in the meantime he must have lost a great deal.

As the coach set off at a very sedate pace, Joan guessed that Pip was too scared to set the horses to more than a trot. She scoured the pavements for a tall muscular fellow with very fair hair, but there was no sign of him—no doubt he had slipped back into that stew of destitution. But for the snuffling of her aunt, and a musky male scent within the coach strengthening her rapidly beating pulse,

Joan might have thought none of it had happened and she'd simply awakened from a nightmare.

But it was real. Her heartfelt wish to assist the Reverend Vincent Walters teach children to read and write at the St George's in the East vicarage school would have very great repercussions. And none of it beneficial, Joan feared.

Chapter Two

Joan massaged her temples to ease her headache, then rolled on to her stomach, pulling a plump feather pillow over her head in an attempt to block out the sound of raised voices.

She had been in the process of replying to a letter from her beloved Fiona when her father's bellows threatened to blow the roof off his opulent Mayfair mansion. Unable to concentrate, she'd abandoned the parchment and pen on her desk and curled up on her bed. Joan realised that her aunt had, despite being asked not to, blabbed to the Duke of Thornley about their disastrous trip that afternoon.

As the noise reached a crescendo, Joan swung her stockinged feet to the floor and felt for her slippers with her toes.

At any minute she was expecting to be summoned by her irate father so brushed the creases from her skirt and tidied straggling tendrils of conker-coloured hair into their pins. She knew the Duke would be livid…with good reason…and she would sooner go downstairs of her own volition than remain on tenterhooks till a sympathetic-looking servant tapped on her door. She knew that she must protect her aunt and Pip—especially Pip—from her father's wrath. In a way she didn't pity Dorothea; she'd asked the woman to keep quiet about the incident, as no harm had been done to them in the end. But it seemed her aunt had not been able to simply rest in her chamber while recovering from her scare.

Joan guessed Dorothea had found her brother in the small library, as that was from where the cacophony seemed to be issuing. Sighing, Joan immediately set off to own up to her father and take her punishment.

'Ah…there you are,' his Grace barked as his daughter entered the room. 'You have saved me the task of sending a servant to summon you, miss. Philip Rook is on his way, as I hear he drove you on this madcap excursion. While we wait for him to arrive let me have your version of this afternoon's folly.'

'There is no need for Pip, or for Aunt Dorothea for that matter, to give an account, Papa,' Joan said. She gave her aunt a rather disappointed look. 'I can tell you what occurred and that it was all my fault.'

'Very noble,' the Duke said scathingly before snapping a harsh stare on his grizzling sister. 'You can turn off the waterworks, madam. You were brought here to chaperon my daughter in my wife's absence…a task as I recall you avowed was well within your capabilities.' Alfred Thornley strode to and fro in front of the ornate chimneypiece. 'There have been other instances when I have had to reprimand you over your inability to control a situation.'

'I do my best, Brother,' Dorothea mewled from behind her lace hanky. 'I tried to dissuade her from having anything to do with the vicar. He is not suitable company for a person of Joan's station…and neither are the brutes with whom he associates.'

'The Reverend is perfectly nice!' Joan retorted. 'And the fact that he dedicates much time to those far less fortunate does him credit.'

'Has Vincent Walters asked you to stump up any funds to assist him in his good deeds?' Alfred demanded to know, depressingly aware of how alluring was his daughter to fortune hunters.

'He has not, Papa,' Joan replied flatly. 'It was my idea to offer to teach the children to learn to read. How else are the disadvantaged ever to better themselves if they are denied skills to make accessible to them shop or clerical positions?'

The Duke's expression softened slightly. 'Your sincere concern for these vagabonds is very worthy, Joan. But you will not correct society's ills by placing yourself in mortal danger.'

'Getting lost was foolish...I admit it. But we arrived home safely,' Joan argued. 'We have so much and take it all for granted. It is our duty to endeavour to brighten the bleak futures facing those youngsters.'

'I cannot gainsay you on that, my dear, but it doesn't alter the fact that I might have been arranging the funerals of my daughter and sister and a member of my staff had things turned bad for you all. The Ratcliffe Highway murders are fresh in my mind, if not yours. You were but a schoolgirl at the time of the heinous crimes, of course,' the Duke pointed out, but less robustly than he might have minutes before.

He despaired of his daughter's impetuousness, but he grudgingly admired her, too, for her independence and benevolence. But from what he'd heard from Dorothea, and he believed it to be the truth, his travelling coach had been almost over-run with beggars threatening robbery and violence. And as a responsible parent he must punish his daughter's bad behaviour.

The door opened and the butler, looking stern, ushered Philip Rook into the room.

Joan guessed that poor Pip had felt the rough side of Tobias Bartlett's tongue; the youth looked terrified to be summoned into his eminent employer's presence for the very first time. In the past the lad had merely seen the Duke in the stable yard from beneath the forelock he tugged. Pip's complexion was alternating between scarlet and white as he stood, Adam's apple bobbing, waiting to hear his fate.

'You, Rook, were driving the coach this afternoon that got beset by a mob,' the Duke stated.

'I was, your Grace,' Pip answered faintly, as his master continued to glare at him.

'Pray why were you doing so and without a footman at least accompanying you?'

Pip licked his lips and blinked a glance Joan's way.

'He was doing so at my behest, Papa.'

Dorothea flapped her handkerchief at her brother, nodding vigorously to indicate the extent of the task confronting her to manage his wayward child.

'And in this way you guessed the escapade might evade my notice, did you?' the Duke suggested drily.

Joan winced as the barb hit home. Nothing escaped her father's sharp mind.

'In fact, had one of the other drivers taken you to St George's in the East you might have avoided getting lost at all and returned home without me being aware of any of it.'

Joan's blush deepened at the hint that she was an incompetent schemer.

'My sister tells me that you were extremely fortunate that one of the locals did the decent thing and steered you out of the rookery before a disaster occurred.' His Grace was frowning fiercely at his novice driver.

'He weren't a local, your Grace, he were Mr Rockleigh.'

The Duke of Thornley had been marching to and fro with his hands clasped behind his back and his head lowered in concentration. Now he halted and pivoted on a heel to gawp at his servant. Joan also stared Pip's way. She'd not believed for a second that her driver had recognised Drew Rockleigh from that one brief meeting, in the dark, over two years ago.

'Mr Rockleigh?' Alfred parroted in utter disbelief. 'Do you mean *Drew* Rockleigh?' The Duke looked to his daughter for a reply.

'Yes, it was him, Papa,' Joan answered quietly.

'You *knew* that ruffian?' Dorothea snorted. 'I believed him to be one of *them*.' She flapped a hand in disgust.

'I believe he *is* now one of them,' Joan said with genuine sorrow trembling her voice.

'You may return to your post, Rook, and you, Sister, may also retire.'

'I certainly did not know the ruffian was your stepson-in-law's friend,' Dorothea avowed while trotting towards the door. 'I swear I got no proper look at him, Alfred…just his back was to me as he leapt down.'

His Grace hurried his sister on her way with a hand flap, but as Joan also approached the exit he halted her with a curt, 'You stay, miss. I have much to discuss with you.'

Once the door had been closed the Duke again prowled about, much to his daughter's relief. Joan had been expecting an immediate dressing down, but it seemed her father was still pondering on the startling news that Luke Wolfson's best friend had been reduced to such poverty.

'Did Rockleigh know your identity, Joan?' Alfred enquired, still pacing.

'He did, Papa.'

'Did you talk about what prompted his fall from grace?'

'No…we exchanged little conversation. It wasn't the time or place for social niceties.' Joan kept to herself that Drew Rockleigh had roundly castigated her for being abroad in the vicinity of Ratcliffe Highway.

'I know some business went bad for him, but never would I have imagined he now frequents a

notorious slum.' The Duke of Thornley sorrowfully shook his head.

'He seems quite able to take care of himself…
but it was horrid meeting him there,' Joan replied.
'I'm sorry, Papa, that I put myself and my aunt
and Pip in peril. But please don't ask me to stop
helping at the school—'

'I ask nothing,' the Duke interrupted. 'I am *telling* you categorically that you will never attend
that place again. And I shall write personally to
your friend Vincent Walters to make it clear that
I hold him responsible for imperilling you.' The
Duke's impassioned speech had turned his complexion florid.

'You cannot! It's not the Reverend's fault that I
volunteered my services. And in any case he did
impress on me that…' Joan's voice tailed away.

'He did impress on you…what?' his Grace demanded.

'He said I shouldn't undertake anything without your consent,' Joan admitted sheepishly. She
didn't want Vincent Walters added to the list of
people she'd caused to be scolded because of her
determination to help those far less fortunate than
herself.

The Duke appeared slightly mollified to know that the vicar had acted correctly. 'I will not write and admonish him, then, if you promise to behave as you should.' The Duke's mind returned to the topic most engaging it. 'Did Rockleigh appear much changed to you?'

'Oddly…no…it took me only a short while to recognise him. Oh, the elements have browned his skin and bleached his hair. His body seemed broader, more muscled…' The memory of that naked torso slick with sweat and blood streaks caused Joan to blush. 'Of course his clothes were very grimy,' she hastened on. 'But he appeared quite healthy, apart from some cuts and bruises to his hands and face.' She noticed her father's deep frown. 'He prize fights to pay for his keep, you see,' she explained.

'*Fights?* What…in the *street*?' Alfred snorted. He recalled that he had once watched his stepson-in-law and Rockleigh sparring at Gentleman Jim's gymnasium and thought them evenly matched. Rockleigh had won the bout and gone on to take a fencing match against Luke, too, that afternoon.

'He pays his way by winning purses, so he said,' Joan added.

'I suppose something must be done to help him,' the Duke rumbled beneath his breath. 'Not so long ago that fellow did us a great service in keeping you safe and keeping confidential another of your hare-brained jaunts; now he has come to your assistance once more. He deserves a reward and methinks that he will be inclined to accept it this time.'

Joan shot a glance at her father. 'You offered to reward him last time?'

'I did, indeed!' the Duke admitted forcefully. 'What occurred wasn't Rockleigh's fault.' He harrumphed. 'I was embarrassed and humbled to learn that I'd wrongly accused him of seducing you, when all the fellow had done was put himself to the trouble of returning you home after you turned up on his doorstep.'

Joan flinched from the reminder of her shameful behaviour and from the memory of her father's attempt to make Rockleigh marry her. He had refused to have her and in the end there had been no need for a forced marriage because the scandal had never leaked out. Only family and the reluctant bridegroom had ever been privy to what had gone on.

'I will set an investigator to unearth him and arrange a payment.' The Duke of Thornley was not simply being philanthropic; his busy mind was weighing up how the possession of a wealthy man's secrets might corrupt a person down on his luck.

A muttered oath exploded between Alfred's teeth as he imagined all manner of disastrous consequences following on from that dratted calamity in Wapping. He dismissed his daughter with urgent finger flicks, pondering on whether the vicar or Rockleigh or both of them might present him with a problem.

When she'd been about fifteen Joan had been soft on her best friend's cousin. Vincent Walters, for his part, had encouraged Lady Joan's attention more than was decent for a fellow of his calling or station in life, in Alfred's opinion. His late wife had reassured him that there was nothing to worry about. Girls blossoming into womanhood liked to flirt at such a tender age, she'd told him, because they were fascinated by the new power they had recently acquired over gentlemen. She'd maintained that Vincent was simply being courteous and kind in his mild responses. By then the Duchess had been quite poorly and Alfred had not wanted to worry his wife by overreacting. Privately he had let the Reverend know by glowering look and barbed comment that he wasn't happy about the situation. In hindsight, Alfred accepted it had amounted to little more than Joan fluttering her eyelashes and the vicar and his relations being entertained to tea more often than was usual. Within a few months his daughter had turned sixteen and had made her come out at her mama's insistence. The doctor had warned that the Duchess might not survive the coming winter weather and his wife had dearly wanted to see Joan launched into society.

During that glittering Season in town Joan had been plagued by admirers. However, Alfred had made sure that the gentlemen's clubs had been rife with talk that the Duke of Thornley considered his sixteen-year-old daughter too young to become a wife and wouldn't countenance a meeting with any suitor for at least two years. But Joan's girlhood crush on the vicar had mellowed into a friendship even before the leaves on the trees turned to gold that year, and shortly after her beloved mama's passing had caused a black cloud to descend on the entire Thornley household.

With a sigh, Alfred wiped a tear from the corner of his eye. He was quite sure that no renewed infatuation with the vicar had made Joan risk the trip to the East End of London. She was a young woman who was too aware of her privileges and society's injustices, and would help those less fortunate when an opportunity arose.

Alfred dragged his mind back to the pressing matter of the real or imaginary threat that a different fellow might present to his family.

Drew Rockleigh had it within his power to ruin Lady Joan Morland. Their unexpected meeting today might have jogged the fellow's memory to the value of the information he held against her. Alfred knew the boxer might even now be pondering making contact with him to quote a price for his continuing silence. He would like to think that conscience and morals would prevent Rockleigh ever stooping so low, but an empty belly could make a sinner out of a saint.

Jerking open a bureau drawer, Alfred found a pen and parchment. He was keen to write to the Pryke Detective Agency to have the matter nipped in the bud rather than wait for it to flourish.

Chapter Three

'What is this?'

'It's a letter, as you can see, sir.' The fellow sneered the final word. He peered upwards along his bulbous nose at the tall blond fellow whose sun-beaten profile was presented to him. Thadeus Pryke attempted to swipe five biting fingers from his forearm, but found he could not budge the bronzed digits an inch.

'I can see that it is a letter. Why give it to me?' The unaddressed parchment, having been examined, was thrust back at the messenger.

'Because I believe you to be Mr Rockleigh... although I hear you're known as *the Squire* round these parts.' Again Pryke's top lip curled. 'My client has asked me to deliver the letter to you.'

'And your client is?' Drew Rockleigh stuck a

slim cheroot in his mouth, then lit it from a match flaring in his cupped palm.

'And my client is…my business.' Thadeus smirked. He was inordinately pleased with himself to have secured such an illustrious patron. He had been an army corporal in his time, before he'd bettered himself and gained employment in his brother's detective agency. But what he really wanted was to set up in business on his own account.

The Squire's precise speech and confident manner proclaimed him to be a man of good stock. The steely strength in his grip, taken together with the battle wounds on his knuckles and cheeks, spoke of his employment entertaining the crowds in a makeshift boxing ring that sprang up illicitly in the neighbourhood, then disappeared equally swiftly. Thadeus knew that the purses could reach quite a sum and attracted talented pugilists from far and wide. There were no holds barred with these men and wily assailants used every bodily weapon they possessed, from head to foot, to gain victory.

'Stay there, while I read it,' Drew commanded. Taking back the parchment, he stepped clear of a group of rowdies who had been loitering outside the Cock and Hen. He'd been on the point of entering the tavern when Pryke intercepted him a few moments ago.

A laugh grazed his throat as his eyes flitted over the few lines of thick black script.

'Have you a pencil?' he enquired of Thadeus, sticking the cheroot back between a set of even white teeth.

The investigator immediately produced one.

Drew scrawled two words across the bottom of the paper, then refolded it and resealed the broken wax with hot ash flicked from his cigar and strong pressure from a calloused thumb. 'Return it, if you please.'

From beneath a pair of wiry brows Thadeus watched Rockleigh's impressively broad back as the fellow strode away into the inn, a pretty blonde tavern wench greeting him eagerly at the doorway.

'Where is he?' the Duke of Thornley demanded to know when the detective returned alone. In his note he'd commanded Rockleigh to accompany Thadeus Pryke to meet him and claim his reward.

Alfred had taken the precaution of garbing himself in a sober suit of clothes and hiring a creaky rig to take him to the Eastern Quarter. He had wanted to blend in with the prevalent atmosphere of lower-middle-class aspiration; lawyers and shopkeepers had colonised an area in Cheapside in which Alfred had instructed his driver to stop. The Duke of Thornley had decided that if his daughter were brave enough to journey into the bowels of the Wapping docks to school children, then he must have sufficient backbone to park on the outskirts to pay the man who had ensured her safe passage home to Mayfair.

His young son and heir was away at school and as much as Alfred adored George, he doted equally on his eldest child, trial that Joan was, because she reminded him of the love of his life— her late mother. He would do his utmost to protect Joan from scandal…and in that he hoped—but was not convinced—that he and the boxer were of a single mind.

Thadeus executed a deep bow, his hat secured beneath an arm. Climbing aboard the rig, he closed the door so they might converse in private. Drawing forth the letter, he proffered it. 'The Squire returned you a message, your Grace.'

'*The Squire?*' Alfred echoed quizzically.

'Beg pardon, your Grace… I have inadvertently used the fellow's nickname.' In fact, Thadeus had intentionally aired the sobriquet in the hope that the Duke would find the boxer risible. The impatience with which his Grace snatched the missive disappointed Thadeus. Whether he was Rockleigh or the Squire, the man was obviously of great importance to Thornley.

Impatiently Alfred broke the seal and gaped at Rockleigh's answer to his offer of fifty pounds' compensation for time and trouble expended on his daughter's behalf. *Nothing required* was the sum of the man's response and he hadn't seen it necessary to add either his gratitude, or his signature.

Alfred slouched back against the upholstery, feeling miffed by the snub. He was a duke with several lesser titles and a number of ancestral estates established in the countryside from Cumberland in the north to Devon in the south. Yet a man who was rumoured to have lost everything in bad business deals, and was reduced to brawling to earn a crust, wanted nothing from him. And Rockleigh hadn't even been sufficiently flattered by the Duke of Thornley's interest in him to come and pay his respects.

Alfred dismissed Thadeus, who on reaching the pavement swivelled on a heel to jerk an obsequious bow. The investigator then rammed his hat back on his head and strode off. Alfred banged on the roof of the rig for the driver to head towards Mayfair. Far from accepting that that was the end of it, he was more determined than ever to have a meeting with Joan's saviour. Curiosity about Drew Rockleigh's decline played a part, but overriding all else was Alfred's prickling suspicion that no impoverished fellow would turn down the opportunity to exploit his secret knowledge. If Rockleigh was playing a long game and heightening Alfred's anxiety with uncertainty, then the tactic was working. The Duke sourly acknowledged that he was tempted to turn the rig about and drive straight into the heart of the rookery to demand Rockleigh spit out how much he did want if the sum offered wasn't sufficient for him to drag himself out of squalor.

He pressed his shoulders against the lumpy

squabs, rueing his missed chance of quizzing his son-in-law over Rockleigh the last time they'd been in each other's company. Luke was sure to know a good deal about his friend's degradation, yet Alfred had not previously been interested enough to probe. He was not one to want to pick over another chap's misfortune. But now things were different.

'I expect your father will put a stop to our meetings now.'

Vincent had sounded sorrowful. He had always been chary of upsetting the Duke of Thornley. His cousin Louise was very friendly with Lady Joan and their mothers were close, too. Years ago, Lady Joan's infatuation with him had initially been flattering, but having the Duke's good opinion was crucial to Vincent. Rich and powerful patrons of the church were hard to come by, and Vincent had been relieved rather than disappointed when Lady Joan's flirtatious behaviour waned as she grew more mature. Vincent was a pragmatic man. He knew there was no real prospect of a clergyman marrying a duke's daughter, so he had accepted early on that their relationship must remain platonic.

'Oh, Papa is just up in the boughs over my misadventure, but he will calm down in a week or so.' Joan gave her companion a smile as they strolled side by side in Hyde Park.

A short distance behind the couple, Aunt Dorothea was stomping along assisted by her silver-topped cane and her maid. The young servant was wielding a parasol to shield her mistress's lined complexion from the April sun.

Joan would sooner just a maid accompanied her when she went out, but her father insisted that she be *properly* chaperoned even though he'd recently deemed his sister unequal to the task.

'I don't think Lady Dorothea cares for me at all,' Vincent said, slanting a glance over a shoulder. 'But for her manners forcing her to respond, I believe your aunt would have ignored my greeting earlier.'

'She took the upset very badly that afternoon,' Joan explained.

On the day in question Joan had entered Vincent's back parlour to find nine children grouped in a semi-circle, sitting cross-legged on the rug.

They'd ranged in age from about six to ten years old. She'd gladly assisted Vincent in chalking letters on the children's slates for them to copy, but her aunt had refused to get involved or to budge from the front room of the vicarage. Dorothea had huddled into her widow's weeds and sat all alone for two hours rather than make herself useful.

'My aunt prefers it when we take a drive round the park, or head towards the emporiums where her cronies congregate. She has a fine time being scandalised by the latest *on dits* during their gossips.'

'No doubt *she* had quite a tale to tell *them* after that drama.'

'I believe my aunt is too ashamed to breathe a word about it…other than to her brother, of course,' Joan added flatly. 'But let's not dwell on what disasters might have been.' She slipped her hand through the crook of Vincent's arm.

She had written to Vincent to inform him that she'd be unable to visit the vicarage again as soon as planned and why that was. She'd only briefly outlined the unpleasant encounter with the beggars because she didn't want Vincent blaming himself. It was not his fault that Pip had lost his way. Sure that her father couldn't object to her and Vincent promenading in Hyde Park, Joan had suggested in her note that they meet up to talk. She and Vincent had been friends for too long to allow a mishap to drive a wedge between them.

Next week the Duke would be reunited with his spouse and Joan was confident he'd be in a better mood then. The Duchess was presently with her daughter in Essex, as Fiona was increasing again and feeling very poorly. Maude had sped off many weeks ago to give support and encouragement, sure the signs were there that an heir to the Wolfson name was on his way.

Her brother-in-law would be immensely proud to have his longed-for son, Joan thought before her mind wandered on…to a person Luke would certainly not be proud of: his degenerate best friend…

An impatient tut escaped her as she realised Drew Rockleigh again occupied her thoughts. Since the hair-raising incident with the beggars she had not managed to forget the dratted man for any length of time, much as she wanted to. His astonishing way of life depressed her the more she dwelt on it. Infuriating though she found him, he deserved better than to end up trading blows in a boxing ring.

'I hope the Duke won't stop you seeing me or make me abandon the vicarage school.' Vincent sounded anxious.

'Of course he won't, on either count! Papa knows that you are a good friend and he is not without compassion for the poor. He will mellow in time.' Joan paused, searching for a new subject to talk about. 'How is Louise liking her sojourn in the countryside?'

Louise Finch and Joan had been close since childhood. Louise's mother and Vincent's mother were kin and, despite one sister marrying a wealthy fellow while the other's husband was a man of the cloth, the women remained close. Vincent had followed in his father's footsteps, but had gained a living administering to a flock in the London stews rather than in a Kentish village.

'I understand from my mother that her guests will be returning early next week. Apparently Louise misses the social whirl and is bored with cattle for company.' Vincent gave a rather disapproving sniff.

Joan bit her lip to subdue a smile. It was the sort

of blunt opinion she would expect from her best friend, yet she doubted Louise had intended her hostess to overhear it.

'I shall be glad to have her back, anyway,' Joan said, patting Vincent's arm in a consoling manner. She gave him a smile and his indignation disintegrated. Vincent was a man of adequate height and build with coppery brown hair and pleasant looks. As they strolled around the perimeter of the lake Joan noticed that they were under observation.

'Your association with me attracts attention, you know,' Vincent said wryly, his thoughts mirroring Joan's. He nodded discreetly at some people craning their necks at them as their barouche passed by.

'No doubt they are recalling how abominably I embarrassed you when I was younger,' Joan teased, making Vincent cough and blush. 'Oh, the gossips should be used to us being friends by now.' She wrinkled her petite nose in a display of insouciance. 'It is more likely those young ladies are staring because they think you handsome and eligible,' she added with a twinkling smile.

'I doubt they would think my bank balance very attractive,' Vincent countered wryly. 'Even the clergy need to pay their bills.' Vincent paused. 'They appear to be returning for a second look,' he said as the barouche again approached.

'Oh, let them look.' Joan sighed. 'That is Miss Greenvale and her cousin. They are heiresses and could spare a few pounds from their trust funds to put towards your new church roof.'

'I fear I'll have no luck there and will carry on collecting rainwater in buckets for the foreseeable future.'

'I'll speak to Papa about releasing some of my money—'

'You must not!' Vincent interrupted sharply. 'I'll not let you do that.' His features softened into a grateful smile. 'You are a very generous and good-natured young woman.' Vincent slanted a glance at the pearly contours of Joan's profile, framed by chestnut curls. 'I hate that you suffered for your goodness. Will you tell me more about this dreadful attack by those beggars?'

'There isn't much to tell…it was over very quickly after we received help…' Joan said carefully. She'd sooner not make much of the incident with Rockleigh.

'Gracious! Over there by the trees is a fellow I

know.' Vincent discreetly waggled a hand indicating to his left. 'He is the Ratcliffe Highway's most successful pugilist. Of course, I rarely attend those contests lest I encourage the men in their barbarism.'

Joan came to an abrupt standstill as her eyes widened on the person who rarely quit her thoughts. He was standing many yards away on a patch of grass fringed by a copse and appeared to be deep in conversation with another fellow. From their position close to shady branches, and their unsmiling expressions, Joan guessed that the meeting was not a social one.

'Is he known to you?' Vincent had heard Joan's quiet intake of breath. 'He wasn't one of the beasts who beset your coach, was he? The fellow is known locally as *the Squire.* One only needs to be in his company for a short while to know he is well bred. He must be badly down on his luck, but I'd be surprised if he stooped to bullying women or begging.'

'No…he would never do that…' Joan murmured with a throb of conviction in her voice. 'He was our rescuer—I told you that we received help. He drove the carriage out of the slum.'

'I'm not surprised he was your Good Samaritan. He's courteous, if brutal, and that's a rarity in the parish. The Squire's got no need to beg as the victor's purses can be considerable.' Vincent looked enquiringly at Joan. 'Shall we speak to him? I'm keen to persuade some of the families to attend the Sunday services more often than they do. The ne'er-do-wells congregate in the Cock and Hen on the Sabbath when they might better spend their time seeking the Lord's forgiveness, or their own salvation.' Vincent clucked his tongue. 'A few of their wives are regular church goers though…'

'Is he married?' Joan blurted out, unsure why the thought of Drew Rockleigh having a wife appalled her.

'The Squire married? Not to my knowledge. He's popular with the *ladies* though…' Vincent cleared his throat to cover his slip. 'Forgive me, Lady Joan…that was most crass…'

But Joan was no longer listening; her eyes had become entangled with a steady tawny stare. Drew stepped away from his soberly dressed companion and the man scuttled into the copse out of sight.

Joan's heart began pounding beneath her ribs

as she watched Rockleigh plunge his hands into his pockets on his casual stroll over the grass towards them. Alert to her aunt's presence, Joan shot a look over her shoulder. 'Lady Dorothea is occupied with Lady Regan, so we can briefly say hello to Mr Rockleigh,' she rattled off.

'Rockleigh? Is *that* his name?'

Joan gave a brief nod, already on her way to meet him and so rapidly that Vincent had to trot to keep up with her.

'My lady… Reverend Walters…' Drew dipped his head, then glanced thoughtfully from one to the other of them.

'You are a distance from home today, sir,' Vincent burst out when his companions stared at one another rather than exchanging a greeting.

'I had an appointment to keep,' Drew informed, sliding his attention back to Joan.

'I must thank you very much for the service you did Lady Joan. I've heard how you helped her and her aunt out of a very unpleasant situation.' Vincent thrust out a hand.

'She wouldn't have been in that unpleasant situation but for you encouraging her into the neighbourhood,' Drew returned coolly, giving the Reverend's fingers a single firm shake.

'I need no encouragement to be benevolent,' Joan interjected sharply, conscious of the vicar fidgeting on being reprimanded. 'I made up my own mind to go to the vicarage school.'

'Against your father's wishes.'

'You are not privy to my father's wishes,' Joan retorted, becoming aware of Vincent's alarmed expression as she bickered with his disreputable parishioner.

'I know your father's wishes, Lady Joan,' Drew said quietly. 'Furthermore I endorse them and advise you to heed them.'

Joan furiously pressed her lips together. So her father had gone ahead and made contact with Rockleigh to reward him for rescuing her. Joan realised such a good deed deserved an acknowledgement; nevertheless, she felt piqued that he'd been venal enough to accept a payment.

'I…um… Lady Dorothea is about to join us, I think. Shall we move on?' Vincent burbled.

'Please go and keep her company,' Joan said, without breaking eye contact with Rockleigh. 'I will be but a moment longer speaking to…my brother-in-law's friend.'

The news that the Squire was an acquaintance of Joan's family caused Vincent's jaw to drop. 'You know Mr Wolfson?'

'I do…very well…' Drew's smile acknowledged the vicar's astonishment on learning he had lofty connections.

Vincent composed himself and with a crisp nod, hurried away over the grass towards Dorothea.

'How much did he pay you?' Joan demanded the moment Vincent was out of earshot. 'Ten pounds?' she guessed. 'Twenty?'

'Your father offered fifty.'

Joan's astonishment caused her full pink lips to part. She moistened them with a tongue flick that drew a pair of lupine eyes.

'So…you were a moment ago conversing with your banker, were you?' Joan asked mellifluously, nodding at the wooded area into which the fellow had disappeared. 'Is he to invest the cash, or pay off your duns with it, Mr Rockleigh?' When Drew remained infuriatingly silent and unperturbed by her barb, Joan prodded, 'Is that sufficient a sum to get you back on your feet or would you like me to play the damsel in distress one more time so you might again test my father's generosity?'

'You know nothing about me,' Drew said quietly. 'And I'm not about to satisfy your curiosity. Go back to your vicar friend and enjoy your promenade, but stay away from Ratcliffe Highway and me. Don't test *my* generosity, my lady, or my patience, because you'll find both lacking next time.'

Joan gasped in astonishment and outrage as he made to walk away from her. Nobody, apart from her papa, spoke to her in that tone of voice. Imperiously she retorted, 'You may halt this instant. I have not finished speaking to you, sir.'

'But I have finished with you…' was sent casually over a shoulder as he strolled away.

'Come here this instant, you impertinent lout.'

He pivoted about and returned so swiftly that Joan skittered back some steps, her heart pulsing in her throat.

'Well? What do you want?' Drew enquired with silky softness.

Joan could think of nothing to say and neither could she raise her eyes to meet those that were singeing the top of her head. His muscled thighs were in her lowered line of vision, encased today in black breeches that seemed as closely moulded to his powerful physique as the charcoal-grey tailcoat he wore. Had she not known what Drew Rockleigh did for a living she might have mistaken him for a businessman rather than a barbarian. Only the faint healing marks on his face and knuckles gave the game away that he was a street fighter.

'You're finding it hard to apologise for your rudeness, are you?' Drew suggested, mockery in his tone, as she continued to glower at the small space of grass that separated them.

'I have done nothing that requires an apology.' To her shame Joan knew that was far from the truth. She'd just been horribly pompous and arrogant and her bewilderment at having allowed him to taunt her to act out of character simply added to her inner turmoil.

'You need not apologise?' he paraphrased silkily. 'I seem to recall having heard that from you before. It was no truer then than now.'

Heat seeped into Joan's cheeks. She had indeed said something similar to him following her outrageous visit to his hunting lodge. With Pip driving the trap, she'd journeyed late at night, seeking Luke Wolfson, but her future brother-in-law had not been there. Rockleigh had found himself in the unenviable position of having compromised a duke's daughter while minding his own business in his own home. Joan had felt ashamed to have caused him trouble, but even when he delivered her safely home and prevented her father chastising her with a slap, a simple 'sorry' had refused to roll off her tongue. Neither had she graciously thanked her escort. She had thought of writing to him and humbling herself...until her father recounted that Drew Rockleigh had refused point blank to salvage her reputation and marry her, even with great financial inducement to do so.

No doubt he would have her like a shot now, Joan thought sourly. The jibe withered on her tongue as she saw his sardonic expression and knew he'd read her thoughts.

'Nothing's changed for me...' he drawled.

'Oh, but I think it has,' Joan replied, bristling with indignation. 'Once you displayed a modicum of gentility and good breeding—now you appear to be just a violent heathen.'

Drew smiled, glanced over her head to where

her aunt and Vincent Walters were pretending not to gawp too obviously. 'The vicar told you he wants to save my soul and get me to attend church, did he?'

'Reverend Walters told me more besides about you,' Joan blurted before she could stop herself.

'He told you *what* about me?' Drew's demand was speciously soft.

'Nothing I want to repeat.' Joan knew she would never explain her comment so spun about, preparing to retreat. She'd discovered he was a womaniser and, tempted though she was to fling it in his face, there were certain breaches of etiquette she baulked at committing. Hot-headed she might be, but Joan hoped she was never vulgar.

'Come…we both know I'm not decent and the vicar's put some embellishment to the fact.' With a single stride Drew strategically repositioned himself in her path. 'We're also both aware that you're no shrinking violet and your reputation won't stand scrutiny,' he purred. 'So tell me what Walters said.'

'What do you mean by that?' Joan demanded.

'I'm guessing he told you I'm an incurable reprobate, best avoided.'

'I'm guessing that you have deliberately mis-construed my meaning.' Joan eyed him warily. 'You commented on my reputation and I'd like to know why.'

'You know why. I compromised you two years ago. Or rather you compromised me. Your father attempted to make me pay for your mistake.'

'Perhaps he did, but you were never in any danger of having to do so, sir. I made it clear from the outset that I'd sooner enter a nunnery than become your wife.'

Drew's amusement turned to silent laughter. 'So you did…but, capital fellow that I am, I saved you from a life of vows and celibacy by rejecting your hand and your father's bribe of lands and riches to go with it.'

'Very noble…' Joan scoffed croakily. 'I trust, despite your unfortunate position, that I can count on you still being a capital fellow?'

'Your secret's safe with me, my lady.' Drew's voice was rich with humour as his honey-coloured eyes flowed with insolent leisure over her figure. 'But that might be all that is…so stay in Mayfair and do your good works there.'

Mingling thrill and alarm streaked through

Joan. She knew if she pushed this man too far she might bitterly regret it…so flight was now the sensible option. Indeed, it was the *only* option because her aunt was marching towards her. Lady Regan was also staring at them and passing carriages were slowing down so the occupants could covertly watch the Duke of Thornley's daughter conversing with a handsome, if ill-matched, stranger. Joan wondered whether any of them had recognised her modestly attired companion as Drew Rockleigh.

'Move aside,' Joan commanded. Chin elevating, she attempted to step past him, but was again thwarted. 'Should my father find out about this he will punish you for your insolence.'

'I should have let him punish you. God knows you're in need of some sense and discipline instilled in you.'

'Why did you not, then?' Joan challenged. She held her breath, unsure why his answer was of vital importance to her.

'Damned if I know…' Drew sauntered off with a low, throaty chuckle.

Joan pressed together her lips, preventing herself again succumbing to an urge to order him back.

She was furious that he'd had the last word—blasphemous, too!—and then walked away from her before *she* could quit *his* presence. But she was also hurt by his final remark. She'd hoped he'd say he'd wanted to protect her from her father's wrath, but perhaps she'd played a minor role in the incident and it had really been a contest of egos between two antagonistic gentlemen.

Chapter Four

'You *must* accompany me to Pall Mall and speak to Lady Regan.' Dorothea's small fierce eyes fastened on her niece's profile. 'Everybody suspected that more than how the Wolfsons do was occupying the two of you. I fielded questions as best I could, so make sure you tell your papa how I tried to protect you from gossip.'

'Mr Rockleigh and I also talked about the beggars who stopped our coach,' Joan offered up one truthful titbit.

'It's your duty to come with me to explain yourself.' Dorothea snorted as a blush spread on Joan's cheeks. 'If you colour up, Lady Regan will know you're guilty of something. And never mention those atrocious vagabonds, I implore you.' Dorothea's nose wrinkled in disgust as she fingered the mourning brooch on her shoulder. 'I thank the Lord that this precious memento of my dear departed husband didn't fall into the clutches of that avaricious wretch.'

'It is not avarice, but cold and hunger that makes the poor act so.'

'You *defend* them?' Dorothea barked, eyes popping in shock.

'No…theft is theft, but I understand how such an environment might corrode a person's honesty and dignity. I know, too, that the rot could be stopped if the disadvantaged were able to share a few of the things that we take for granted.' Joan cast a damning eye on her aunt. 'Helping slum urchins to better themselves through learning to read and write is surely a step in the right direction; I find it inconceivable that any decent person would ignore the need for children to be given a basic education.'

Dorothea gulped indignantly at the pointed reminder of how she'd sat sulking in the vicar's parlour rather than assist with the lessons that day. 'Those vile people would have robbed and murdered us but for Mr Rockleigh's intervention. They should be horsewhipped…every one of them,' she warbled dramatically. 'Say nothing about any of it to my friends; they will find it abhorrent to know we came close to such taint.' Dorothea waggled a cautioning finger. 'Of course, the dreadful tale of what occurred is bound to circulate eventually now you have told the vicar all about it.' She sent her niece a blameful glare. 'So you will come and have some tea with us?'

'I'm afraid not; I shall go straight home.'

'You are the most selfish miss!' Dorothea hissed. 'Your father will be livid to know you have been consorting with Rockleigh again.'

'He won't mind me having a conversation with my brother-in-law's friend.' Joan sounded more confident than she felt. 'Besides, there is no need for Papa to be bothered with any of it.'

'Had you been with the Rockleigh of old...*then* I would agree. But the fellow is now in the gutter and you would do well to remember that before accosting him.'

'I did no such thing!' Joan protested, although she recalled approaching him rapidly. She settled back into the squabs to stare sightlessly at passing scenery. 'Would you have recognised Mr Rockleigh had the vicar not told you his identity?'

'Oh, indeed I would have!' Dorothea trilled. 'I

got a good look at him this time.' She studied her niece's reaction. 'Such handsome features aren't disguised by a heathenish tan, are they?'

Joan was saved from finding an answer; she'd suddenly realised that the coach was about to sail past the turning to her home. She rapped on the roof, determined to use her chance to escape.

'Baldwin's has in some fine new silk. You will want to choose from the bolts before all the best shades are sold out.' Dorothea made a last attempt to keep her niece's company.

Ignoring Dorothea's angry huff, Joan said farewell, then alighted without waiting for the groom to open the door. Having hopped down, she immediately set off in the direction of Upper Brook Street.

Dorothea's friends knew that Drew Rockleigh and Luke Wolfson were chums without Joan having to take tea with them and tell them so. The *ton* also knew that one man lived in luxury while the other… Her train of thought faltered as she realised she had no idea where Rockleigh resided. The idea that he took bed and board in a slum was outlandish considering who he was…or rather who he had been. He didn't seem unfed…far from it; his strong solid physique spoke of nourishment as well as exercise. Vincent Walters had spoken of high-value purses being won by the victors such as the Squire, as he'd called Rockleigh.

Her aunt's cronies would have quizzed her mercilessly so they could repeat details of Rockleigh's disgrace in scandalised whispers. Joan wasn't privy to his secrets, but if she were, she'd not betray him.

It puzzled Joan why she felt rather protective of a man who exasperated her, mocked her and also alarmed her. But Rockleigh had, not once, but twice now done her a great service. The need to act fairly and return a favour was quite understandable, as her father had recently pointed out. And what else could there be feeding her growing obsession with him?

Preoccupied, Joan entered her home. On looking up, she spotted her stepmother's maid and some of the other servants hurrying towards the cloakroom laden with garments. Then her darting eyes pounced upon the woman herself. Maude had been tweaking her flattened coiffure into shape in front of a mirror spanning the length of a fancy console table. Packing cases and port-

manteaux lined the walls and a convoy of footmen were converging on the vestibule to transport
their mistress's vast amount of luggage upstairs
to her chamber.

'Oh, it's lovely to have you back and sooner than
expected.' Joan rushed to Maude to give her a hug
that was warmly returned.

'How is Fiona? Is she better now?' Joan eagerly
asked, breaking free of the older woman's embrace.

'Your sister is much brighter, my dear, so I decided to get myself from under their feet. The physician has assured Fiona that the queasiness will
ease as the babe grows.' Maude linked arms with
her stepdaughter. 'Come, I am parched and want
some tea. Let us sit in the rose salon and have a
chat. Then I must snooze for a while and look re-
freshed for your papa when he gets in.' She sighed
contentedly. 'I have missed you both, you know.
Tobias tells me that Alfred is at White's and won't
return before we dine so there is plenty of time
for us to catch up with all the news.'

'And how is my lovely little niece?' Joan asked,
removing her bonnet. She ran five tidying fingers
through a tumble of dark chestnut curls.

'Oh, that tot is destined to be a tomboy. Diana likes sticks and stones to play with rather than a doll to dress.' Maude sounded nostalgic while speaking of her granddaughter. 'Fiona was the same as a youngster: she would crawl about the garden to catch worms and snails as pets while her little sister behaved prettily.' The woman shuddered, glancing searchingly over a shoulder. 'Tobias told me you'd gone for a drive with your aunt,' she commented as they strolled over marble flags.

'Dorothea has journeyed on to Pall Mall to browse the emporiums and meet Lady Regan in a teashop.' Joan sighed. 'I opted to come home. I cannot abide dawdling about those places just for the latest gossip.'

'You and Fiona are alike, you know.' Maude chuckled. 'My eldest would never shop for new dresses either. It was always Verity who loved to have the seamstresses fluttering around her hem with needles and pins.'

'I find the idea of being like Fiona very agreeable.' Joan sounded wistful. Her stepsister was indeed fortunate to have a doting husband and an adorable daughter to cherish plus another little one on the way.

'She has sent you a letter; it's in my portmanteau. Fiona spoke about you constantly, asking me this and that and when will you visit. She was disappointed you did not accompany me.'

Joan would have very much liked to see her sister and brother-in-law, but when Maude had left for Essex over a month ago Joan had been suffering with a chill and too unwell to travel.

The refreshment arrived promptly after the two ladies had settled themselves in the rose salon.

'So what scandals have I missed while away?' Maude sipped from delicate bone china, her lively eyes displaying her eagerness to have some gossip.

'Miss Richards has been jilted by her fiancé,' Joan related after a cursory racking of her brains.

'That doesn't surprise me! He was a fortune hunter and has probably got wind of her father's ship sinking off China.'

'Has it?' Joan's eyes widened. 'What cruel fate. Who told you of it?'

'Luke had heard the news on the grapevine, then Fiona told me about another fellow who has been greatly reduced in circumstances. I understand that was entirely his own fault, though.'

Joan put down her cup, then waited till the maid had deposited some cakes and disappeared before asking hesitantly, 'Was Fiona referring to Drew Rockleigh?'

Maude airily waved a tartlet she'd immediately selected and bitten into. 'Rockleigh is out of favour and never mentioned. The culprit is another fellow who lost his house on a turn of a card to a professional gambler.'

'How careless...' Joan gulped her tea. She wished she'd not mentioned Rockleigh now because she feared her stepmother would pick up the thread of the conversation and she was confused as to how to continue. She was still smarting from his maddening attitude to her earlier. She was also still feeling embarrassed about her unpleasantly haughty response to his provocation. Yet, despite it all, there was within her a restlessness to see him again that was so powerful she felt tempted to fly to the stables, find Pip, then return to the slum and demand answers to the questions bedevilling her.

'Fiona is aware that her husband's friend has had

a dreadful time of it.' Maude popped some stray currants into her mouth. 'Luke refuses to discuss Rockleigh because he is very angry with the ingrate.' Maude sighed. 'These men! They will get themselves into scrapes with their bad habits.'

'He didn't gamble away his money!' Joan had immediately leapt to the ingrate's defence.

'Did he not?' Maude sounded surprised. 'What *did* he do?'

'Um…I'm not sure,' Joan admitted. 'Papa heard that some business went bad for him.'

Maude helped herself to another cake. 'I see… but Drew always seemed a devil-may-care charmer to me.' She arched an eyebrow at Joan. 'I recall he paid you rather a lot of attention at their wedding reception.'

'For the short time he attended,' Joan countered. Fiona and Luke's wedding breakfast had been a wonderful celebration held in the ballroom that occupied a sizeable amount of the first floor of the Duke of Thornley's town house. Wistfully Joan recalled Drew looking heartbreakingly handsome that evening. He had asked her to dance, causing fans to stir amongst the ladies present.

But by ten o'clock he had gone. Joan had been

piqued enough by his abrupt disappearance to discreetly try to find him. Her search had taken her from the card room to the supper room and then to wander down the stairs. In the vestibule she had heard two dandies, lounging against a marble pillar, laughing that Rockleigh's mistress had waited over two hours outside for him in a carriage. Joan had melted away into the shadows in a whisper of lemon silk, not wanting those chortling young bucks to spot her. She'd felt a fool, pining for a man who clearly wanted to be elsewhere and had danced with his host's daughter out of politeness.

And that had been the last time Joan had been in Drew Rockleigh's company…until very recently.

'Why is Luke angry with him?' Joan enquired. According to her sister, Drew had been a true friend to Luke when they were growing up and Luke had been unhappy at home. 'Is Rockleigh no longer deemed fitting company since my brother-in-law settled down to a staid family life?' Joan hoped Luke's loyalty ran deeper than that.

'Not at all!' Maude wiped crumbs from her lips with a napkin. 'Luke *wants* to be friends. Apparently he offered his chum a loan to get him back on his feet, but Rockleigh flatly refused to have it. Drew is now living like a degenerate, consorting with quite the wrong sort of people. Luke is out of patience with him.' She frowned. 'It is inconceivable that somebody would willingly remain in the gutter. It might be all exaggeration.' Maude's expression turned optimistic.

'I fear this time the gossip might not live up to the reality, ma'am,' Joan said quietly.

'You know the ins and outs?' Maude was intrigued enough to push away the tempting plate of tartlets and give her stepdaughter her full attention.

'I might as well own up, for no doubt Papa will regale you with details of my latest scrape.'

'Indeed, you must, if you wish to have my assistance in the matter,' Maude answered with a wink.

Five minutes later when the saga about the beggars and Drew Rockleigh's heroics had been related, Maude was looking much less amiable.

'Oh, Joan!' the woman wailed. 'I wouldn't have gone off to Essex for so long if I'd known you'd get embroiled in the vicar's ragged school. There's always a price to pay for doing a good deed, as my late husband would say.' Maude sorrowfully shook her head. 'I've always sanctioned your friendship with the vicar as he is kin of the Finches and I know your late mama liked him. Alfred is sure to remind me of *my interference* when he gets home.'

'You know you have my father wrapped about your little finger.' Joan managed a fraudulent smile, inwardly wincing at having caused yet another person's upset. She'd not wanted to bring tears to her stepmother's eyes, but equally she would never regret teaching some slum urchins their letters.

Thus far her stepmother had been her ally. Maude would gently chide her husband over keeping a too-strict rein on his eldest child. Her own daughter, she would remind him, had braved the hazards of travelling hundreds of miles in the seeking of employment and in the end the adventure had enriched Fiona's life rather than ruining it.

The Duke would listen and nod. He would heed Maude in most things. In this particular case he had no need to humour her though, as there was great truth in her boast that Fiona's courage had been well rewarded: Joan's stepsister had travelled to Devon to take up a position as a governess when her life was at a low ebb and instead had fallen straight into the loving arms of her future husband.

'Oh! That is your father back now.' Maude had agitatedly gained her feet at the sound of voices in the corridor.

Joan had also heard the Duke's baritone mingling with her Aunt Dorothea's shrill treble. She was itching to speak to her father in private to discover why he'd found it necessary to reward Rockleigh with as much as fifty pounds. But now Maude was home husband and wife would want time alone, so Joan would have to wait her turn for an audience with him.

She was wrong on that score. Her father strode into the rose salon with his sister trotting in his wake. 'Ah, capital to have you home, m'dear,' he addressed his wife with a fond beam. A moment later Alfred's beady gaze was turned on his daughter. 'It seems you and I must have another serious talk, miss,' he announced.

Over his shoulder Joan could see Dorothea's fingers nervously plucking at the skirts of her widow's weeds. So her aunt had blabbed about the encounter with Rockleigh in Hyde Park and had doubtless put her own fantastic interpretation on it.

'I should like to speak to you, too, Papa,' Joan replied stoutly.

'You will have an immediate opportunity to do so, miss, never fear,' the Duke retorted. He turned a softer gaze on his wife. 'Why do you not retire for a while, Maude, and I'll join you shortly?' He raised her fingers to his lips in tender salute. 'Off you go, now. There is no point in bringing you in on this half the way through. I'll explain it in private, for deuce knows there are bits that stretch the bounds of credibility and might need oft repeating.'

Maude glanced at her stepdaughter, seeking a small signal that Joan had no need of her support. Satisfied by a smile, the Duchess greeted her sister-in-law by clasping Dorothea's thin hands before quitting the room.

'I should like permission to retire, too, Alfred,' Dorothea piped up the moment her niece's fierce grey gaze veered her way. 'My headache is worse. I have missed an appointment with Lady Regan because of it.'

Joan guessed that it wasn't a migraine, but the

thought of awkward questions being fired at her over the teacups that had caused the woman to abort her social engagement.

A grunt of agreement sanctioned Dorothea's request. Before his sister quit the room the Duke said, 'Now my wife is home you will no doubt wish to hurry back to your own hearth, Dorothea. Tobias will see to it that you have every help to get packed up to leave the moment you are ready.'

'Indeed, I should like to be back in Marylebone, Alfred.' Dorothea's puckered lips formed a thin line at the termination of her services. 'My nerves have been stretched beyond bearing these past weeks.' A blameful gaze landed on her niece.

'My bank draft for your trouble will no doubt soothe them, my dear.' Alfred followed up that dry remark with an unmistakable nod of dismissal. He then sat down. Having shaken the teapot, he poured tepid tea into his wife's abandoned cup, then took a gulp.

'So…explain yourself, if you will,' he commenced testily, jabbing a glance Joan's way. 'You had a meeting this afternoon with Rockleigh in the park, under cover of a stroll with your vicar friend, that much I know.' He waved an impatient hand at his daughter's immediate protest. 'I'm not so easily duped by the use of a beard. I've some personal experience of a clandestine tête-à-tête from my own youth, you know.'

'It was no arranged meeting!' Joan burst out. 'I was promenading with the Reverend Walters and we came upon Mr Rockleigh with a companion.'

'A companion, eh?' The Duke seemed interested to hear that. 'And who was this person?'

'I've no idea. He was dressed like a clerk; when Mr Rockleigh caught sight of us they parted and the fellow disappeared into the trees. Why on earth would you believe I'd plot an assignation with a man I don't like?'

'So…it is all an innocent coincidence. There are no lingering passions between you in danger of rekindling?'

Joan spluttered a sound that hovered between amusement and amazement. 'If you mean *pleasant* feelings, then, no, there are not! Nor were there ever any. And I don't know why you'd think differently; we were constantly at one another's throats when you tried to force us to wed. And I have just said I have no liking for him.'

'Mmm…love and hate are close kin. I recall you

both protested too much,' the Duke commented reflectively. 'You mooned about for a while and as for Rockleigh…most fellows would have accepted a token of my gratitude and esteem if only to humour me. But he wouldn't take a penny, then or now. I applauded his lack of avarice two years ago, but this time I'm uneasy about it.'

'But you recently gave him fifty pounds, didn't you?' Joan sounded perplexed.

'Is that what he said during this *private talk* you had?'

'Yes…no…' Joan amended in confusion. 'He told me you'd offered him that amount and I assumed he'd taken it.'

'I did offer it, but he would not have it. He also refused to come and thank me for my most generous gesture.' Alfred was still smarting over the snub.

'You wanted a street fighter to come *here*?' Joan's dark brows shot together in disbelief.

'Of course not, my dear,' Alfred answered tetchily. 'I travelled to his territory and waited in a carriage in Cheapside. The detective I engaged delivered the note asking him to meet me and claim his reward.' Alfred snorted in indignation.

'Rockleigh dismissed me as though I were a no-body! Deuced cheek of the man!'

Joan nibbled her lower lip while digesting that astonishing fact. People—even those with wealth and standing—kowtowed to her father, bowing and scraping to earn his favours. But Rockleigh was a breed apart, it seemed.

'So…what are we to do about all of this?' the Duke muttered to himself as he got up from the sofa and began prowling the Aubusson carpet. 'I'm hoping *the Squire,* as my man Thadeus Pryke named him, is as honest and sincere as was Drew Rockleigh, but I'm not sure.'

'What do you mean, Papa?' A shiver of appre-hension rippled through Joan. The Duke of Thorn-ley was rarely lacking in confidence, or at a loss to know what to do about any situation.

'Rockleigh is cognizant with our secrets. He has not once hinted to me about your youthful in-discretion since you committed it and in the past we've often met at clubs and functions. But he is a different person now; who is to say *the Squire* will not seek to capitalise on what he knows? A man who has lost wealth and rank might claw his way back into society by whatever means present themselves,' Alfred concluded bleakly.

Joan realised that her father's attitude was horribly cynical, yet a similar fear had tormented her when Rockleigh had reminded her of her disgrace. *'Your secret's safe with me, my lady...but that might be all that is...'* A sultry gleam had been in his eyes, leading her to believe that lust was behind the threat. But perhaps the base desire he had was not for her, but for the riches lodged in her father's bank vault. 'He promised not to betray us, Papa,' Joan said forcefully in an attempt to reassure herself as much as her father.

'Promised? You talked about your disgraceful behaviour two years ago?' The Duke had stopped roaming the room to bark questions at his daughter.

Joan nodded, inwardly berating herself for having brought her heated exchange with Rockleigh to such a dangerous point. The vicar had told her *the Squire* was a womaniser and she'd been unable to resist hinting at what she knew. He'd retaliated by bringing up the subject of her brazen visit to his hunting lodge.

'If he means to blackmail me...' The Duke left

the rest unsaid, but his florid physiognomy told of the impotent rage he felt at the idea becoming reality. 'He is no longer friendly with your brother-in-law so there is no loyalty at stake to make him hesitate.'

'He will never risk you calling his bluff, Papa. A gentleman accused of seduction is not completely off the hook.' Joan managed a wan smile, but her rapid heartbeat made her quite breathless.

'It seems Rockleigh is no longer a gentleman and I doubt he gives a toss for fair play or etiquette.' The Duke headed towards the sideboard to use the decanter. The cognac he poured was shot back in a single swallow. 'Of course he might welcome marrying you now to get himself out of the mess he's in.' The Duke rubbed his chin with thumb and forefinger, adding rather wistfully, 'If I truly believed that beneath the Squire's scruffy exterior still beat Drew Rockleigh's heart, then I'd hear him out if he called.'

A few of Joan's slender fingers stifled her horrified laugh. 'Well, thank heavens he made it clear he wants no more of me now than he did then.'

'That must have galled,' the Duke said gently, eyeing his daughter's proud profile. His little Joan was easily wounded; indeed, when he'd told her two years ago that Rockleigh had declined several thousand acres of prime Devon farmland, together with a handful of Mayfair freeholds, rather than contract to marry her, Alfred had thought she might blub. Of course she had not...pride had seen to that. His daughter had concealed her humiliated expression. Then she had acted as though Rockleigh's slight was to her liking. Just as she was doing now.

'I don't know why the matter cropped up,' Joan rattled off airily. 'Our lucky escape from a forced marriage was of little importance then or now.'

'Yet crop up, it did,' Alfred said. 'And who raised it?'

'It wasn't raised...just hinted at.'

'By whom?' The Duke stubbornly insisted on knowing, even though he could tell that his daughter desired the subject to be dropped.

'I don't recall, Papa.' It was a fib. Joan could remember everything that had occurred during her meeting with Rockleigh. She'd wanted to know whether a street fighter regretted turning down the chance of netting a fortune and a duke's daughter. And she'd received an answer without asking the question. *'Nothing's changed for me...'* he'd drawled while looking privately amused that she might have thought otherwise.

'Do you believe him corrupt, Papa, and capable of blackmail?' Joan asked solemnly.

For a moment the Duke said nothing, simply shaking his head slowly from side to side. 'I always liked the fellow; Rockleigh was not only your brother-in-law's chum, but a friend to you and me when he dealt so coolly with your misbehaviour. But now...who knows? An empty belly might turn a saint into a sinner...'

Chapter Five

'You are lucky, Joan! Nothing thrilling ever happens to me.'

'Lucky?' Joan spluttered, gently extricating herself from her friend's welcoming embrace. 'You think it fortunate to be set upon by beggars while an elderly relative swoons at one's side?'

'I almost swooned with boredom in Kent,' Louise Finch riposted. 'There was nothing to do in the evenings but play bridge with my elderly relatives. I did attend a jig at the local assembly rooms, but I can't recommend a country affair. The ladies were quite standoffish and all the gentlemen had ugly clothes and loud voices.'

'Not so different then from the people we are used to,' Joan commented wryly as they strolled past two young bucks in garish waistcoats, quaffing champagne and chortling at their own jokes.

'Speaking of coarse fellows...' Louise winked slowly. 'Vincent mentioned that a pugilist nicknamed *the Squire* acted the hero, putting an end to the skirmish in Wapping.' She grinned on noticing Joan's heightened colour. 'A gentleman down on his luck who is acquainted with your brother-in-law, is how Vincent described him. I'll wager your Mr Rockleigh is a very handsome rogue.'

'Handsome is as handsome does...' Joan bit her lip, feeling uncharitable. Her saviour might fight for a living, but just minutes spent in Rockleigh's company proved him to be mannerly and intelligent. And protective...and provocative. Intriguing, too, she realised; she certainly couldn't stop thinking about the infuriating individual.

Joan forced her concentration to another gentleman as they strolled on towards the supper room. She was miffed that Vincent had blurted out her news before she'd had a chance to tell Louise in her own way about the drama.

Within hours of his aunt and cousin arriving home from visiting his family in Kent the vicar had made a point of paying a call on the Finches. He'd been eager to report how one of the Duke's coachmen had taken a wrong turning, landing his female passengers in a dreadful pickle. Louise had listened, open-mouthed, to her cousin's account, but had been keen for more gory details. The invitation to the Wentworths' ball, propped on the mantelshelf, had provided a prime opportunity for a chinwag with the main protagonist. Louise was confident that Joan would attend as the Duke and Duchess of Thornley were chummy with their hosts.

Moments ago the two young ladies had spied one another through the throng of guests. Simultaneously they'd left their groups to have a fond reunion beneath the scintillating chandeliers.

Joan linked arms with Louise and they began to perambulate the edge of the dance floor, avoiding the sets forming for a quadrille.

'This is something else I've greatly missed,' Louise said. They had arrived in the supper room, where a dining table was spread with silver platters filled with delicacies. 'Country fare leaves much to be desired.' Louise popped a marchpane pineapple into her mouth, enjoying it and licking her lips before adding, 'Vincent's people are nice folk, but I couldn't live on broth and stew as much as they do.'

'I enjoy a good pheasant casserole.' Joan fondly remembered the hearty meals served up at Thornley Heights, her father's primary ancestral seat. During dismal Devon evenings, when the winds sometimes blew so loud that it seemed banshees inhabited the chimneys, she'd loved to curl up by a roaring fire with a book, feeling cosy and content after a satisfying repast.

'Who is that young lady? She keeps staring at us,' Louise hissed, holding a napkin to her lips. 'I've not seen her before.'

Joan had been choosing titbits from the buffet, but stopped to glance over a shoulder. Her grey gaze collided with a pair of china-blue eyes, then the stranger flounced aside her face. The girl was buxom and fair-haired, although a sulky twist to her lips marred her pretty features. By her side was a couple Joan guessed to be her parents. The woman was very similar in looks and colouring; the fellow dark-haired and heavy jowled. 'I don't recognise any of the family. Perhaps they are just arrived in town.' Normally Joan might have taken more notice of newcomers, but since her friend had brought up the subject of the beggars moments ago her thoughts had been back in Wapping. She wanted to know what Rockleigh might be planning to do. In common with her father, she longed to believe him still honourable, despite his hardship, yet niggling doubts were chipping away at her peace of mind over his trustworthiness.

'Ah, there you are, girls.' Maude had sailed up to join them with Mrs Finch in tow. 'Oh, those look tasty.' The Duchess began filling a plate with an assortment of tiny *vol-au-vents*.

Hot on their tails came Aunt Dorothea's thin bombazine-clad figure. She announced her presence with a cough.

Since the Duke had sent his sister back to her own home, Joan had seen nothing of her aunt. She felt rather mean thinking that the respite had been very welcome.

'I promised Lady Regan that we would have a chat to Mrs Denby and her daughter.' Dorothea swivelled her eyes to indicate the newcomers. 'My friend has kindly taken the girl under her wing.' Inclining closer, Dorothea muttered, 'Sooner hers than mine, I can tell you.' The widow's loaded comment soon gained her companions' interest.

'What is amiss?' Maude darted a glance at the strangers. 'Is there some scandal?'

'Indeed there would be! If news of it circulated.'

'Surely it already has, if you know of it,' the Duchess pointed out.

'Oh, I have given Lady Regan my word not to tell a soul.' Dorothea observed that several quizzical looks were turned on her. 'Of course, I may confide the sorry tale to people I know I can trust.' She gave her niece a hard stare.

Joan and Louise exchanged a look of muted amusement.

'Well, don't leave us in suspense,' the Duchess prompted in an undertone. 'I must say Mr Denby appears bored rather than embarrassed.' As the fellow glanced her way Maude attended to her plate of food. 'I expect he might prefer to play faro while the ladies mingle,' she whispered. 'I'll ask Alfred to speak to him later about a game of cards.'

The Duke of Thornley had come to find endearing his second wife's gauche social manners. Maude found nothing strange in expecting him to befriend lesser mortals. And neither did he since she'd entered his life like a breath of fresh air.

'Oh, that is not Mrs Denby's husband.' Dorothea's explanation emerged from behind her quivering fan. 'She is a widow. Mr Saul Stokes is Cecilia's guardian. The girl has just turned eighteen, although she made her come out last year and just as well she did!' Dorothea added darkly. 'For I doubt she'd shine this Season.'

'She is surely old enough to do without a guardian,' Maude responded. 'My two girls were independent from an earlier age.'

'And so was Louise,' Mrs Finch piped up, keen to join the conversation.

'Since her debut Cecilia has been a terrible trial to her mother.' Dorothea pursed her lips. 'The chit needs a father's discipline. If she were mine I'd disown her…after I'd taken a stick to her back.'

Maude's widening eyes prompted her sister-in-law to hurry on. 'A while ago the minx was caught on the Great North Road, attempting to elope with a groom.' Dorothea employed her fan so energetically her companions also received its benefit. 'Of course, the family are adopting a united front, but then they would.' The widow gave an emphatic nod. 'Mrs Denby will want the little hussy sporting a wedding band as soon as may be.'

'What a dreadful thing for her poor mama!' The Duchess darted horrified eyes to Cecilia's profile. 'Mr Stokes caught up with the lovers in time then, you say.'

'Oh, *he* didn't save the day…it was her uncle brought her back and she behaved like a harpy all the way, so I've heard. At one point she tried to jump from his speeding carriage so he bound her hand and foot.'

'Her uncle seems the better choice to keep her in check,' Maude ventured.

'He's sunk out of sight following some trouble.'

'Bad blood the lot of them,' Patricia Finch summed up with a sniff, turning grateful eyes on her well-behaved daughter.

Louise was still single at twenty-one, having rejected the only proposal that had ever come her way when she was seventeen. At the time Patricia had been exasperated to lose a future son-in-law with so little consideration given on Louise's part. Her daughter had said she needed no time to think: the fellow wasn't right for her. As he had gone on to duel over a Covent Garden nun, then flee abroad to escape arrest, Patricia had to admit that Louise—despite her tender years—had been the wiser of the two of them on that occasion.

'Your friend is taking a special interest in the

girl, you say?' Maude glanced through the open dining-room doors. Lady Regan, an influential, veteran hostess, was settled on a sofa with her entourage around her. She didn't seem to be putting any effort into welcoming the Denby family herself.

Maude could pull rank on every female present, should she choose to, but she had not long been elevated through marriage to the peerage. She knew that there were those present who resented her good fortune and thought her an upstart. Her husband's sister was a prime example, as was Lady Regan.

'Is your friend related to the Denbys in some way?' Maude was keen to understand why a snob would lend her name to nobodies.

'I believe her ladyship's husband has asked her to be of assistance in the matter.' Dorothea raised her sparse eyebrows. 'Mr Stokes is Lord Regan's friend, I understand.' Dorothea hurried on. 'Vouchers for Almack's have been procured for Cecilia. The little hussy is luckier than she deserves to be.'

Having listened with mounting interest to the older ladies' debate Joan realised she felt rather sorry for Cecilia Denby. She was sure the strangers knew they were being gossiped about. There but for the grace of God went she. She'd acted recklessly when a similar age and Joan knew she'd no excuse, other than a hankering for an adventure, for having done so. Cecilia, on the other hand, could claim love as a purer motive for her outrageous conduct.

'Shall we say hello to them?' Joan suggested with a bright smile. On impulse she set off towards the Denbys and some hissed words of restraint told her that her stepmother and aunt were not far behind.

'I've come to introduce myself,' Joan blurted, giving a little bob and one of her hands to shake. 'I'm Lady Joan Morland.' For an awkward second it seemed her friendly overture might be rebuffed, then the older lady extended her gloved fingers.

'How nice of you to take the trouble to speak to us. We know few people here this evening. I'm Mrs Denby and this is my daughter, Cecilia.'

'Mr Stokes at your service, ladies,' the gentleman trumpeted with a stiff bow.

After the other introductions had been politely made the silence lengthened. 'There is a fine selection of dishes on the dining table,' Joan rattled off. 'Would you like to sample a few, Miss Denby?'

'I've no appetite.' Cecilia sighed.

'The lemonade is very refreshing, too.' Maude attempted to keep the conversation going. 'I should like another glass.' Her smile drooped when the gentleman present made no courteous offer to fetch it for her. She had hoped to get rid of Mr Stokes for a short while as he seemed to be a barrier to a more informal chat with the Denby women.

'It is very warm in here…might I walk with you, Lady Joan?' Cecilia flicked open her fan to cool her pink cheeks. 'I noticed you and Miss Finch were strolling in the ballroom earlier.'

Joan crooked an elbow in an affable way. 'Let's go and watch the dancing.' Her sympathy for Cecilia increased as she realised the poor thing was desperate for an excuse to escape her guardian's eagle eye.

'Your mama and I will walk on the terrace for a few minutes, then join you,' Mr Stokes announced sternly.

Cecilia gave a nod of acceptance, then the trio of young ladies set off towards the ballroom.

'Who are *they*?' Cecilia was observing, from under her lashes, the two boisterous young fellows.

'Henry Laurenson and his chum Ralph Woodley,' Joan supplied, noticing from a corner of an eye that Henry had turned to watch them as they passed by.

'I'd like it if he asked me to dance,' Cecilia whispered, slanting a subtle glance at Henry. 'He's very handsome...I wonder if he's charming, too.'

A soft-chinned, auburn-haired fop was not to Joan's taste and she could tell from Louise's comical expression that her friend wasn't smitten either. But Joan had been a flirt with Vincent and, although she'd been younger than Cecilia at the time, she could recall the heady excitement of attracting a gentleman's attention and acting in a way designed to make his eyes pursue you from place to place.

'Will your guardian object if you are asked to dance?' Joan had noticed Henry straightening his colourful waistcoat in a purposeful way.

'I don't care what *he* thinks,' Cecilia muttered,

stabbing a sour glance back over a shoulder to where her mother and Saul Stokes had been standing. But they had already stepped through the billowing curtains on to the terrace.

'And your mama?' Joan drew to a halt and gazed questioningly into the girl's blue eyes.

Cecilia shrugged. 'She'll follow his lead; she's his puppet. But I'll not jig to his tune. I'd willingly dance with *him*, though…and I think he is about to ask me.'

'Might I beg an introduction and a dance?' Henry had slipped into Cecilia's path to bow low over his extended hand.

'You may, and I would like to,' Cecilia replied and immediately slipped her gloved fingers onto his sleeve.

'Well…let's get the formalities over with first,' Joan rattled off, resisting an urge to snatch Cecilia's hand away from her admirer's arm till etiquette had been observed.

'Good, that is out of the way,' Cecilia said the moment Joan had introduced them. She gave Henry a beam and a nudge towards the dance floor.

Henry looked delighted, obviously finding engaging Miss Denby's lack of modesty.

Joan smothered her chuckle with a tiny cough as the couple went off. Cecilia's mama obviously did have a trying time controlling her daughter.

'Would you care to gavotte, Lady Joan?' Ralph enquired with a bashful grin. 'Or perhaps Miss Finch might like to partner me.'

'I'm sure she would,' Joan said with a twinkling smile for her friend. 'Alas, I must find my stepmother and fetch her a glass of lemonade that she asked for some time ago.'

Joan did go in search of the Duchess, but found that she and Mrs Finch had quit the supper room. Thinking they might have followed Cecilia's people on to the terrace, Joan headed in that direction.

Chapter Six

A refreshingly pure fragrance of jasmine and rose was wafting from the blooms trailing over trellises, welcoming Joan into the evening air. Indoors, she'd found the atmosphere heavy with cloying French scent and cigar smoke. Strolling to the balustrade, she gazed out over the darkling lawns edged by shadowy shrubbery. The perimeter of the vast garden was staked at intervals by burning torches that cast undulating shapes on to those promenading beneath a star-studded sky. But of her stepmother and Mrs Finch, or of Mr Stokes and Mrs Denby, there was no sign.

Joan pivoted on her satin slippers, settling her slender hips against the iron railings. While her friends were dancing she could go back inside and seek her papa's company…but she knew he would be with his chums, enjoying a brandy and concentrating hard on the cards in his hand. The Duke took gaming seriously. It amused Joan that he was miserly with his wagers despite his skill and stack of sovereigns. Besides, she had no desire to quit the soothing twilight yet and return to the ballroom. She felt a twinge of guilt at having abandoned her friend. She hoped Louise wouldn't mind too much; during their friendship—that had started properly in the schoolroom—they had mischievously indulged in teasing one another. The Finches and Morlands were friends of long standing. Joan's mama and Louise's mama had also known one another as children. They'd been of similar stock, but whereas one young lady had gone on to wed an aristocrat, the other had settled on a plain mister of comfortable, rather than great, means.

The difference in their husbands' status had made no difference to the two women who'd continued their friendship much as before. And Maude had settled into a similar, cosy amity with her predecessor's old friend when she became the Duke's second wife.

Feeling at a loose end, Joan descended the wide stone steps, endeavouring to keep her silk skirt from collecting dew from the lawn as she traversed it. A fountain was playing to her left and the sweet sound lured her towards it. She stripped off her lace gloves, enjoying the sensation of light spray on her warm fingers.

Mingling with the tinkling of the water was a hum of low voices. Joan was about to move away when she heard spoken aloud the name that seldom quit her mind and it rooted her to the spot. Usually Joan would have died rather than be found eavesdropping on a private conversation, but on this occasion she had no hesitation in moving quietly closer.

Taking a cautious peek about a privet hedge, she glimpsed Mr Stokes and Mrs Denby locked in an embrace. Joan sharply jerked back her head before she was spotted, but pressed an ear against the bush to catch any further mention of Rockleigh. First came the unmistakable sound of a passionate kiss interspersed with little moans from the lady. Joan's cheeks were burning, her stomach squirming in embarrassment, but still she stayed right where she was and was soon rewarded for her courage.

'We must put matters right. My brother is no

fool and his retribution will be harsh when it comes, my love,' Mrs Denby whispered.

'Rockleigh can do nothing where we are concerned,' the man scoffed. 'And if your dear brother were the paragon of wisdom you imagine him to be, Bertha, I would not have managed to so easily dupe him.'

Joan smothered her hissing intake of breath with her fist. Her quick intelligence sifted through what she'd just heard, plucking out the facts. Drew Rockleigh was Bertha Denby's brother! And Mr Stokes had somehow managed to deliberately trick him! Joan strained to hear the rest of their conversation, but the voices were growing fainter. Her uncontrollable need to discover more propelled her forward an inch. Cautiously she again peeped about the privet and was furiously disappointed to see that the lovers were strolling sedately towards the terrace.

Flabbergasted, Joan immediately questioned what she'd seen and heard. But she rejected the notion of having imagined it all and cupped her face with her palms while fiercely concentrating on the puzzle.

If Drew Rockleigh and Mrs Denby were brother

and sister, then Cecilia was his niece. *He* was the uncle who had dragged her home when she'd attempted to elope with a groom! Joan could understand now how the girl had been apprehended: Rockleigh didn't seem to be a character easily thwarted once he set out to do something.

Yet…she'd just overheard Cecilia's guardian crowing about besting him. Stokes must be a fraudster who had cruelly impoverished Rockleigh! And the victim's own sister had assisted in the plot. Joan didn't believe that Cecilia was also an accomplice. The swindlers would conceal dangerous information from such a scatterbrain.

'Joan! What are you doing alone in the dark?'

Joan nearly jumped out of her skin at the sound of her stepmother's voice. Stepping away from the fountain, she waved a hand that still quivered from the shock she'd received.

Maude daintily stepped over the lawn towards Joan, tutting all the while. 'The grass will spoil our new slippers,' she complained.

'The turf is barely wet,' Joan reassured, forcing herself to act normally although her mind refused to concentrate for long on anything other than the dialogue between Mrs Denby and her lover.

'What were you doing over there by the fountain?'

'I was…um…taking the air and looking for you to see if you still fancied a glass of lemonade,' Joan replied truthfully. She quashed the urge to immediately confide in somebody. She was privy to something dangerous and thus must think very carefully before divulging a word of it, even to those she loved and trusted. But she was certain that a dreadful crime against Rockleigh *had* been committed.

'I don't know why you imagined I'd be loitering in the shrubbery.' Maude sounded bemused. 'I was having a chat to my friend Rosalind Wentworth. Her godson is just back from his Grand Tour and will attend Almack's next week. Apparently he is seeking a wife as he has just taken his birthright. We could obtain vouchers for that day.' Maude's smile drooped when the exciting news of a rich young earl seeking a countess prompted not a single comment from her spinster stepdaughter. Joan was a vivacious beauty, but at twenty-one, she'd been out for five years and hadn't received a single proposal. Even her doting papa sometimes seemed concerned over his daughter's lack of interest in becoming a wife and mother at her age, yet he confessed to having scared off more than half-a-dozen would-be suitors when Joan first made her debut.

Distracted though she was, Joan realised conversation of sorts was required from her. 'Louise and Miss Denby were asked to dance,' she rattled off.

'And you were not?' Maude barked, sounding vexed.

She knew that her stepdaughter would sooner remain on the shelf than settle for a marriage of convenience as Maude had when accepting Alfred's proposal. Maude understood and applauded youthful idealism about romance. She, too, had wanted a love match the first time round and she had got it with her daughters' father. She knew, too, without rancour, that Alfred had dearly loved Joan's mama. But against the odds the two of them dealt well together and their mutual affection strengthened with every passing day. But Joan was not getting any younger and if she didn't hurry up she might miss out on choosing her soulmate.

'Would you have *liked* to dance?' Maude rephrased her question when Joan seemed to have gone into a dream world.

'Oh, Ralph Woodley asked me to partner him, but I let Louise have her toes squashed,' Joan answered.

'No great missed opportunity, then.' Maude smiled wryly. She knew the Woodleys and Laurensons. The heirs to those dynasties were woefully immature. Nevertheless, they were personable enough young gentlemen and had the sort of prospects that ensured their mantelshelves were stacked with invitations.

'Henry Laurenson definitely wanted Cecilia as his partner.'

'Did he, indeed?' Maude slanted an enquiring glance Joan's way. 'I wonder how her guardian will take to knowing that. Of course, considering what Dorothea has told us, if a solvent bachelor comes up to scratch the family should give thanks and immediate consent. Some might approach her without a marriage proposal on their minds though,' Maude rumbled beneath her breath.

'You think she'll be propositioned if rumours spread about her aborted elopement?'

A genteel lady usually feigned ignorance of

gentlemen's mistresses. But Joan had just heard a fellow admitting to a worse sin than attempted seduction, so she refused to act twee. Although barely ten minutes had passed since she'd listened to the lovers talking, their words had reverberated in her head a thousand times, firing her awareness of a terrible injustice having been perpetrated. Rockleigh might rub her up the wrong way, but he was fundamentally a decent man—Joan was sure of it—and she wouldn't wish his kin on her worst enemy.

'If your Aunt Dorothea knows the girl's ruined you may mark my words that many others do, too,' Maude finally responded in a doom-laden voice. Linking arms with Joan, she allowed her stepdaughter to assist her up the terrace steps.

As they entered the ballroom the first person Maude spied was Saul Stokes striding towards his ward and her dance partner. The orchestra was in recess and the couples were dispersing. Cecilia and Henry were still on the parquet chatting, and it was noteworthy, Maude thought, that Miss Denby's hands were still being held by her admirer.

'Mr Stokes could do worse than encourage Henry to call,' the Duchess whispered. 'That young man has an estate in Sussex and several thousand a year despite being barely dry behind the ears.' She returned Mrs Denby a nod as the woman looked their way.

Joan avoided clashing eyes with Rockleigh's perfidious sister, shielding with her lashes the disdain darkening her pupils. She knew she mustn't risk arousing the couple's suspicions that their treachery was out.

Louise was heading her way and Joan gave her friend an apologetic smile. 'Have you suffered bruises, my dear?'

'I have not.' Louise gave a whimsical smile. 'Mr Woodley told me he has been taking dancing lessons since last we took to the floor together. I have to say I was quite impressed.'

'Were you, indeed?' Joan's surprise was overlaid with amusement. A moment later her eyes had again narrowed on the man who'd plotted against Rockleigh.

Stokes looked very bumptious while steering his ward away from Henry as though a viscount's heir were beneath his notice. Henry seemed forlorn rather than affronted at the snub. A moment before disappearing into the crowd the object of his affections smiled over a shoulder at him.

'Come...we must find your mama and tell her that Ralph Woodley is making eyes at you.' The Duchess took Louise's arm.

'I think I shall find Papa and beg some coins to stake at the tables,' Joan excused herself.

While winding a path through the crowd she spotted the Denbys. The little group appeared as they had earlier in the evening: Cecilia's face was etched with boredom, Bertha seemed preoccupied while Stokes looked pleased with himself... as well he might, Joan thought fumingly. She felt greatly tempted to fly over to Cecilia's guardian to tell him she knew him for a crook, simply to wipe the smirk off his mouth.

But she would not—must not—mention a word of what she knew, so snapped her eyes away. Neither must she tell her father; he would have the troublemakers ejected from the party and under investigation in the morning. It was imperative she didn't succumb to the need to unburden herself. Her father was doubtless too deep into his cups now to be logical, so she'd wait till he was before relating news of such magnitude.

A burning rage filled Joan's chest when she dwelled on the trickery employed against Rockleigh. They had parted company frostily just days ago, yet her instinct was to fly to his rescue, in the way she knew he had naturally protected her from harm when the mob surrounded her coach. It was only fair that she should do what she could to help, believing as she did that one good turn deserved another. Joan also believed that devious people should get their comeuppance and it seemed from what she'd overheard emerge from their own mouths that Stokes and Bertha Denby were indeed up to their necks in deceit.

'Might I speak to you, Papa?'

'Not now, my dear; I have a raging toothache and a very sad duty in front of me in Devon.'

Joan was startled by that abrupt announcement. 'You are going to quit town for Thornley Heights?' she asked, skipping to keep up with her father as he strode along the corridor with a hand cupping his swollen jaw. She'd been loitering in the breakfast room, picking at a plate of kedgeree, hoping he might join her. Maude rarely emerged from her chamber before noon so Joan had been optimistic of having an opportunity for a private talk with her papa about the intrigue concerning Rockleigh. But rather than partaking of his breakfast Joan had heard the Duke giving instructions to the staff about carriages and teams of horses. When she'd realised she'd waited for him in vain she had rushed into the corridor to catch him before he went out.

'I'm travelling to the West Country this afternoon, my dear, and it's devilish inconvenient in the middle of the Season. Your stepmother is being understanding, though. The journey must be made.' He sighed. 'I wouldn't have it otherwise.'

'What on earth has happened?' Joan peered into her father's frowning face.

The Duke suddenly came to a halt and patted his daughter on the shoulder. 'I hoped to avoid bumping into you, coward that I am. I know you have always had a great fondness for that fine gentleman and I didn't want to see you upset. But then you must know eventually so delaying is no use at all.' Alfred ceased his rambling explanation to blurt, 'Just after dawn a messenger arrived with news that Old Matthews has passed away.

I must return and deal with the matter of his funeral. He served me, and my father before me, and I couldn't in all conscience miss seeing him being laid to rest with every honour and tribute.' Alfred grasped his daughter's hands to give them a squeeze on hearing her sorrowful gasp. 'I hope his remaining family come to the wake; I should like them to accept a token of my gratitude and esteem following their loss.'

'It is our loss, too, Papa,' Joan choked. 'You will replace him, as you must, but I fear you will not again have his equal.'

'Well said, my dear...well said, indeed.' Alfred nodded solemnly.

Joan blinked tears from her eyes. 'He has left many colleagues and friends behind who will mourn him.'

'It shouldn't come as a surprise that a man of seventy-two has gone to meet his maker, but it has,' the Duke said. 'Never would he consider retiring to an estate cottage and time and again I tried to press him to it.'

Joan gave a watery chuckle, recalling how the old fellow would insist he'd sooner keel over in the butler's pantry than be pensioned off. It seemed he had got his way.

'Do you want to come with me to Devon and attend the funeral?' the Duke asked gently, brushing wet from his daughter's cheek with a thumb. 'I'll wait while you pack a case, if you like.'

Joan shook her head, a lump blocking her throat. Distressed as she was to know of their faithful servant's passing, she'd chosen to stay in town because warning Rockleigh about his scheming kith and kin seemed more important to her. 'I know you will do a fine job of conveying our condolences, Papa, and then when we travel west in August I'll visit his resting place and lay flowers,' Joan gave a composed smile. 'He liked Michaelmas daisies, as I recall.'

Alfred gave his gruff-voiced girl a tender smile. 'Was it important, my dear?'

Joan pushed her damp handkerchief back in a pocket and frowned at her father.

'You said you wanted to speak to me,' his Grace prompted. 'Is it something to do with the Rockleigh business? I have that constantly on my mind, too.' The Duke sighed. 'But on balance I think him a good fellow. Besides, good or bad, it will all have to wait till I return.' Alfred pulled out his pocket watch and frowned at the time. 'I won't loiter in the West Country once the wake is over. I've a mind to ask Luke to shed some light on his friend's bizarre behaviour.' He looked expectantly at his daughter for her comment.

'Oh…it was nothing vital, Papa… I *was* going to speak to you about Rockleigh, but as you say, if we are to judge him on how he has treated us in the past, on balance he seems a good fellow.'

'I have a minute or two if you want to get something off your chest, my dear…' the Duke kindly offered, rubbing his aching jaw.

'There's no need for you to tarry, Papa. I shall come to my own conclusions.' Joan hadn't the heart to distract her father from his sad duty even though she was eager to have his help in calming the thoughts whirling in her head. She took a deep breath. 'You ought to have that tooth seen to before you go. It will pain you dreadfully else.'

'It does hurt like the devil.' Alfred gingerly prodded his gum. 'Perhaps I'll not wait for the sawbones to turn up. He'll not injure me any less than will a servant who pulls it. I've a mind to find Pip—he's a strong lad—and fetch a pair of pliers from the stables.' Alfred purposefully re-traced his steps towards the servants' quarters.

'Be careful with the pliers, Papa!' Joan called after her father. 'And get Mrs Lewis to prepare you a healing poultice to use on the wound.' Knowing that her father would probably forget to send for the housekeeper, Joan went herself in search of the woman to give instructions for the poultice to be prepared and given to her father before he left for Devon.

Once Mrs Lewis had given her stout assurance that she wouldn't allow his Grace aboard the carriage until he'd packed the medicinal wadding against his gum, Joan felt able to return to her room and to the other problem that constantly occupied her.

Perched on her comfy feather mattress, she found the letter from Fiona that Maude had brought home from Kent. She reread it, smiling at her sister's humorous observations about the trials of bearing and rearing children. Folding the parchment, Joan carefully replaced it in a drawer. Her sister and brother-in-law would be sad to have the news about Old Matthews. The couple would also be shocked and upset to learn that

Drew Rockleigh had apparently been betrayed by his family.

Once he knew about it Luke would surely want to assist his friend, despite their recent differences. Joan pondered on whether to contact her brother-in-law asking for advice, much in the way her father had recently mentioned doing. According to Maude, Luke had turned prickly towards Drew so might not respond as quickly as Joan wanted; patience was not a virtue she had mastered.

Springing off the edge of the bed, Joan prowled to and fro before settling down on the dressing-table stool. Resting her elbows on polished yew, she cupped her sharp little chin in her palms and stared at her reflection. For some minutes she sat quite still, searching for the required courage in the clear grey depths of her large eyes.

She knew she must not directly approach Drew Rockleigh; she had learned at least one lesson from her past mistakes. She had tempted fate before, avoiding danger and ostracism only because he had protected her and brought her discreetly home from that jaunt. She would not trifle with her family's illustrious name a second time. Settling back on the stool, she worked a comb through the glossy tumble of chestnut curls that caped her shoulders. A tiny smile heralded a burgeoning idea. She put down the tortoiseshell and got up.

If she were to use her father's method and use a go-between to make contact with Rockleigh, then she could meet him discreetly and tell him what she'd overheard. The idea that if she did nothing and allowed the plotters to scheme further against him, worsening his situation, was anathema to Joan. She found it hard to accept that the distinguished handsome gentleman who had danced with her at her stepsister's wedding breakfast was now reduced to fighting for a living. She'd seen the marks on his face and hands…seen blood smeared on his body…and the idea of any innocent victim suffering physical pain stabbed at her heart. She couldn't sit back and perhaps leave it too late to nip in the bud a plot still in its infancy. His sister had seemed worried that Drew might uncover their deceit…well, Joan wanted to make absolute sure that he did! And that he had a fighting chance of pulling things to right before it was too late!

Thadeus Pryke! Joan pounced on the name of

the fellow her father had said he'd engaged to deliver his letter. It surely could not be that difficult to find out where Pryke had his detective agency and arrange a discreet meeting to take place.

Chapter Seven

'What is it this time?'

'I've another missive for you, sir.' Thadeus Pryke held out the parchment with sly obsequiousness, having discerned irritation in the Squire's voice. The little blonde who'd been waiting by the Cock and Hen the last time he'd met the Squire was again hovering close by. She was a pretty wench and lured Thadeus's eyes.

Drew gave the girl a few coins, dug from a pocket, and an order for some food to be purchased from the inn. Constance flounced off towards the hostelry and Rockleigh handed back the unmarked letter, having given it barely a glance. 'You may relay to his Grace that my reply is as before and there's no need for further correspondence.'

The Squire's attitude caused Pryke to blink in

astonishment. For a down-and-out to reject the patronage of a worthy such as his Grace the Duke of Thornley was madness in Thadeus's opinion. He ruminated on whether Rockleigh might be more amenable to a tête-à-tête on learning that no portly aristocrat awaited him on this occasion. Miss Morley, as his client had introduced herself, was not as attractive to Pryke as the gaudy jade who'd disappeared into the tavern, but she was comely enough. Buttoned-up spinsters were not to his taste, nor did he imagine them to be to the Squire's.

'Is there something else?' Drew hesitated in joining Constance when he noticed the smug-faced detective loitering.

'I'm not here on the Duke's account, sir.' Thadeus cleared his throat and inclined closer. 'My client is a lady; I must respect her wish not to name her, but do as she bade and give you this.' He ceased hissing in the recipient's ear and rammed the parchment against Drew's open shirtfront.

Within seconds of breaking the sealing wax an oath exploded between Drew's teeth. He snapped hawkish eyes to Pryke's face. 'You've not brought her here?' He glanced over the man's shoulder as though to locate a stationary carriage.

'I know better than that with female clients.' Thadeus looked and sounded affronted. 'Cheapside…that's where I instructed the hackney to wait.'

'Who's with her?' Drew barked. 'Don't tell me you've left her there alone in a public conveyance!' He cursed fluidly on seeing the man's guilty floridity.

'The driver will watch out for Miss Morley's safety,' Pryke spluttered, neglectful of his rule to shield the lady's identity. 'She is used to the hazards of travelling without a maid, being of straitened circumstances, I would say.'

'Would you?' Drew purred, turning such a ferociously sardonic stare on the investigator that the fellow visibly wilted.

Thadeus rubbed a hand about his mouth, regretting having accepted this job. He didn't want the prize fighter landing him a facer and the Squire looked angry enough to do it. From that he deduced that Miss Morley must be of considerable importance to him. Warily Thadeus took a step back, positioning himself outside the reach of a dangerous-looking sinewed forearm that had a cambric sleeve scrunched back to its bronzed elbow.

Miss Morley had turned up at his office without a companion of any sort. From her deportment Pryke had guessed she was genteel. From her plain attire and the nature of her request he'd also surmised her to be no better than she should be. No decent woman would be seeking out a fellow such as the Squire. Pryke had immediately glanced at the chit's belly to ascertain whether the urgent nature of her business with Mr Rockleigh was growing by the day.

'Take me to her...now!' Drew snarled. With Pryke leading the way the men set off. When the puffing detective could no longer set the pace, Drew loped ahead, barking questions over a shoulder to get accurate directions.

At regular intervals Joan had been lifting the leather blind at the window of the hackney cab to peer into the gloom. Although in reality it was probably no more than three-quarters of an hour since Pryke started off towards Wapping it seemed to her that she'd been waiting an age for the fellow to reappear. She hoped he'd return with Rockleigh: she wanted to explain everything face to face rather than commit to paper the bizarre tale of how she'd come to suspect people close to him had plotted his downfall.

She fidgeted against the squabs, nervousness putting cramps in her belly. She realised that there was no certainty that Rockleigh was in the locality this evening, or that he would agree to a rendezvous. He had refused her father's invitation to meet…yet female intuition persuaded Joan that if he received her summons he *would* come, and quickly.

On his perch atop the hackney sat the jarvey and Joan could hear him grunting a tuneless song beneath his breath, interspersed with some whistling. The horse was restless, probably ready for his hay, Joan thought pityingly. Again she peeped out of the window, but no sign yet of the detective's dumpy figure approaching on the deserted street. Or of a tall athletic figure purposefully striding along.

The night sky was heavy with stormy nimbus, bringing dusk descending early. Apart from the lamplighter Joan had seen nobody…and that was a blessing, she realised, remembering the ruffians who'd terrorised her the last time she was this way. Dropping the leather into place, she sat back and sighed, feeling uncomfortably warm and moist from the humidity in the atmosphere. Undoing her bonnet, she discarded the straw on to the seat beside her, then slid her fingers through damp tendrils of hair on her brow. Her light cloak also felt cumbersome and she shrugged it from her shoulders before stripping off her cotton gloves to air her palms. She'd dressed modestly so as not to arouse suspicion about her true identity. She'd concealed from Pryke that she was the Duke of Thornley's daughter. The investigator would charge her an extortionate amount if he knew she was titled and she only had her allowance with which to pay him. But the main reason for her subterfuge concerned her fear of disgracing her family. Never again must she risk doing that!

Now her father was en route to Devon, Joan had decided no good would come of advising him of what she'd done after the event. There was a slim chance she'd misconstrued what she'd overheard and was about to make a fool of herself. Oddly she hoped that was the case. Sooner that, she realised, than discover Rockleigh had been easily hoodwinked by the likes of smarmy Stokes.

Joan darted her eyes to the horizon as a shimmer of lightning silvered the slate-grey clouds. She knew that she wanted to be home in her bed before the worst of the weather set in. It seemed the jarvey did, too, for his singing had stopped and Joan could hear him blaspheming at the delay. He began grumbling to the whinnying horse. Peg, as he called her, had resumed stamping and snorting, making the carriage rock.

As far as Maude was aware Joan had missed supper and retired early to nurse a migraine. Her stepdaughter had then slipped out through a side door at twilight dressed in plain dark clothes, walking swiftly away from Upper Brook Street. When sure she would not be spotted Joan had hailed a hackney to take her to Mr Pryke's office. If her stepmother remained untroubled by her absence the deceit would not be too bad a sin in Joan's eyes. She knew her conscience would suffer, but she deemed the lie a small price to pay to achieve what she had set out to do. Neither had she told her maid about her clandestine trip. Anna would have insisted in accompanying her and Joan knew that the meeting between herself and Rockleigh must remain completely confidential. Anna, though younger than herself by a year, was a mature character and would be determined to protect her mistress. Although Anna was fairly new to the household the two of them had got on well from the start. Pip and Anna had also struck up an immediate friendship that had blossomed. Joan knew that some below stairs gossiped about the sweethearts, believing a lady's maid should look higher for a mate. Joan wished the couple well, understanding that for some people only fate and their hearts could determine with whom they fell in love.

With a sigh Joan again scoured the gloomy, empty streets. If the detective didn't return in the next minute or two, she'd instruct the jarvey to get going. Mr Pryke would have to make his own way back to his abode.

Earlier that day Pryke had conquered his surprise at hearing her request and given her an insolent inspection. Arrangements had been made for her to return to his office that evening. On arrival Joan had been pleased to see that he had a carriage ready and waiting for the trip. She was relieved, too, when he'd observed etiquette and hauled himself up to sit beside the driver. She'd not wanted his shifty eyes constantly on her, or the obligation to find conversation in case an unbearable silence built between them…

'What in damnation do you think you're doing?'

Joan almost jumped out of her skin as Rockleigh leapt into the hackney, rudely curtailing her reflection. Slamming the door behind him, he plunged on to the seat opposite.

'I thought I warned you to stay away from me, my lady,' he growled, a dangerous glitter in his tigerish eyes as they tore over her petite form.

Joan jerked herself upright, annoyed to have instinctively cowered from him. She was vexed, too, that he had jumped down her throat when she'd put herself to some trouble on his account. 'You may show me a little more courtesy, if you please, sir! I'm here to do you a favour!' she snapped.

'Are you, indeed?' he queried softly. His hands slid on muscled thighs to his knees as he inclined closer. 'Let me know what it is then; if it's to my liking, perhaps I'll not return you to your father so speedily this time.' Drew's voice was as subtly amused as his half-smile.

Joan felt the colour rising in her cheeks as his hooded gaze flowed more leisurely over her buttoned bodice. 'To return me to my father on this occasion would take more time and money than I'll warrant you're prepared to spend,' she returned acidly.

'You think I can't afford your company?'

'I know you can't,' Joan retorted hoarsely, avoiding a pair of preying eyes that now challenged rather than laughed at her. 'The cost of travelling to Devon is considerable.'

'His Grace is at Thornley Heights, is he? And you thought in his absence you'd masquerade as Miss Morley and come to do me a favour.'

'The Duke has been called away due to a bereavement. Had he not, he would have come here in my stead,' Joan said firmly, hoping it was the truth. She could not be certain that, having heard the tale, her father *would* have sought another meeting with Rockleigh. But without doubt the Duke would abhor the idea of criminals bankrupting a person who'd in the past proved to be his friend.

Instinctively Joan touched her cheek as her blush deepened. The wretch thought she had a fancy for him…which she did not, she impressed upon herself. Her fingers were returned to her lap and calmly clasped together. 'If your conceit is leading you to think my interest in you is personal you are utterly mistaken.' She turned to fully face him. 'You have done us good turns in the past, Mr Rockleigh, and refused payment for it. Thus I thought it only fair to help you now that an opportunity has arisen.'

Drew rested his powerful shoulders against the squabs. As though becoming aware that he was partially unclothed he slowly began doing up the shirt buttons open from tanned midriff to throat. When that was accomplished he rolled down his sleeves with slow deliberation. For an odd reason that small act of good manners made Joan's heart tip over.

'Your father would never have agreed to you journeying alone after dusk and if he finds out about it I imagine you'll taste the back of his hand.'

'He wouldn't hit me,' Joan said hoarsely.

She knew that they both remembered the time when her father would have done so but for the man lounging opposite preventing the Duke's open palm stinging her cheek. Never before and never since had her papa raised his hand to her. In the interim she had behaved as she ought. But now Drew Rockleigh had once more been reluctantly embroiled in one of her escapades and her father would be livid if he found out about it.

'Neither do I believe that the Duke of Thornley would send his daughter to act for him.' Drew crossed his arms over his shirt ruffles. 'I think he's ignorant of this opportunity you've found to be charitable, my lady.'

Joan pursed her lips, exasperated by his attitude. It seemed to her that he wanted to throw back in her face any assistance before knowing what it was! 'If I have inconvenienced, or embarrassed, you by offering to alleviate your awful predicament, then just go away again!' Joan flicked an imperious hand at the door. 'I'd as soon return home before travelling becomes hazardous.' An ominous rumble of thunder endorsed her fear that the storm was rolling closer.

'What awful predicament am I in, Joan?' Drew's tone still hinted at mockery, but it was gentle now and the finger that traced fire on the back of her hand was feather light…less a caress and more a way of gaining her attention.

Slowly, Joan withdrew from his reach, but the sensual tingle on her skin remained.

'I know you've had rotten luck,' she blurted. 'My father told me that business turned bad for you, but perhaps there's a reason behind it that you know nothing about.' She waited for his comment, but the quiet continued and his expression gave nothing away. 'I attended the Wentworths' ball a few days ago and while there met two ladies I believe to be your relatives.' A flicker of emotion crossed his features, but thick black lashes soon shuttered his eyes. 'Have you a comment to make?' Joan prompted.

'What do you want me to say? That I'm sorry you had to breathe the same air as my kin?'

'Of course not!' Joan tutted. 'A Mr Stokes was accompanying them.' She'd gained a reaction the moment she'd mentioned Cecilia's guardian; Drew leaned closer, again, propping his elbows on his knees. His steady stare was hypnotic, entrapping Joan's eyes while he quietly brooded on what she'd said.

'I gather you've somehow worked out for yourself I'm related to these people rather than having had it confirmed.' His neutral statement broke the spell.

Joan nodded vigorously, feeling she was making progress in solving the puzzle. The crux of the matter was approaching so she shifted nearer to him. 'There was some talk about a Miss Denby and her mother. I went to say hello as they were all alone in the supper room.' She paused, wondering how to phrase that *the talk* about his niece could escalate into trouble for Cecilia. 'Lady Regan and my aunt are friends and during the evening it came out that her ladyship is assisting Miss Denby's rehabilitation following…an unfortunate episode.'

A cynical smile acknowledged her diplomatic reference to Cecilia's aborted elopement. She needed no further proof that the Denbys were his kin. 'Later, I was walking in the garden,' she rattled off. 'I overheard a conversation between Mrs Denby and Mr Stokes.' A rush of blood stung her cheeks at the memory of being privy to their passionate encounter.

'You were eavesdropping on my sister and her lover?' Drew suggested drily.

'I...I was not!' Joan stammered out the fib. She had purposely strained to hear every syllable uttered by the couple. 'Well...I did, actually,' she admitted sheepishly. 'And you should be glad of that!' She sent him a frown. 'I heard your sister mention you. Then Mr Stokes started talking and it became apparent why you have been reduced to earning a living the way you do.' Joan's expression turned wary. She was unsure how he'd react to knowing she'd discovered things about him that he might prefer remained hidden.

'They were stupidly discussing a fraud out in the open, were they?' Drew sounded contemptuous rather than embarrassed.

Joan's soft pink lips parted in surprise. 'You *knew* about their scheming?'

He sent her a smile that was as good as an affirmative.

'They think you do not!' Joan exclaimed, scouring her memory for the words she'd overheard. 'Mr Stokes said... "If your dear brother were the paragon of wisdom you imagine him to be, Bertha, I would not have managed to so easily dupe him."' Having parroted the villain's boast, Joan sat back, waiting for Drew's reaction.

'Well…paragon of wisdom…is overdoing it a bit,' he said. 'But I'll take the praise, even from her.'

'You think it a joke?' Joan demanded, exasperated by his attitude. She looked him over: tall, handsome, a fine figure of a man despite his lowly status. But most people who had known his luxurious life would be devastated to fall so far. 'Do you not care that they have ruined you?' she demanded. She had anticipated him thanking her for alerting him to such treachery.

'What I care about is that you should remain unharmed by this,' he countered sternly. 'Did they spot you close by?'

Joan shook her head vigorously, setting her glossy curls swaying. 'They were too wrapped up in each other and I made sure to keep out of sight.'

'You must never speak of this to anybody but me. Do you understand?'

'Of course, I wouldn't tell a soul, other than my papa,' Joan replied. On seeing his expression darken, she added quickly, 'You can trust him. He will help you, I'm sure. And Luke is bound to want to offer assistance, too…'

Drew leaned forward, gripping her hands and jerking her closer to him. 'You tell nobody, Joan. Please forget all about this. As I've said I wish you'd never heard those two talking about me.'

'Well, I'm glad I did! I'm not bothered about them,' Joan stoutly declared, wrenching herself from his restraint. 'I'm used to being in the midst of criminals. I'm from the West Country, as you know, and the smuggling gang that used to infest the coast were always making trouble. Papa and I strove to get the ringleader punished and eventually he was arrested.' She gazed earnestly into Drew's shadowy hazel eyes. 'When I turned up at your hunting lodge, unannounced, I was urgently seeking Luke Wolfson's assistance against those murderous rogues.'

'Yes…I discovered that later,' Drew said ruefully. 'If you'd have told me at the time, I'd have offered my help in his absence.'

'I couldn't…I didn't know you then, I was unsure whether to trust you…'

'And now?'

Joan nibbled her lower lip, drawing a sardonic smile from him as her silence continued.

'I'm not sure whether I can trust you either, my lady.'

'I think you know you can!' Joan returned indignantly. 'If I didn't honestly want to help you, I wouldn't have come, would I?'

'No, you would not,' Drew gently said, offering an olive branch. 'And I'm grateful to you, but you should not have come here.'

'But can't you see I'm a boon to you? I'm already practised at bringing villains to justice. My father will tell you how we outwitted the smugglers. Mostly it was Papa's doing, but I had hand in it, too.' Her breathless boast made him smile wryly and Joan tingled with self-consciousness. After a moment's concentration Joan demanded, 'The man I saw you with in the park…is he involved in this mystery, too?'

'In a way he is…but he's assisting me in another matter, too.' Drew sat back, rubbing a hand about his unshaven jaw. 'I want you to forget about all of this, Joan. It's kind of you to offer to help, but I have things in hand; there's no need for you or your family to worry on my account—'

'I think you should set the authorities on to the crooks,' Joan interrupted. She slid forward on the seat, tempted to shake him by the shoulders in her zeal to prod him into action. 'How *can* they ever rectify making you suffer like this?'

A corner of Drew's lips tilted and, taking her hands, his thumbs caressed over soft skin. 'You've risked a lot to come and tell me about this, and I'm grateful,' he said gently as though praising a child. 'But I meant what I said; you must forget about it.'

'You *will* get them arrested?' Unconsciously, Joan squeezed his long fingers in an attempt to hurry his decision.

'In due course they'll get their comeuppance…'

'I'd like a better response than that!'

'Such as?' A single long finger turned her chin back towards him when she averted her eyes. 'Forget about them,' he commanded huskily. 'Dwell on us…'

Joan flicked moisture to her lips with her tongue-tip and immediately his eyes devoured her innocent enticement.

'I…I thought you'd be fired with resentment and vengefulness when I told you about it.' She gestured impatiently and with a jerk liberated her chin. When he ruefully lowered his face to his clasped hands, Joan's niggling ire increased. It seemed her daring and her cash had been squandered after all. She'd engaged a detective so she might warn him and had had her assistance rejected. 'You enjoy being a pauper, do you?' she taunted. 'Will you carry on fighting in a boxing ring because Stokes has beaten you? Perhaps in time you'll find the nerve to confront him over it.'

'You don't know anything about it…and now I think it's time you went home.' Drew rammed his back against the seat, regarding her steadily from between close ebony lashes.

'I *will* go home, Mr Rockleigh, not because you say so, but because I'll waste no more time on a coward. You may stew in your own juice!' She glared at him, waiting for him to get out. When he didn't she nodded at the door to hurry him.

The only movement he made was to rap on the roof to set the vehicle in motion.

'What are you doing?' Joan demanded, contradicting his order with a hefty bang of her own. It had the desired effect and the hackney shuddered to a standstill. 'You may get out and let Mr Pryke get in.'

'I'll take you back to Mayfair.'

'I shall return in the same company as that in which I arrived.'

'Pryke's been dismissed from duty.'

'By whom?'

'By me.' Drew signalled with a fist for the carriage to set off.

Joan called out this time for the jarvey to rein Peg in. Her storm-grey eyes clashed on a lazy stare. 'There is no need for you to accompany me and I'd greatly prefer that you did not. There is a risk we might be spotted together and stir up trouble.'

'I think that particular horse bolted two years ago, my dear.'

'Two years ago you were a gentleman and it would not have been quite so dire had it got out that you'd compromised me.'

'That's not how you saw it at the time.' Drew's eyes swerved to the window as lightning flared behind the blind. 'As I recall, you considered it a calamity and said you'd take vows rather than wed me.'

'Now you have turned into a ruffian that convent seems yet more appealing. So take yourself off.' Joan whipped her face from his silent laughter. This time when he knocked for the hackney to set off she did not counteract his command simply because she knew he wanted her to. 'My brother-in-law would be disgusted to know his friend is too craven to exact retribution from the crooks who've swindled him.'

'Luke would also be upset that you've been slum visiting.'

'Under the vicar's protection and for a good cause,' Joan parried.

'The vicar's protection proved not much use as I recall. Now that your father has forbidden you teaching the children, am I your new charity case, my lady?'

'No, you are not! Those youngsters were far more deserving than you. Had I known what an ungrateful wretch you are I'd not have wasted a second of my time on you.'

'Now you do know there's no reason for you to ever return here, is there?'

'Nor shall I!' Joan flared, her fingers clenching in her lap.

The longer he sat in silence, simply gazing at her with a ghost of a smile moulding his narrow mouth, the more incensed Joan felt. But there was constrained levity in her tone when she next spoke. 'If we had been forced into that arranged marriage, my father's name would have protected you from such clever felony as Stokes has perpetrated. Oh, dear...' she sighed '...how you must be rueing not taking me when you had the chance.'

'Oh...I regret that,' he drawled silkily. 'But as for marrying you...' He waited till she turned an affronted expression on him, then slowly shook his head.

Joan clenched her fingers at the insult, but she managed an insouciant little shrug. 'It is all over and done with and now of little interest.'

'You brought the subject up.'

'Perhaps, but I'll hear no more of your degradation now I understand that you enjoy living like a heathen.'

'Again...you brought it up, my lady.' His hands were spread in mock appeal.

A temptation to lunge forward and slap him bedevilled Joan. She was certain he was acting indolent simply to rile her. 'Why do you not go and join your new friends in the slums? I really cannot abide your company a moment longer.' She leapt up, about to hammer on the roof for the hackney to halt, but her raised arm was gripped and she was jerked forward, falling against him.

'And why do you not give that busy tongue of yours a rest...or better still...tell me honestly why you came to find me?' Drew kept her struggling form pinned to his torso. 'You'd risk your father's wrath and all manner of opprobrium, would you, simply to warn a heathen of a plot against him?'

'Yes!' With her puny fists Joan battered a chest that felt like granite, trying to squirm away, but he suddenly shifted sideways on the seat and brought her down on her back beside him.

Drew braced an arm over her so she was trapped against the upholstery. Slowly his face descended and, mesmerised, Joan watched his mouth until it blurred out of focus. But he didn't kiss her; his lips skimmed her hot cheek, the faintest tickle of bristle scouring her skin.

'Do you know what I think, my lady?' he murmured against her small sensitive earlobe. 'I think my conceit is making me believe your interest in me *is* personal. I think you're as eager to taste me as I am to have you.'

'I'm not...' Joan gasped. 'You're wrong...'

But she lay still, barely breathing, racked with

terrible excitement as an artful touch of his mouth made her shiver. She felt his lips brush her throat as they curved in a smile, acknowledging her acquiescence. Her eyes closed as he nuzzled her warm flesh and his fingers started to work their magic against her hip and belly, smoothing and stroking till her back was arching against the seat.

Joan's lips parted on a moan and she turned her head, seeking him, but still he didn't kiss her and eventually her lids fluttered up, her storm-grey gaze merging with his feral eyes.

He lowered his head, waiting till she ceded and rose to meet him, placing her lips on his.

He worked her mouth in a slow narcotic rhythm that was so enervating to Joan that she sank, sighing, back to the seat, unable to resist allowing him any liberty. His hands moved to her bodice, unbuttoning slowly, tormenting her with the opportunity to stop him before he'd untied her chemise to expose plump creamy breasts.

'Hold your clothes open for me,' he said softly but with intractable authority.

She did as she was told, pulling back the edges of linen so his two hands could rove and caress her flesh before shaping it to receive his mouth.

He suckled hard and fast, drawing a squeal of mingling pain and pleasure from Joan that caused him to soothingly circle the tight little nubs with his tongue.

'Hush, my lady,' he murmured, smothering her whimpers with his wooing mouth. 'Come...quietly now...or I'll have to stop...'

In wordless answer to that threat, Joan shook her head and wound her arms about his neck, keeping him close. Every skilful slide of his lips made her heart race faster and there was an unbearable heat in her veins that only his caressing fingers could cool. The next time his tongue probed her mouth she met it with a touch of her own.

'What next for you?' he whispered roughly. 'Come...your heathen is here to oblige you, my lady, show me what you like...what you want...'

Joan could not answer, but her hands fluttered to her chemise, peeling apart the gossamer lawn once more so swollen rose-tipped breasts were naked beneath his blazing gaze.

A soft grunt of praise rewarded her obedience, then she shuddered in ecstasy as his long firm fingers curved over the sensitive flesh, massaging in light orbits till her back bowed and her shoulders supported her. His mouth swooped and this time two of his fingers stopped her squeal, plunging and retreating fractionally between her lips till her gasps faded and her tongue welcomed those two strong digits and their gently erotic dance.

Joan felt her knees being parted, felt a rush of blissfully tepid air bathing her feverish nether regions as he shoved up her skirts and caressed her thighs. His fingers trailed onwards into the tight little curls beneath her drawers and a jolt of sensation hit Joan as he edged a fingertip into her, then withdrew to smooth the pulsating tip of her womanhood with dew.

And then he stopped.

Chapter Eight

Abrupt incandescence had brightened the interior of the coach for a second and been followed by an almighty thunderclap. Rain began battering the roof, but it was the cruelty of losing him that penetrated Joan's sensual daze. Then seemingly from a distance she discerned Peg's frightened whinnying over the elemental din.

Drew had leapt to his feet a mere moment before the carriage began juddering to and fro. With fast, impersonal efficiency he straightened Joan's attire, then put her upright. As the vehicle again swerved crazily she huddled into the corner of the seat.

'Stay there!' Drew barked, pointing a commanding finger at her as though anticipating she might also leap from the swaying contraption. A moment later he'd forced open the door against the gale and disappeared into the howling night.

The hackney came to a stop so sharply that Joan had to cling to the door handle to keep seated. Seconds later she'd poked her head out of the window, blinking against streaming rain to see what was happening. Drew was holding Peg's bridle and soothing the terrified mare as she fought to liberate herself. The jarvey was agitatedly yanking at a splintered wheel, water tipping from the brim of his hat.

With a groan of dismay Joan sank back against the squabs, forking ten fingers into her hair. 'Oh, what have I done?' she cried into her forearms, eyes screwed shut. Her mortifying wantonness was blocking out even the immediate danger of Peg bolting. Suddenly her duty to her family was at the forefront of her mind. She had yet to make a safe return home and to slip upstairs without being spotted. Or had she been missed and the mayhem already started? Joan prayed that the storm hadn't woken her stepmother. If Maude had sought her company during the bangs and crashes only to find her bed empty, the woman would by now be in hysterics.

Joan had left the house when the threatening tempest had been merely a purplish cliff on the horizon. She'd dismissed the risk as minor...and compared to the self-inflicted ache of shame that throbbed beneath her breastbone, it had been.

But strangely, though her cheeks blazed at the memory of what they'd done, Joan didn't regret having come to meet him to tell him he'd been tricked. She would do it again. But never again would she allow...no, encourage...him to seduce her.

She must insist he quit the coach and allow her to travel alone the remainder of the way home. Abruptly it struck Joan that poor Peg might be too skittish to be of further use. If so, she'd have no option but to alight and find another cab and not many would be for hire in such frightful conditions. Her frantic planning was interrupted as the door was jerked open and slanting precipitation spattered the interior of the cab.

'Put on your cloak and hat and we'll shelter in the inn across the road.' Drew beckoned urgently, keeping his face lowered to shield it from the downpour.

Joan had no intention of entering such a place

with him, but she did quickly don her outer things, tying her bonnet strings with quivering fingers. 'I shall shelter here, thank you, till the worst blows over!' she replied stiltedly, turning her back on him.

'The jarvey wants you to get out.' Drew swiped a hand over his rain-fogged vision. 'The mare is highly strung and has taken fright before. The dimwit should never have brought her out on such a night. He's unharnessing her.'

Joan groaned in consternation on learning that; the flapping blind and the tattoo on the roof were proof that the foul weather was far from finished. Another enormous roll of thunder made her shrink back into the furthest corner of the cab. But frightened as she was, she now had full possession of her wits. She'd sooner take her chances waiting out the storm in the lurching vehicle than be bedded on a tavern mattress.

Perhaps he'd imagine she'd see it as the height of gallantry if he purchased a chamber in which to finish what he'd started on a hackney's cramped seat. A mingling of thrill and dread raced through her; they both knew he had the power to conquer her morals and upbringing and make her beg him to touch her again once they were alone. Joan noticed that he was holding out a hand to help her alight. Spontaneously she slapped it away with all the strength she could muster.

With an oath Drew reached in, grabbing her elbow. He tugged her resisting form towards him just as the nervous mare leapt forward, causing the coach to rotate on screeching wheels.

Joan tumbled out of the carriage against Drew, momentarily clinging to him. When she strove to be free of him he didn't immediately let her go. His hand smoothed her wet cheek in a show of reassurance that she sensed was prompted by the peril he presented rather than that Peg was wreaking.

'Go and wait in that doorway,' he yelled over the screaming wind. When she looked mutinous he spun her about and gave her shoulder a little push.

Joan hared across the road, hopping over fast-flowing rivulets on the cobbles that would soak her shoes. She got under cover, then swung about, squinting through damp lashes at the two men working together. The jarvey was holding on to the mare's harness while Drew uncoupled the horse and vehicle. With a fascination she didn't understand she watched the muscles in his shoulders and arms moulding a shirt made transparent by the downpour. When the job was done Drew violently shook water from his head while all around him rain bounced and bubbled in the puddles.

The night had grown chilly and Joan wrapped her arms about her soaked form to keep warm while she waited for…she knew not what. But she guessed trouble was afoot and she felt unbearably guilty at the prospect of wounding her father when this catastrophe broke. But she wouldn't cry. She had landed herself in this terrible mess and somehow she must pick herself out of it.

The shadows in her little hidey-hole suddenly darkened. Joan glanced up to see Drew had joined her. He stood in the entrance, blocking her view of the street and everything else. At that moment she was only aware of him, looming over her, and of her racing heartbeat. She blinked, staring at rugged slippery features, his long fair hair swarthy with water. But it was the sight of his shirt stuck fast to the rocky contours of his torso that wedged her breath in her throat. Just minutes ago that solid expanse of chest had been warmth beneath her fingers.

'Is…is the mare under control?' she stammered the first thing that came to mind.

He smiled, a sarcastic tilting of his lips, and she knew he wasn't just thinking of the four-legged creature he'd tamed.

'I hope so…' He glanced over a shoulder. 'Her master's led her into the inn's courtyard. If he can stable her there for a while she'll calm down.'

'Good…' Joan said huskily.

'Come inside the tavern; you can't stay here.'

He held out a hand to her but she ignored it and shook her head. 'I must get home. My stepmother will be frantic with worry and raise the roof on finding me gone.'

'And your father will have my hide if he finds out I've left you sheltering from a storm in a shop doorway.'

'He's a better reason to kill you than that!' She felt hot and bothered to have flung that at him. It had been no ruthless ravishment…he'd asked her to join in the erotic game and she'd willingly done so.

'I'm sorry…I shouldn't have touched you. Trust

me…there's no need to be frightened. I'll get you home unharmed.'

It was a softly spoken apology, yet she'd heard it above the clamour of the storm. He sounded sincere, Joan thought. But she knew better than to risk worsening this fool's errand she'd embarked on. 'You needn't humour me!' she snapped, indignant that he could treat her as though she were a child when a short time ago he'd desired her… touched her…as a woman. They both knew he'd nothing to apologise for. She could have told him to stop. But he'd been the one to call a halt when her moans became too loud. Still she'd imprisoned him with her arms, urging him to carry on.

'Be sensible, my lady, you'll catch your death if you stay outside,' Drew muttered in exasperation when she backed off from his outstretched hand. 'If you insist on staying here, I should keep you warm. You're shivering.'

Without warning he embraced her, briskly and roughly rubbing his hands along her back to chafe her. To object to such impersonal handling seemed superfluous and as Joan felt her sluggish blood prickling into life she realised she had indeed got colder than was wise. Then the ministration changed…his hands coaxed rather than nursed and, despite every good intention not to succumb, Joan felt her flesh begin to yield and move against his palms.

'Don't…don't you dare…' she whispered, plea hoarsening the words. Still she couldn't prevent her hips swaying forward as his fingers spread at the base of her spine.

'Come inside the tavern and have a hot drink,' Drew said harshly, stepping away. 'I'll find transport as soon as it quietens down.'

'I'm not entering that place, but you may fetch me a hot toddy, if you will. And I'd be obliged if you'd purchase me a ride of any sort. Please tell the innkeeper to do what he can to provide a gig and driver. A stable lad will do and I'll pay handsomely for his trouble and yours.' Pulling coins from a pocket, she held them out to him.

Drew looked at the money, then at her. His devilish eyes never quit her face as he said, 'Thank you, my lady, but I'm at your service in every respect…no payment required.'

Joan crouched down, lowering her chin to her knees and hugging herself to keep the warmth he'd rubbed into her cold bones. His expression had been hard with mockery, but he was angry, too, that she'd treated him like a hireling.

She heard his suffocated curse as he turned away, but didn't look up till she heard fast footfalls splashing away over the cobbles.

From beneath a fringe of damp lashes Joan watched him sprint across the tavern courtyard and disappear before she uncurled and stood up. Hurrying to the front of the porch, she darted searching looks to and fro. The rain had eased and the lightning had retreated to the edges of the heavens. She took a deep breath; Drew Rockleigh hadn't finished with her yet, of that she was sure. But she had most definitely ceded the fight. She had set out intending to befriend him and instead had got a tiger by the tail.

On impulse she hoisted her drenched skirts and ran in a westerly direction over the glistening cobbles. Many street lamps had extinguished beneath the wind's battering; only intermittently did she spy candles peeping between the edges of curtains at cottage windows. As she turned a gloomy corner she hunched against a stone wall, breathing heavily because a stitch was needling beneath her ribs. She heard a vehicle, glimpsing an approaching hackney whose driver had been brave enough to venture out. With a surge of hope she waved, forcing her weary legs onwards, but it passed her by, its passenger glaring at her.

She knew that a lone woman out at night would attract no good attention. A milk cart, churns clanging on the back as it negotiated a rut, trundled to a crossroad and Joan flew forward to beg a lift as it seemed to be heading her way.

Then the sound of galloping hooves caused her to hesitate and spin about. A horse came into view...

Suddenly Joan whipped frantic glances to and fro, searching for a hiding place. Spying an alleyway, she sped into it, having realised who the rider might be. She waited, her heart in her mouth, wondering if he'd seen her fleeing figure.

He had! The animal was being reined in to a walk, its clopping hooves ringing on stone. Deep in the crevasse between two high walls Joan pressed her back to gritty brick. Straining her ears, she heard the unmistakable sound of leather creaking as a rider dismounted.

'I'm tiring of this particular game, my lady.'

'Than why do you not leave me alone and go

away?' A distant lightning bolt outlined his silhouette at the mouth of the lane.

'Because I know you don't want me to.'

'You are the most arrogant and conceited wretch alive.'

'Perhaps…but I'm still gentleman enough to insist on seeing you indoors. So, come here. I'll ask just the once. You may ride in front of me, or behind, or over the saddle. Your choice.'

Joan didn't deign to answer him, but she knew he meant it from the tone of his voice. And she'd not turn up in Mayfair thrown across a nag like an old blanket. She put up her chin and walked steadily out of her dark sanctuary and into the wan light of an emerging moon. Haughtily she attempted to avoid his eyes, but found she could not. A black-diamond gaze mocked her feeble attempt to escape him as wordlessly he lifted her, then mounted behind, hauling her back against him to prevent her falling off. He kicked the horse into action and it leapt forward, making Joan gasp and cling to him. She relaxed after a while, sheltering her face against his shoulder as the pounding rhythm of the journey, and her nervous exhaustion, caused her eyelids to droop.

* * *

It seemed mere minutes later that he halted at the top of Upper Brook Street and dismounted, lifting her down immediately. 'Nobody's about… you're unseen,' he growled.

Without another word he swung into the saddle. But the horse remained motionless till he'd watched her petite figure hurry out of sight into the grounds of her father's mansion.

Drew turned the animal he'd appropriated from the tavern, spurring it into action. Seconds after rounding a corner at a gallop his raging emotions were no longer controllable. He vaulted from the chestnut's back almost before it came to a standstill. Wildly he strode to and fro, then threw back his head to roar a curse at the storm-washed heavens. He was a damnable fool. It had taken time and effort to set up the scheme to trap Saul Stokes and his gang of crooks and he knew he'd have to act swiftly to end it because of his obsession with Lady Joan Morland.

He'd had a similar lust for her years back when she'd arrived at his hunting lodge one evening, searching for Luke Wolfson. Drew recalled that he'd believed her to be an exquisitely pretty new recruit to the cathouse that operated a mile or so distant, close to the Devon coast. Then she'd told him more about Wolfson and it had become clear that she honestly knew his best friend. *Lady Joan* hadn't been role-playing to excite his interest, but using her legitimate title. Drew had sobered up quickly and called for a carriage once he understood that he'd confused a peer of the realm's daughter with an opportunistic doxy on a home visit.

When he'd escorted her back to Thornley Heights her father had gone into a rage—as was to be expected from a man who'd discovered his maiden daughter being returned at dawn by a stranger.

Despite her infuriating reluctance to explain herself, and the explosive altercation with her father, Drew had rued parting company with the enchanting chit so speedily. The Duke of Thornley had accused him of sullying his daughter with a callous seduction, so he might as well have got hung for a sheep as a lamb. But although Alfred had offered to make him rich as Croesus the moment he signed a marriage contract, there was no inducement that would make Drew turn both their lives miserable. For all his cynicism towards wedded bliss, he still held taking vows a serious business, though he'd no intention of entering the married state himself.

A harlot might have brought him up, but Drew liked to think that his stepfather's influence weighed on him equally with his mother's. Joan was sweet and innocent and this evening he had been on the point of stripping her of those tender qualities along with her clothes. Despite his conscience bothering him he couldn't quash a burning need for her that was making him want to hurtle back to catch her before she escaped.

He hunkered down, arms stretched out and head lowered to them, dragging controlling air deep into his lungs while wondering if his early upbringing had corroded his soul. A wink of lightning on the horizon heralded the storm's cessation. Drew raised his eyes to smile at it. He'd been close to the point of no return in that damned coach, then nature came to his rescue, knocking some sense into his head before he did something they would both have deeply regretted. She might have surrendered quickly, but she'd been frightened enough to run from him as soon as the web of desire in which he'd had her bound disintegrated.

But…she'd tasted sweeter than honey, he ruefully reminded himself, and the throb in his loins wouldn't let him forget it. He wanted more of her. But he'd leave her be because it was over now… it had to be.

In a fluid movement he rose to his feet and ran a hand over the nose of the placid horse before mounting it.

'I thought I might expire from the fright of those thunderbolts!' Mrs Finch thumped her ample bosom in emphasis. 'I've not known such a storm since I was a little girl. And of course childhood exaggerates the experience.' She glanced at her hostess. 'You say you slept right through it, Maude? Most odd! I thought the worst might pass us by, but suddenly it was right overhead and loud enough to wake the dead.'

'I'm a very deep sleeper,' Maude replied, taking a treacle biscuit from the plate. She indeed did go out like a light at bedtime. Since the Duke had left for Devon, his wife had found a tot from the decanter helped ensure unbroken slumber. There was no great passion between the couple, both in the autumn of their lives, but Alfred was a fine companion and Maude missed having his warm presence lying beside her. Although she understood the reason for his absence, she wanted him back as soon as maybe.

'And you, my dear?' Mrs Finch glanced at Joan, chatting with her daughter on the sofa. 'Were you disturbed by the celestial fireworks?'

Joan put down her teacup. 'Indeed I was, ma'am. It was an…extraordinary night.' Joan fidgeted at the memory of that *extraordinary night*. She hoped the other ladies didn't notice her growing pink; if they guessed what was on her mind they'd blush, too, especially her poor stepmother who could be excused for swooning on the spot! Joan had thanked her lucky stars that Maude *had* slept through the tempest.

After Drew had set her down Joan had avoided the main entrance and dashed to the side of the house. She'd managed to slip in through the servants' quarters, but not unassisted, as she'd hoped. The door she'd left open had been locked, no doubt by a vigilant footman. But Pip had been making his stealthy way out of the house just as Joan had been attempting to make her way in.

They'd crept into one another in the dark quadrangle, stifling their squeals of surprise. Pip had blinked in disbelief on seeing Joan's damp and dishevelled state. He'd quickly shown her which entrance to use. The youth didn't ask her business and Joan returned the favour, although she'd guessed, from Pip's dry attire, that an attic tryst with Anna probably provided the reason for him being up and about at such an hour. She had planted a finger on her lips and Pip had given a nod of understanding. The young groom had doubtless wondered why his master's daughter was abroad on such a filthy night. The upset with the beggars would still be fresh in his mind and Joan imagined Pip might link the two incidents, and come up with Drew Rockleigh as a possible connection. She'd been out after dark with that gentleman once before when she should have been tucked up in bed and Pip knew about it because he'd driven the gig that had taken her to Rockleigh's hunting lodge. But she trusted Pip to keep his lips sealed on what he suspected.

Joan's brooding was interrupted as the door

opened and a visitor swept into the rose salon before the maid had a chance to dodge past and warn them of Lady Dorothea's visit.

'I have come on an errand for Lady Regan,' Dorothea announced.

'How nice,' her Grace replied with an inflection reserved for her sister-in-law's pomp. 'Have you time to take tea with us or must you quickly report back to her ladyship?'

'Indeed I shall have tea; I am able to tarry a short while as Lady Regan is presently with her modiste.' Dorothea smiled magnanimously, removing her black gloves and bonnet.

Although her husband had expired over fifteen years ago Dorothea was still particular about wearing deepest mourning. Maude found it quite odd, especially as Alfred had told her that his sister had been unhappily married. His late brother-in-law had divided his time between his wife and his mistress, the Duke had recounted, with the paramour getting preferential treatment. Dorothea had produced no offspring whereas his mistress had given birth to four. Dorothea's attitude towards her late husband might lead a person to believe the woman lamented the loss of a paragon of virtue rather than a selfish adulterer. She treated his memory to every respect and showed no sign of ever having despised him, although apparently she had, quite violently.

'So what errand might we help you with?' Maude asked while the maid served more tea.

'Lady Regan is holding a salon tomorrow afternoon and would like us all to attend.' Dorothea's eyes shifted to the two young ladies, listening politely. 'She has invited the Denbys and especially wants Lady Joan and Miss Finch to come along, too, so they might get to know Cecilia better. The girl is in need of some friends of her own age to take a drive with and go to the shops and so on.'

Maude's usual response to Lady Regan's invitations was to quickly find a reason to be unavailable.

'I think that sounds agreeable,' Joan interrupted the preliminary to her stepmother's declination. 'I'd like to see Miss Denby again and I expect that Louise would, too.' She gave her unsuspecting friend a little nudge.

Louise smiled gamely, but shot a quizzical glance at Joan.

'It is quite an honour for you girls to be asked.'

Dorothea primly folded her hands in her lap. 'Her ladyship is not one to regularly have young people about her.'

'So…why is she keen to cosset Cecilia Denby? She's only eighteen and seems rather a henwit, if I might speak plainly.' Maude frowned.

'Her ladyship is generous and charitable to a fault,' Dorothea replied.

The Duchess and Mrs Finch exchanged a glance that disputed that comment.

'Well…that is settled then; we shall go to Lady Regan's tomorrow and get to know Miss Denby better.' Joan hoped her stepmother wouldn't take offence at her assertiveness.

'I'm not sure I wish to know the chit any better.' Patricia's sniff preceded, 'She was flirting outrageously with Henry Laurenson with no thought to how it looked.'

'She was just letting off steam,' Joan said mildly. 'It seems Mr Stokes keeps a strict eye on her.'

'Unsurprisingly…' Maude sighed, selecting another biscuit.

Joan didn't want the ladies to rescind agreement

to the visit, so quickly stood up. 'I think I shall take a stroll in the conservatory,' she announced.

'I'll come, too,' Louise piped up, guessing that her friend had something to tell her in private.

Chapter Nine

On learning how greatly Maude adored growing things, the Duke of Thornley had commissioned a magnificent glasshouse as his second wife's wedding gift. The Duchess's fond husband paid adventurers to bring all manner of flora from the foreign lands they visited, setting his team of gardeners to nurture the exotic blooms for his wife's pride and joy.

A pleasing floral fragrance was in the air and the linnets in gilded cages up in the rafters filled the warm space with a natural melody.

Joan often sought this little sanctuary when in a reflective mood. When feeling nostalgic, she'd sit on the little bench and think of her beloved late mama, wrapping herself in wistful memories of the final months they'd spent together. The Duchess of Thornley had been far more excited than she had over her debut. Joan had indulged her frail mama's every whim, wearing the gowns that the Duchess preferred to those she liked herself. She went to every function her mama wanted to attend, without demur, although some had not been at all to her taste. She'd assured her mother she was having a fine time, yet she'd been crying inside.

Her parents had wanted to keep the news of the Duchess's ill health from her, fearing she would be too upset to grant her mother her final wish and make her come-out.

But for all their attempts to protect her Joan knew her mama didn't have long to live. She'd learned of the awful truth through a closed door; it had been another occasion when muted voices uttering a name had brought her to a halt, straining to hear a conversation that would shock her to the core. That afternoon had remained etched into her mind—even the weather had mocked her with its bright February sun on that darkest of days.

Inside the room her parents had been talking about her in low sorrowful voices. The Duchess had expressed concern that her daughter—even more than her son, who was too young to comprehend—should be sheltered from knowing she was dying.

The sound of her father weeping and her mother comforting him had made Joan hurry blindly away to seek the sanctuary of her own room. Henceforth when her mother coughed and grew thin and pale, Joan accepted without question her mama's mild explanation that a lingering chill was to blame, playing her part in the poignant deceit. Although she had wanted to rave at the pain of it, she did not. She would have done anything, told any lie, to make her mama's last days as joyous and carefree as possible. At night she had muffled her tears with the blankets and in the mornings had risen as bright as a lark to go on outings with a smile pinned to her lips.

'Have you caught a chill?' Louise sounded concerned when her friend gave a lingering sigh that was followed by a sneeze.

Joan dabbed her nose with her handkerchief. 'I expect I've taken in a bit of pollen.' She touched a fingertip to the silky petals of a gardenia.

'Is your cousin holding the children's reading class this week at the vicarage?' Joan busied herself watering some plants with a small copper can, determined to cheer up. 'I should like to be of help again, if he'll have me.'

'I thought the Duke had banned your further visits, following the incident with the beggars,' Louise cautioned.

'The Duke *is* hundreds of miles away, and besides, Pip now knows which route to take to avoid Ratcliffe Highway. I'm sure Papa would not object *too* much.'

'It is good of you to offer to tutor them, Joan, but Vincent has abandoned those lessons.'

'Why has he done so?' Joan swung about with the copper can poised in mid-air. The vicar had been teaching the children before she volunteered to help; she was sure he wouldn't have given up on the school simply because her father had vetoed her attendance.

'The bishop sent Vincent a letter expressing disquiet about the vicarage being used as a ragged school.' Louise raised her eyebrows. 'Mama and Papa were talking about it over breakfast. Apparently Vincent caved in straight away on the matter, as his living depends on it.'

'Your cousin should be praised rather than condemned,' Joan said pithily, putting down the watering can amidst a forest of ferny leaves. 'How did the bishop find out about it?' Sudden enlightenment caused her to sigh. Her father had doubtless pulled strings with distinguished ecclesiasts. If the ragged school were closed, there would be no further need for her to travel to the stews and risk her life and reputation undertaking charity work. The bishop wouldn't want a horror story circulating that a duke's daughter had had been assaulted by ragamuffins due to her association with a clergyman of the diocese.

Joan pinched her nostrils to contain another sneeze erupting. She suspected she *had* caught a cold from the drenching she'd got on that stormy night.

Though they were close Joan hadn't told Louise about what had happened, knowing her friend would be rightly shocked to hear what she'd done. If her rendezvous with Drew ever came to light she'd have no choice but to disclose her motive for it and expose Stokes as a fraudster. But she could no longer lie to herself about the real reason she'd gone to see him: *I think you're as eager to taste me as I am to have you,* he'd taunted her and her denial, though immediate, had easily been proven fake.

Joan knew her life had changed...*she* had changed; Duke's daughter or no, she'd become enslaved by a street fighter. And it was driving her mad...

Every waking hour—and there were very many now sleep seemed impossible—was filled with memories of Drew Rockleigh and the feelings he'd awakened in her. She'd gone to meet him with the best of intentions, but now believed she'd only made matters worse for them both.

He'd refrained from accusing her of meddling, courteously praising her instead. She'd sensed his annoyance stemmed from a genuine concern for her welfare because she was privy to a crime. From that Joan deduced Stokes to be a dangerous man as well as a crooked one. At the outset, she'd intended to extract a promise from Drew that her visit to his hunting lodge would remain their secret. In the event she'd forgotten to mention the incident that concerned her papa so greatly that he constantly fretted on it. Ironically, that episode was of less importance now she'd behaved with even greater abandon with Drew Rockleigh.

She thanked heaven that her father knew nothing of that!

The memory of their shared passion had intensified rather than faded as the days had passed. At night, undressing and donning her negligee caused excitement to shiver through her. Silk slipping against her skin might have been phantom lips tracing her flesh. The yearning for him to touch her again was pitching her into uncertainty over whether what they'd done was right or wrong. Her upbringing could only present one answer to the conundrum, but she was a woman as well as being a duke's daughter. She had the same feelings in her body and soul as did Anna, who no doubt revelled in her beau's caresses during secret meetings with Pip. But what was Rockleigh to her? Certainly he was not her beau. He'd not murmured a single affectionate word to her that night as he'd disrobed her to touch her intimately. But he had spoken to her in a way calculated to crumble her defences and heighten her response to him. Even now, those gruff commands could make a mingling of shame and excitement heat her blood.

Weeks ago the vicar had told her that the Squire

was popular with women; Joan knew it had been no exaggeration. But was there a young woman who received tender words as well as artful kisses and caresses from him?

'Are you listening to a word I'm saying?' Louise tilted her head, gazing at her friend's distant expression till Joan gave her an apologetic smile. 'I thought you'd engineered our escape to the orangery so we might have a gossip about seeing Miss Denby later in the week. Are you after all the grisly details of her thwarted elopement?'

'No!' Joan clucked her tongue. 'Well…maybe…'

'I should like to hear more about it, too!' Louise giggled. 'I imagine the groom she ran off with was terribly handsome and the uncle who saved her dreadfully strict.'

Joan smiled quite wistfully. 'Perhaps we may find out,' she said.

'Your aunt takes a delight in organising things, doesn't she?' Cecilia frowned. 'She was busy with Lady Regan earlier, planning our timetable for tomorrow. We are to go to a museum and then for a drive in the park, I believe.'

'Are we?' Joan gave her companion a smile,

though feeling miffed that Dorothea had seen fit to make arrangements without consulting her.

'Never fear…I shall say I've got a migraine so you can escape.' Cecilia sounded glum. 'My patroness is trying to surround me with ladies of unblemished character in the hope that some of their goodness might rub off on me.'

'I've no intention of escaping because I'm sure we shall have a nice time,' Joan *did* want to get to know Cecilia better, but none the less felt a fraud for tacitly claiming a spotless reputation. If a hint of what she'd recently been up to slipped out, she'd be ejected from this elegant salon quicker than would Cecilia.

'Are you just pretending to be making friends with me?' Cecilia laid a card, pouting when Maude smiled apologetically, then trumped it with the King of Hearts.

'I think we could very easily become friends,' Joan returned truthfully. She deliberately played a bad hand, hoping to also go out of the game. Seated around the baize-topped table were a number of Lady Regan's middle-aged guests and there'd been no real opportunity for the two younger ladies to chat privately. Joan was waiting for an opening in their conversation that might allow her to mention Cecilia's uncle. Thereafter some clues might emerge as to why Bertha Denby and Saul Stokes had plotted against him.

'Shall we peruse the bookshelves and find a suitably erudite tome to pore over while we chat?' Joan gave a subtle wink and it had the required effect of cheering Cecilia up.

'Oh, yes, let's; I should like to stretch my legs and have a gossip.' Cecilia pushed back her chair.

'It is a shame Miss Finch is unwell and couldn't come.' Cecilia flicked the pages of an atlas she'd just slid from a mahogany shelf.

'She has a very sore throat,' Joan explained, feeling guilty that she hadn't suffered a bad cold after her drenching, but had spread the germs to Louise.

'Mr Laurenson's friend liked Miss Finch, didn't he?' Cecilia peeked from beneath her lashes at Joan.

'I believe they enjoyed dancing together,' Joan replied neutrally, pondering on how to get the information she wanted without seeming inquisitive.

'I enjoyed dancing with Henry,' Cecilia burst out

in a whisper. 'Oh, he asked me to call him Henry,' she explained, having read Joan's expression.

'But perhaps you should not...just yet,' Joan advised gently. 'If a lady and gentleman become too familiar too soon, it often leads to trouble.' Joan wondered what on earth Henry Laurenson had been thinking to encourage such behaviour. Then she remembered what her stepmother had said about Cecilia attracting the wrong sort of admirers. Joan hadn't heard rumours that Henry was in the market for a wife, but she *had* seen him sauntering along Regent Street with a member of the petticoat set on his arm.

Joan glanced at their hostess, seated on a velvet sofa. Lady Regan was flanked on one side by Dorothea and on the other by a dowager viscountess. Today, sedately sipping tea, they looked harmless enough, but beneath their soft kid gloves were claws that could sharpen in an instant. Bertha Denby seemed content to perch on an armchair close by, although she was keeping a close eye on her daughter. Thankfully Saul Stokes was absent from the all-female gathering.

'I don't care what people think about us,' Cecilia muttered. 'I like Henry very much and he called me a beguiling beauty. He doesn't care about my bad reputation.'

Joan glanced swiftly at Cecilia. 'You *told* him you'd run away?' she rattled off in an aghast whisper.

'I did…but I didn't need to…he already knew.' Cecilia's lips twitched in a smile. 'You know I'm ruined, too. Everybody does…they just pretend otherwise because Lord and Lady Regan give us their support.'

About to fib and deny knowing about the scandal, Joan realised she'd already let the truth roll off her tongue in an unguarded moment. 'I'd heard a tale about an aborted elopement,' she admitted very quietly.

Cecilia began turning pages again, her mouth twisting bitterly. 'I did love Robbie and thought I'd made good my escape, but he had to spoil it for us.'

'He?' Joan echoed. Her heartbeat quickened in anticipation of a mention of Drew Rockleigh.

'My guardian,' Cecilia muttered.

'I expect your mother had your best interests at heart.'

'She only cares about herself.' Cecilia darted a stinging look Bertha's way.

'Your uncle caught up with you, I believe?' Joan wanted to discover what Rockleigh's part in it all had been before Bertha joined them. On turning her head, she'd noticed the woman staring at them, then purposefully depositing her cup and saucer on the table as though about to gain her feet.

'I certainly tested his patience that day.' Cecilia sighed.

'You like him even though he brought you back?' Joan was unable to contain her surprise.

'Mmm...ever since Papa died Uncle Drew has been generous and kind. He's chastised me on occasions, but I know I've deserved it. I certainly did when I ran off. But I don't see my uncle now.'

'Why not?'

Cecilia seemed to be on the point of answering, but instead pressed her lips together, her cheeks glowing.

'You two young ladies seem to have a lot to chat about.' Bertha had sidled up quite quickly and placed a hand on her daughter's arm.

'We've been talking about our excursion tomorrow,' Joan smoothly interjected. Though she was itching to tell Drew's odious sister what she thought of her she forced a placid smile to her lips.

'Let's hope the weather is clement.' Bertha glanced at the drizzle spattering the window. 'Lady Regan has said we may use her splendid landau if it is fine...' Her voice faded away as the door opened and their host ambled in.

Joan noted the immediate change in mother and daughter brought about by Lord Regan's appearance. The man's wife acknowledged him from the sofa with a dip of her turban, but he ignored her and started towards the trio of ladies by the bookshelves.

'Capital to see you, m'dear.' Bertram Regan clasped Cecilia's fingers and gave them a clumsy shake. He then turned his beam on Mrs Denby, who seemed better pleased to have his attention.

'How's the gel settling in with her new friends?' he asked, giving Joan a glance. 'You're Thornley's daughter, aren't you?'

'I am, sir.' Joan dipped him a polite bob.

'Good choice...good choice, indeed,' Lord Regan praised, patting Mrs Denby's arm. 'She's got nice pedigree and is just the ticket to be dancing attendance on little Cecilia.'

Joan felt amused rather than annoyed on hearing that. But both *Little Cecilia* and her mother fidgeted uncomfortably at their host's implication that a duke's daughter might toady to a woman of inferior age and rank.

'The rain has stopped—shall we stroll on the terrace for a breath of air?' Joan suggested, hoping for another chance to get Cecilia alone so they could resume their talk. From her new friend's expression she gleaned that Cecilia would like nothing better.

'Cecilia has yet to sit with Lady Regan before we leave. Come…let us join her for a while. You must let her ladyship know how greatly you appreciate having the use of her landau.' Bertha linked arms with her daughter.

Looking disappointed, Cecilia allowed her mother to steer her away, Lord Regan trailing in their wake like a faithful lackey.

'Stranger and stranger, don't you think?' Maude muttered with a frown. 'I know Dorothea told us that Lord Regan and Mr Stokes are acquainted, but I think his lordship's show of favouritism to the man's ward was too much. What do you make of it?'

'I'm not exactly sure what to make of it,' Joan replied, gazing through the window of the coach as they rattled on their way home, having left the gathering.

But of something Joan was certain: she and Maude were not alone in their confusion, or their suspicions, about an old roué paying attention to a pretty young blonde. The other ladies present had also noticed it while pretending not to.

Lady Regan's reaction to her husband's fawning over the Denby women had also been closely monitored. If their hostess had been annoyed about her spouse's behaviour, she'd kept it concealed and graciously allowed mother and daughter to sit either side of her on the sofa. Lord Regan had quit the room not long after entering it without bothering to pass the time of day with anybody else present, including the woman he'd married.

'I could hazard a guess as to what it's all about, but I'd best not air such thoughts,' Maude rumbled darkly.

'Perhaps we are reading too much into it. Lord

Regan might simply want to help his friend Stokes settle Cecilia.' Joan tried to sound convincing.

Maude gave her stepdaughter an old-fashioned look. 'It's not *settling* the chit the old lecher's keen on, if you ask me,' she blurted. 'Oh, fiddlesticks.' Maude waggled a hand. 'You're not an idiot or a child and I'll not treat you as either. You're older than my Verity was when she got married and I discussed such things with her, Fiona, too, of course.' Maude paused. 'You may tell me to be quiet at any time if I embarrass you, Joan. But in my opinion it is cruel for a mother to allow her girls to embark on adult life with no inkling of what…or who…might ambush them.' Maude gazed earnestly into her stepdaughter's limpid grey eyes. 'I know I can never replace your own mama, my dear, but I feel as close to you as I do to my own children, so may I stop beating about the bush and talk plainly to you, woman to woman?'

'Please do, ma'am.' Joan's smile held warmth and gratitude. 'I want to be treated as an equal rather than be wrapped in tissue as though I might break, as Papa tends to do to me.' A wry little chuckle preceded, 'I promise not to have a fit of the vapours either if you tell me that gentlemen are not always honourable when pursuing ladies they fancy.'

Maude leaned closer and clasped Joan's fingers. 'Your papa means well; he dotes on you and would protect you from all harm. But, alas, we cannot keep our offspring in our pockets out of harm's way. We must prepare them for the world and the villains in it.' She sighed. 'That's enough of my blathering; but I'd like it if in future you'd call me Mama…only if you want to, of course. It's so much nicer than ma'am.' Maude raised her step-daughter's fingers, fondly brushing them against her cheek before letting them go. 'Now that's out of the way, let's have that gossip.' Maude settled back against the upholstery. 'In my opinion, Lord Regan has his eye on his next conquest and is after Cecilia under his wife's nose, and perhaps with her blessing.'

'That had occurred to me, too,' Joan admitted. 'But surely her mother and guardian would not be complicit in it, especially as it will eventually come out. Cecilia will then be a notorious *demi-rep*, barred from polite society.'

Maude shrugged. 'It's not unheard of for a rich man to flaunt his mistress or even set up a *ménage à trois* with her and his wife. And it's quite common practice for a sullied young woman to be found a rich protector so the family might wash their hands of her.' Maude frowned. 'Stokes might have made any offer from Lord Regan conditional on her retaining her good name. If they were to marry her off, Cecilia would continue to be accepted. Many a penniless fop would take her and turn a blind eye to her lover if paid well enough to do so.'

'I doubt Cecilia will agree to any of it,' Joan announced flatly. 'She has her own mind and is still smitten with Henry Laurenson.'

'Is she, indeed?' Maude's eyebrows shot up. 'Well, that young man is no penniless fop and, though he might act the clown on occasion, I doubt he'd take kindly to being cuckolded by a fellow old enough to be his grandfather.'

'It *is* possible his lordship might have a philanthropic motive.'

'Do you think so?' Maude asked.

The ladies exchanged a dubious look, then fell quiet, gazing out of the windows as the coach rattled on its way through the grey damp streets of Mayfair.

When they alighted from their transport in Upper Brook Street thoughts of Drew Rockleigh again occupied the forefront of Joan's mind. What would he make of the theory that Lord Regan had an unhealthy interest in his niece? Cecilia had spoken warmly of her uncle and if Drew returned that fondness, he would be sure to hate the idea of his niece becoming an old man's mistress.

Had Joan been more alert to her surroundings she might have noticed that she was being watched. Standing on the opposite side of the road was a fellow with a hat tipped low over his eyes and his shoulders hunched up to his ears.

From beneath the beaver's brim the gentleman observed the two women ascend the steps of the Duke of Thornley's mansion then disappeared into the house. A moment later he gleefully rubbed together his palms with a satisfied grin.

Chapter Ten

The combatants circled one another, squinting against the setting sun as their dodging and feinting turned them towards the west. The gypsy lunged forward, swiping sweat from his eyes with one meaty fist while the other lashed out. He was driven back by a jab from his opponent, but no second blow capitalised on the first and the stocky Romany managed to shake himself awake and deliver a right hook. It appeared to fell the Squire; he stayed down on one knee despite raucous shouts from the crowd urging him to get up and fight.

But he'd no intention of doing that and let the referee count him out.

'Was the sun blinding you? Or are you losing your touch, do you think? I've not seen you go down so quickly before.'

'Perhaps I am past my peak at this game,' Drew

replied, wincing as Constance dabbed at his cut face with a wet rag.

'Benny said he'd like to crack as many heads as you do.' Constance gave a cheerful smile while dunking the bloodied cloth in the bucket of water beside her, then wringing it out.

'Your brother would do better to forget about boxing and get himself a job on the docks.' Drew knew that Benny Cook idolised him and was proud that his sister was a prize fighter's concubine. The lad would often badger him for a sparring session on the cobbles outside the Cock and Hen pub.

'Benny doesn't want to be a stevedore; my little brother likes easy pickings.' Constance chuckled wryly. 'Out of the three of us it was only my sister wanted regular work on the docks. Sonia, God rest her, did earn a pretty penny at it, too. For the good it did her!'

Drew removed his paramour's hand from his cheek as her storytelling caused her to become over-enthusiastic in cleaning his wounds. Constance had been his mistress for several months and though he was about to put her off he wanted to do so kindly. She was an amiable companion and an adequate lover. He also appreciated her artless character and the fact that she slept with him because she liked him rather than for the cash in his pockets.

Wisely, Constance Cook hadn't joined her elder sister, servicing seaman in taverns along the Thames. It was a dangerous profession: disease and violence were never far away from a popular harlot mixing with rough trade. Two years ago Sonia had got between two navvies fighting over her and had been stabbed to death at the age of nineteen, the age Constance was now.

The Romany came over to shake Drew's hand. As the men clashed eyes Drew saw that the victor suspected the fight had been thrown. But the bulging purse was gripped tight in the fellow's torn fingers and he sauntered off with his entourage, enjoying his shoddy fame. It stuck in Drew's craw that he'd let a second-rate boxer get the better of him, but he wanted it to appear that his withdrawal from the neighbourhood, and the sport, was due to his loss of form rather than let people speculate.

The spectators started to disperse, leaving just Barnaby Smith, the boxing agent, dismantling the ropes of the makeshift ring. Intermittently he glared over at the loser of the bout, muttering beneath his breath about the Squire's inexplicably bad technique.

Drew was sitting on the low wall outside the Cock and Hen tavern while suffering his mistress's attempts at patching him up. Constance had been working at the hostelry since the age of fourteen, but she seemed in no hurry to get to her job now the contest was over. People made thirsty from bellowing their advice at the boxers had repaired to the tavern to pack the saloon bar. The harassed landlord glared at Constance from the doorway, but his employee simply tossed her untidy blonde curls and turned away. The landlord, in common with everybody else in the neighbourhood, knew that the young woman had the Squire's protection. While she retained it Charlie Clarke was chary of upsetting her...or him.

'I hope you're not badly hurt after that fight, Mr Rockleigh.'

Drew got to his feet as Vincent Walters approached, having just emerged from a cottage across the square.

'I'm well enough, Vicar, thank you for your concern.'

The last time they'd spoken in Hyde Park their exchange had been prickly, but Vincent bore no grudges. 'It must be disappointing for you to get nothing but bruises for your trouble.'

Drew shrugged easily. 'It's the nature of the business. I've had a good run at it.'

'How is Old Blackie, Vicar?' Constance referred to the ancient blacksmith who still lived at his redundant forge.

'He's rallied well, but the Lord only knows for how much longer he can find the strength to draw breath.' Vincent had been comforting the gravely ill fellow that afternoon. Old Blackie, as he was nicknamed, had suffered a nasty attack that had robbed him of full mobility and yet still he clung determinedly to life.

'I expect he's not yet ready to meet his maker, or his dragon of a wife.' Constance smiled. It was common knowledge that the blacksmith's late spouse had ruled him with an iron fist. 'He'll curl up his toes in his own good time.'

'Indeed he will,' Vincent replied, rather charmed by the young woman's blunt philosophy. He glanced at Rockleigh, wondering whether to mention their mutual acquaintance. But the Squire's hard-eyed stare seemed to caution him not to talk about Lady Joan Morland. With a nod Vincent took his leave and walked on in the direction of the vicarage.

'Come…let's go home.' Constance tugged at Drew's arm to make him rise. 'Out of sight I'll do a better job of making you feel better.' She nuzzled his bristly cheek.

'I'm in need of a drink and you are needed in there.' Drew disentangled himself from her clutch, nodding at the tavern's doorway. He'd no intention of Constance losing her employment on his account; in a short while he'd no longer be around to provide for her because his time in Ratcliffe Highway was finished. But that wasn't the only reason he felt immune to her seduction: the sensation of another woman's smoother skin and sweeter lips were constantly tormenting his mind and body, and although he was damned if he knew why he should feel faithful to Lady Joan Morland, he did.

'Have you tired of me, Drew?' Constance asked as though she'd read his thoughts.

Drew carried on winding a bandage about his bleeding knuckles. 'Why do you ask?'

Constance shrugged, twirling a pearly tress about a finger. 'I've not know many toffs down on their luck, but Mayfair or Wapping, I reckon you men are all the same, anyhow. You feed a girl a good dinner, then sweet talk her into bed, and so it goes on until your eye lands on your next fancy.'

From beneath her sooty lashes, Constance watched his impassive profile. 'Your eye's already landed on somebody else, hasn't it?'

Drew continued fixing the bandage, but jerked his head at the door of the pub. 'Time you started work, Connie. I'll have a mutton pie and a quart of ale, if you please.' He gave her a slow smile. 'And you can treat yourself to the same; there, I've done my job of feeding you, according to your rules.'

Constance tutted, flouncing to her feet. It was his way of telling her to mind her own business about his private affairs. He might joke with her now, but she knew he'd turn cool if she got too impertinent in her questioning. She had learned little from Drew Rockleigh other than his name and not to pry into his past. For all she knew he might have a fine lady waiting for him when he got back on his feet.

Drew watched his mistress's curvaceous figure disappear into the saloon, then looked about at his seedy surroundings that nevertheless had been his birthplace. From where he sat he could see the ramshackle house where his mother had reared him and his sister in their early years. He'd never discovered who'd sired him; he doubted his late mother had known either. When he'd been a boy Rosemary Wilding had attempted to satisfy his curiosity about his deceased father by telling him she'd been a soldier's child bride. Drew hadn't swallowed his mother's yarn, although he knew she'd been very young when he was born.

If his father *had* been Private Wilding, Drew couldn't remember him at all, but he could recall a succession of scruffy, sly-eyed men who'd turn up at night, bringing a smell of the sea and a fistful of coins, with them. Then the curtain would be drawn across the room they all shared and he'd see no more of them and try not to hear their grunting either.

Once Drew had been obsessed with knowing his sire's name, but now he no longer cared enough to want to find out. His paternal line was certain to be tainted with coarseness and devilry. And perhaps he, too, had villainy in his veins, despite his stepfather's good influence during the latter part of his childhood. His sister had also been beneath Peter Rockleigh's care for more than a decade, yet Bertha was indisputable proof that bad blood would out.

Drew stretched his legs in front of him, conscious that the honourable gentleman who'd bestowed on him his name and an education, then all his worldly goods, should dominate his memories. But still his eyes and his thoughts wandered back to the hovel in which he'd spent the first nine years of his life with his mother and sister.

Abruptly he stood up and entered the pub, elbowing a path through the rabble to a table in the corner. A moment later a rat-faced fellow slid on to a stool opposite.

'Rum do that, the Squire losing to a fat tinker,' the fellow snarled sarcastically.

Drew shrugged. 'Win some…lose some.'

'I reckon you could've knocked him down after ten minutes. Now I'm out of pocket.' Barnaby Smith had a ferocious glint in his eyes. 'I'd put a tidy bit of blunt on you to win. And I reckon you must've wagered on yourself to lose.'

'Unfortunately I didn't,' Drew replied truthfully with a hint of a smile.

Barnaby's hand slithered across the table to the coins by Drew's elbow, but his wrist was gripped in vice-like fingers before he could snatch them. 'So, you're quick enough when you want to be.' Smith wrenched himself free.

'You'd do well to remember it.' Drew pocketed his money. He took a gulp from the ale that Constance had plonked in front of him along with his mutton pie.

'The next fight I line up for you, I'll want a bigger cut to make up for it.'

'I'm retiring.'

'Then I'll take payment now—' Barnaby didn't get to finish his threat. Drew had anticipated the man's move and pinned his sleeve to the rough-hewn table top with a blade before Barnaby could whip his own knife from his pocket.

'You'll be sorry you crossed me,' Barnaby Smith hissed.

Drew gave him a quizzical look, but yanked the

knife from the wood, allowing the struggling fellow to surge to his feet and stalk off.

Before Smith left the tavern he jerked his head at the landlord. With a shifty glance to and fro, Charlie Clarke shuffled from behind the counter to converse quietly with Smith by the exit. Drew dropped his gaze to his tankard, apparently uninterested in the conversation between the two men. But he saw money change hands and Barnaby pocketing the cash as he went out of the door.

Constance had anxiously watched the dangerous altercation between her lover and the boxing promoter. She had been on the point of taking the vacant seat when Barnaby Smith got up, but her boss had been glaring at her. While she was collecting empty pots she'd been keeping an eye on Drew as he ate and drank a few yards away. Forlornly, she noted that he rarely looked her way and continued brooding into his tankard.

He'd made a good living off these shabby streets in the past months and Constance was sad that it seemed his skill had deserted him. But she reckoned the fault wasn't in his fists, but in his head.

Drew had seemed different after the swanky

coach took a wrong turning into Ratcliffe Highway. Then the fellow from the detective agency had started coming round looking for him. Drew had been casual about the fellow's first visit, but angry on the next occasion Thadeus Pryke had turned up.

Constance had been cheering Drew on when the coach got ambushed that day. The Squire had thrown in the towel, bringing the boxing match to a premature halt, before driving the coach and occupants to safety. Her brother Benny had been one of those who'd clambered on to the coach and he'd described the young lady passenger as a real corker. Constance had assumed Drew had felt obliged to help his own kind, but now she wondered if there had been something more personal in it.

Drew drained his ale, while thinking of Lady Joan Morland—something he seemed to do with damnable regularity, he sourly mocked himself. As far as his business and his pleasure were concerned she'd messed him up. He wanted her more than he'd ever wanted any woman, yet however readily she might succumb to his seduction he knew there could be no real future for them. Sometimes he felt like damning the consequences and that he'd go ahead and propose to her. But he knew his conscience wouldn't allow him to tie her to him dishonestly.

Bearing in mind his upbringing, he knew it was laughable to imagine a boy from the slums marrying a duke's daughter. He'd not risk seeing disdain in her eyes when she learned the truth. People knew that Peter Rockleigh had married their widowed mother and that the estimable fellow had reared her children as though they were his own. But nobody knew that Rosemary Wilding had been plucked from the gutter to be his mistress before the besotted fellow made her his wife. When the marriage was announced a romance had been concocted of the couple, both having few friends or family, meeting and falling in love at a coastal town while taking the air for poor health. It was a plausible tale; Peter Rockleigh had been at Brighton suffering lung disease and he did have a dearth of relations. Apart from her children, Rosemary had no kith and kin who wished to acknowledge her, and by then had been frail from disease got from servicing low-life. But she'd never seen the water at Brighton, just the Thames where it flowed through the East End of London.

Had Joan's father been acquainted with his past, Drew suspected he'd have been ejected from Thornley Heights on the night he had delivered the man's daughter safely home. In the event he'd been offered a serious talk about a marriage contract and a drink from the man's decanter.

Drew had felt attracted to her from the start, but the feelings she aroused in him ran deeper than lust now. She was sweet and honest, beautiful in character as well as looks. If he took her as his mistress, he risked not only sullying her reputation but destroying her relationship with her family. And he wouldn't do that. She'd reignited a fire in him that he'd believed he'd doused years ago... yet the memory of her had remained a ghost at the back of his mind. But she was no longer just a phantom lover and the memory of her taste and shape made him burn to finish what he'd started.

His palms grew hot from the thought of her silky body moulding against them. A redolence of lavender and rosemary seemed to be teasing his senses, reminding him of when he'd buried his face in her thick lustrous tresses on that coach seat. He curled his fist about the empty glass to cool it, a sound of frustration rasping in his throat. He wanted to believe that Joan would forget about the conversation she'd overheard between Stokes and Bertha. But she wouldn't. She'd fret over it, then unburden herself to somebody in her family because she wanted to help him and couldn't do so alone. Her father or her brother-in-law would be her first ports of call. As the Duke was out of town Drew wondered if he would soon hear from Luke Wolfson.

The only people alive who knew of his sordid lineage were his sister and his best friend. Luke's unhappy early life had made him respectful of a person's wish to leave questions unanswered and skeletons in the cupboard. Early on in their friendship they'd made a pact not to delve for clues about each other's histories, but wait until information was volunteered. As for Stokes, he knew, of course, that Bertha was a harlot from the wrong side of town and had capitalised on it. But Drew imagined his sister would have been too ashamed to admit to her lover that she was the spawn of a dockside whore and an unknown tar.

Saul Stokes was likely to turn vicious when cornered. The villain already had a catalogue of misdemeanours to his name, but he'd so far stayed a step ahead of the law, evading arrest. With luck a rope awaited the villain, though, and Drew knew it was his job to hurry him to it.

'There is a gentleman caller for you, my lady.'

Joan had been lounging on her bed, idly sorting through the pieces in her jewellery box to find some silver earrings that needed repairing, when Anna tapped on the door.

Quickly she swung her feet to the floor and stood up, her insides tightening. Surely Drew would not have risked coming here to see her? She craved a meeting with him and she was sure he wanted the same…but not here.

Earlier in the week her museum trip and drive in the park with Cecilia had proved unfruitful; Mrs Denby had been between them the whole time, monitoring what was said and preventing Joan unearthing a morsel of information from Drew's niece.

'Did the visitor give his name, Anna?'

'He did not, my lady. He said it was a confidential matter. He is waiting in the small library, but I can have him shown out...' the maid suggested diplomatically.

'No! I shall be down directly,' Joan quickly replied. 'Is the Duchess at home?'

'Her Grace went out with your aunt, about fifteen minutes ago.'

Joan imagined her thoughts coincided with Anna's: it was an odd and fortuitous coincidence that her stepmother had left the house only minutes before her visitor turned up. It was more likely that he'd waited for the Duchess to leave before knocking on the door.

After Anna left Joan frantically set about tidying her crumpled appearance. Her nervous fingers pressed creases from her dimity skirt, then attempted to secure stray tendrils of glossy hair in their pins. She tilted her face to inspect her reflection in the dressing-table glass. A moment later she rushed from her chamber as it had occurred to her that, given time to think, he might rue his arrival and leave before she'd had a chance to speak to him.

'Mr Stokes! What...what do you want, sir?'

After hurtling down the stairs Joan had managed to steady her pace when entering the small library. The sight of the swindler, standing with his chest puffed out and his hat beneath his arm, brought her to an abrupt standstill.

It took just a few seconds for the ramifications of this man's presence to penetrate Joan's disappointment. His smug expression increased her suspicions that he'd not called to arrange a social engagement with his ward, but rather to stir up trouble.

'Did my stepmother invite you to call?' she asked pointedly. 'I wasn't aware you had our address.'

'I am here on your account, not the Duchess's. As for knowing where to find you... I'm happy to say I received that information from a relative who observed you entering these premises with her Grace earlier in the week.'

'And why would that sighting seem to you to be serendipitous?'

'I believe we will come to that in a moment, *Miss Morley*.'

Joan's heart ceased beating and colour fled from her cheeks. The only way that Cecilia's guardian could know of her alias was from Mr Pryke.

Stokes struck a pose, thick forefinger pressing his lips as though he were considering something important. 'May I call you by your correct name now the intrigue is over, *Miss Morley*?' He almost winked at her when adding conspiratorially, 'If the intrigue is unfinished and you'd sooner continue with your alias, you've only to say.' He licked his lips suggestively.

'I would sooner you immediately leave, sir. There is no reason at all for you being here. A servant will show you out.' Joan quickly approached the bell pull, but his next words, gruff with faux humility, prevented her yanking on it.

'I beg your pardon for this intrusion, but if my cousin's services as a go-between are no longer required, I will conclude his business for him, then take my leave.' Again the sly smile undulated on his mean lips.

Joan felt her hackles rise at the same time that lead settled in the pit of her stomach.

'Your cousin?'

'Thadeus Pryke. He has recently been employed by you and your father, I understand. Through your patronage he has become privy to some sensitive information. The poor fellow feels out of his depth and unsure what to do about it, so has enlisted my help.'

'I imagine you refer to my family's acquaintance with Mr Rockleigh.' Joan felt anger overcoming her apprehension. For two pins she'd tell the odious fellow that she held some sensitive information, too, about him! But she must bite her tongue because Drew had demanded her silence and she would not let him down. 'We are not ashamed of our friendship with a street fighter. You may tell your cousin he can rest easy on that score and that our business is concluded. Had I known Mr Pryke to be too timid to conduct his own affairs I would not have employed him.' Joan gestured angrily at the door, indicating he should leave.

'But the business is not finished, my lady,' Stokes purred. 'I am here to present my cousin's bill and when I receive payment then it will be over.'

'I've already settled his account.' Joan felt ice stalk her spine. So the crux of the matter was money...or blackmail to be more precise.

'Ah...but that was remuneration for escorting *Miss Morley* to meet Mr Rockleigh. Since then both Thadeus and I have undertaken more for you, have we not?'

'Explain!' Joan burst out, marching closer. 'I've not asked him to perform other duties. And as for you…I owe you nothing!'

'Well, you may not have *asked*, my lady, but being two diligent fellows we have used our own initiative on it.' He slid an insolent look at her. 'Mr Pryke took you to meet the Squire, unaware of your true identity and the real nature of your business with the boxer.' He resumed perambulating over oak boards. 'My cousin agreed to act as an escort, but not to be a keeper of secrets, and now that he has told me about it my conscience is also burdened.' Stokes swivelled on a heel. 'You see, we are sure your father would be horrified to discover that you and a street fighter are *intimate* friends.' Stokes propped his jowls on a fist, adopting a reflective air. 'I know your father is at present away from home, but soon he will return. A great scandal is just a whisper away.' He sighed. 'Thankfully the cab driver is ignorant of your identity and we must keep it that way or a great calamity would ensue, would it not. The fellow has related at length on how you found the

Squire's company very pleasant.' Again Stokes moistened his lips while a lascivious gaze flowed over Joan. 'Rockleigh didn't hold you against your will; that might give your poor father some relief. Nevertheless, should he ever find out about what you got up to with the rogue in a Hackney cab he is sure to be greatly distressed...'

'Enough! I have the gist of your vile attempt to blackmail me, sir, never fear.' Joan's complexion had alternated between scarlet and white as she'd listened to Stokes's threats and lewd innuendo. She put a hand out to steady herself against the library table as fury and embarrassment rendered her light headed. She knew exactly what the cab driver had overheard; her little moans and sighs of that night constantly ebbed and flowed in her memory. She sucked in air, standing straighter and tilting up her chin. 'You mistake my character if you believe I will bow to blackmail and pay you. However, I do not mistake *your* character, Mr Stokes. I know you for what you are. So go away. My word will be believed over yours and I am willing to put that to the test.' Joan sought support from the furniture again while uttering her brave boast.

'All in good time will I leave you be, my lady,' Stokes snarled, abandoning all pretence at civility and respectfulness. 'I can guess at what you refer to. I had a suspicion that somebody was close by when Mrs Denby and I were conversing in the Wentworths' garden. It was you, wasn't it, eavesdropping like a common servant?'

Joan felt guilty blood sting her cheeks, but she wouldn't give him the satisfaction of prodding her to lie and deny it.

Stokes snorted scornfully. 'You may think you know me, but I know you equally well. High born, perhaps, but you're as much a trollop as that lightskirt of the Squire's.' Hearing about her rival brought a flicker of emotion to cloud Joan's eyes, making him smirk. 'Ah, perhaps you did not know about his pretty little ladybird; the Cockney Blonde is quite devoted to him, so Mr Pryke tells me.'

Joan *did* know about his women. The vicar had let that slip weeks ago, but still she felt as though a knife had been plunged beneath her ribs. So Drew Rockleigh had a pretty blonde mistress who was devoted to him. She wondered if the poor thing realised he was unfaithful to her. Abruptly Joan saw their passionate encounter for what it had been: a tawdry liaison borne of opportunity and lust on his part and silly infatuation on hers. Rockleigh had done the decent thing and apologised to her, then brought her home safely; but he'd galloped away without a backward glance, doubtless keen to return to his Cockney Blonde's bed. That night, while restless and bombarded by sensual memories, her mind had concocted a love affair from it because that's what she'd wanted it to be.

Joan hurried to the door, but she hesitated in pulling it open too soon. The last thing she wanted was for a servant to overhear *any* of this conversation.

'And never forget, my lady, that I also have influential friends.' Stokes had strutted up behind Joan to hiss in her ear. 'Lord Regan and his lady wife dance to my tune. And I can make you do so, too. After you have handed over one hundred guineas for my silence I shall not trouble you, or your father, again.'

'One hundred guineas?' Joan echoed in disbelief, spinning about. She had imagined he might demand a few guineas, but not a hundred of them. And she also knew that whatever Stokes said

about leaving them in peace, he would be back again and again for more money.

'My calculation reflects the value of the information I hold. It is money well invested if you consider the severity of the consequences should my lips unseal.' Stokes inspected her boldly. Her prettily dishevelled dark hair trailing on rosy cheeks made Lady Joan look ready for bed. The thought of tumbling a duke's daughter held a piquant appeal for an ambitious fellow determined to better himself. But he concentrated his efforts on getting the money, although he did give Joan's arm a clumsy caress.

Joan recoiled from his stubby fingers, glaring at him. 'My father will have you horsewhipped should he find out you have attempted to touch me and blackmail me, Mr Stokes. Take yourself off and I'll say no more of your disgusting impertinence. And make sure to never return.'

She had spunk, that was obvious, Stokes realised. But her hauteur couldn't disguise the fear in her eyes. She would never risk her tryst with the Squire becoming common knowledge; her duty to her family was paramount.

When Thadeus had related to him that a young

woman had engaged him to take her to the Squire, Stokes had relished hearing about it. Thadeus had gone on to tell him that the cab driver had overheard Rockleigh calling the woman *my lady*. Thadeus was an investigator used to searching for a common denominator in odd coincidences. Two people had approached the detective to set up a meeting with Drew Rockleigh and after a few days of surveillance Thadeus's hunch had paid off handsomely. The Duke of Thornley and Miss Morley lived beneath the same elegant roof. Thadeus had guessed his Grace had been attempting to buy off his daughter's swain, but the girl was besotted enough with her lover to risk secretly seeking him out. Saul had quickly bullied Thadeus into allowing him to intervene; his cousin was a coward who'd not risk crossing a powerful aristocrat. Saul had no such qualms when scenting a small fortune in the offing.

Thadeus might blab out his business, but Saul was secretive about his own and only fed his cousin the information he wanted him to have. Few people understood how he accumulated his cash or his connections, but Saul had even surprised himself in managing to pin a duke's daughter beneath his thumb. He looked Joan over with spiteful satisfaction.

'A duke's daughter fornicating on a coach seat with a street fighter,' he tormented. 'His Grace will become a laughing stock because of his wanton child.'

Joan could take no more; least of all because of the truth in his malice. She jerked open the door. 'Leave this instant. Get out,' she whispered.

Stokes smiled, dipping his head politely as though they had just concluded business amicably. 'You may contact me through my cousin to pay what is due. I will tell Thadeus to expect your early visit, Lady Joan…or your father can expect mine…'

Chapter Eleven

In equal parts Bertha Denby resented and envied her elder brother, and always had.

Even as children, growing up in a slum, Drew had seemed high and mighty to her. Not for him the rough and tumble in a gutter with the other snotty-nosed imps scrabbling for farthings tossed by passers-by. As soon as Drew was old enough to do a day's toil he'd earn his pennies honestly rather than beg. He'd boasted, too, that one day he'd be an officer in the Hussars, not a common soldier taking the King's shilling.

Their affluent stepfather had bought Drew a commission in the Hussars, but even had he not, Bertha believed her brother would still have achieved his ambition; it wasn't in his nature to give up on something.

Drew had always been able to discipline himself and rise above squalor and adversity. Bertha was sure she'd guessed how he'd acquired such worthy qualities: he was a guttersnipe with a distinguished sire. His character had been passed on from an admiral, or the like, whereas she had been a lowly seaman's spawn. Their mother had been indiscriminate in her choice of client; when the ships docked and the navvies crowded the wharves, Rosemary would sooner lure a fellow with gold braid on his shoulders, but in their absence, anyone would do.

Spitefully Bertha reminded herself that with Saul's help she'd finally tumbled her half-brother from his pedestal, snatching the riches left by Peter Rockleigh that Drew had refused to share with her. Now she was the one living the high life in Mayfair while he was back where he started, in a hovel.

Their stepfather had done his best to turn her into a lady, but he'd been doomed to failure from the start. If Drew was his father's child then she was her mother's: a harlot through and through. But she hoped her own daughter would turn out to be different, although Cecilia was already showing worrying signs of wantonness. Bertha knew she must soften Saul's grip on his ward, for he would praise her flaws when it suited him to do so.

Cecilia yearned for Henry Laurenson to pay a call, but Saul had other plans for the girl and believed rich pickings were to be had from Lord Regan before she was married off.

Her brother and Luke Wolfson had been close friends before their estrangement and the connection through marriage to the Morlands remained. The grapevine between mutual acquaintances might provide too much information to Lady Joan. She seemed a spirited and inquisitive young woman. Bertha had overheard Joan questioning Cecilia about her family at Lady Regan's and there were things that should remain concealed. Much as she loved social climbing, Bertha realised it might be wise to keep her daughter apart from the Duke of Thornley's daughter.

'I should like to see Lady Joan again, Mama. Shall we invite her and her friend to tea this afternoon?'

Bertha flicked the pages of a journal, then lifted her eyes to Saul for his reaction to Cecilia's request, hoping it would come in the negative. In addition to her other reservations, the establishment they'd taken on for the Season wasn't grand enough for them to entertain a duke's daughter. Stokes signalled with a glower that he disapproved of Cecilia's idea.

'It is short notice, my dear,' Bertha said, standing up from her armchair. 'We are attending Lady Regan's soirée. It is time to choose a dress to wear.'

'I don't want to go,' Cecilia cried. 'Her husband gives me goosebumps when he creeps up behind me. I don't like either of them.'

Saul surged to his feet, flinging aside *The Times*. 'Lord Regan is showing interest in your future, and you would do well to encourage him rather than scoff.'

'My papa wouldn't have forced me to go,' Cecilia protested. 'I wish Uncle Drew were still here. Where is he? Why has he disappeared?'

'He has troubles, that's all you need to know,' Bertha said quickly.

'It's not fair! Once he was like a papa to me. I should be told why he has gone away.'

'It's none of your concern,' Stokes snarled, raising a hand as though to slap his ward. He clenched his splayed fingers, remembering himself, and instead pointed at the door. 'Go to your room and get ready for your outing.'

Cecilia glanced at her mother, but got no assistance from that quarter. Bertha had already reseated herself and resumed looking at the journal. With a contemptuous snort Cecilia stormed from the parlour.

Joan was undoing the strings of her bonnet when her stepmother's rapid footsteps echoed on the vestibule's marble flags.

'Louise is feeling a bit better, but her cough lingers,' Joan reported. She'd returned home from visiting her friend's sickbed and believed Maude must be eager to discover how the invalid did.

'That is good news,' Maude rattled off, smiling wanly. 'Your papa has arrived home,' she hurried on. 'The Duke is not at all well, Joan. The physician has been sent for.'

Joan let her gloves and bonnet fall to the console table. 'What ails him?' she demanded anxiously.

'He believes that the gumboil has poisoned his blood.' Maude flapped a hand. 'I have scolded him for not remaining at Thornley Heights to recover from the fever.' Worriedly, she paced to and fro. 'You know how obstinate he can be when he gets a maggot in his head over something. He said he had to come home to attend to a pressing matter and requested you go to him on your return.' Maude gazed searchingly at her stepdaughter. 'Are you aware of this *matter* he speaks about? Alfred said it was nothing for me to fret over. But how can I not if he is suffering for it?'

Joan comforted her stepmother with an embrace despite demons of her own squeezing her heart. She could guess what had made her father dash back to Mayfair. But had his Grace only known it, he could count Rockleigh as the lesser threat now Stokes had come after her.

Guilt and fear raged through Joan, turning her body alternately hot and cold. She dearly loved her father and if he were to relapse, or, God forbid, die because he'd sped home thinking he must cover up her past misdemeanours, she would never forgive herself. And neither, she guessed, would Maude should the woman ever find out about it.

Warning the Duke of a looming calamity would be sure to do him untold harm. Joan knew she had only two options: pay Stokes off and hope never to see him again—if she could get her hands on enough money—or enlist Rockleigh's help in defeating him. He was also embroiled in the matter after all! In fact, he was to blame, having instigated the passion that Stokes now held over her head like the Sword of Damocles!

'Alfred has sent me away, saying the sight of my Friday face makes him feel worse.' Maude began dabbing at her moist eyes. 'I fear he is delirious not to want his wife at his bedside at such a time.'

Joan squeezed her stepmother's hands in comfort. 'Papa is just being Papa. He'd sooner you were spared the distress of the sickroom.' She had walked the short distance to and from her friend's town house in Grosvenor Square, feeling quite light-hearted as the golden orb dropped to paint a sunset on the horizon. Since Stokes's visit a few days ago Joan had convinced herself that the man would never risk having his swindle exposed and neither would he cross the powerful Duke of Thornley. With her papa now ill in bed the danger seemed terrifyingly real again.

'You must not upset him either.' Maude affectionately rubbed colour back into her stepdaughter's pale cheek. When Joan had returned she'd had a healthy glow gained from the blustery outdoors.

'We must both buck up.' Joan forced a smile. 'Papa is as strong as an ox and stubborn with it. He will be up and about again by the end of the week, you'll see.'

Following a light knock on the door, Joan tiptoed into her father's chamber. Tobias Bartlett was stationed on one side of the huge four-poster bed and a maid was on the other, dipping a cloth in cool water to bathe the patient's brow. On noticing his daughter Alfred waved away the solemnfaced servants, urgently beckoning Joan.

'Oh, Papa!' Joan whispered as she drew closer and saw the crimson flush spotting his cheeks and the brightness in his eyes. The Duke was propped on pillows and his rasping for breath worsened as he tried to struggle up to greet her. 'Why did you not rest in Devon till well enough to travel?' Joan gripped the dry palms he held out to her.

'I am well enough to travel…or I wouldn't be here, would I?' he weakly joked.

'Indeed you are here, back with us, and must rest in bed and heed the doctor's advice when he comes and tells you to stay just where you are.' She raised his knuckles to her lips.

'A concoction or two and I'll be right as rain,' the Duke wheezed, pulling the blankets this way and that as though he would fling them off and rise. 'Mrs Lewis is mixing up some noxious brews for me.' He chuckled huskily. 'Kill or cure, that'll be my choice.' With surprising strength he suddenly drew Joan closer to the edge of the bed. 'Has Rockleigh been a nuisance in my absence?' he whispered, his burning breath fanning his daughter's cheek.

'He has not, Papa,' Joan replied quietly. 'There is nothing for you to fret over where he is concerned, I promise.'

'You've not seen him then?'

'I have…but…he was agreeable,' Joan's heartbeat slowed to a dull thud as erotic memories flowed into her mind. She felt ashamed even having such thoughts in her father's presence.

'So what did he do to please you?' The Duke's lips twitched in an optimistic smile.

'We spent only a short time talking and parted quickly. It was dreadful weather and I wanted to avoid the storm,' Joan carefully picked a path between truth and lie and embarrassment. 'Did Old Matthews's funeral go well?' she said, changing the subject.

The Duke gave a tired nod. 'A capital send off for him. A good crowd of people in the chapel, and a fine wake afterwards…' He started to cough.

'Hush…that is enough talking for now. Shall I fetch you a powder to help you sleep, Papa?'

'No need, my dear, the sawbones is here.' The Duke's red-rimmed eyes veered past his daughter to the fellow entering with the housekeeper. Mrs Lewis was carrying a tray laden with bottles and cups. 'No doubt between them they'll fill me full of potions fit to fell a thirteen-hand nag.' Alfred patted his daughter's arm. 'Off you go now, my dear. You have put my mind at rest over it all.' He sighed, sinking back against the pillows. 'I wish I'd not tortured myself over it while away, imagining all sorts of chaos. Perhaps I *should* have stayed where I was in Devon for I feel weak as a kitten now…'

Having reported to Maude that the Duke seemed to be rallying, Joan returned to her chamber, alternately fretting over her papa's health and the risk of Stokes smearing her name before she could come up with a plan to stop him. A moment later she glanced out of the window and her anxiety soared.

Despite Stokes having pulled his hat low over his eyes his identity was obvious. Joan wondered if her tormentor intended loitering until he believed the coast was clear to call on her again. He suddenly bowled off along the street, but Joan's respite was brief; it had occurred to her that he might have watched her sick father being helped into the house by footmen earlier. If that were so, the villain would be calculating how to turn the Duke of Thornley's weakness to his advantage.

'I will tell Thadeus to expect your early visit, Lady Joan...or your father can expect mine...' Those had been his parting words to her on the afternoon of his blackmail. Indeed, he had not waited long before returning to spy on the house. Now her father's health was at stake Joan knew *she* daren't wait long before acting.

'Lady Joan! Um...please, do come in,' Vincent Walters stuttered, striving to cover his blushing confusion at the astonishing sight of the Duke of

Thornley's daughter on his step at seven o'clock in the evening.

'I'm sorry to turn up unannounced, sir,' Joan began breathlessly. 'But I'd be grateful for your assistance in an urgent matter, if you don't mind.' Given her mooning over him when younger, Joan spoke in a way designed to quash any suspicion Vincent might have that her inappropriate visit was romantically motivated.

She was far from feeling mellow. The sight of Saul Stokes boldly stationed outside her home that afternoon had sent Joan into a horrible state of uncertainty. She'd paced about in her bedroom, inwardly debating whether to pay an unchaperoned visit on the vicar and enlist his help. She'd considered writing to him, but that would simply create a delay, prolonging her inner turbulence and making more likely the odious villain carrying out his threat to contact her sick papa. Impulsivity had suddenly overwhelmed her and Joan had bolted down the stairs with Anna in tow to find Pip and a carriage. But now she had arrived at her destination her negligence in protecting her own, and her family's, good name was pricking at her conscience once more.

The elderly servant who'd opened the door was squinting her disapproval, heightening Joan's misgivings. She gave Mrs Pickles a polite nod and stepped over the threshold. The woman had obviously remembered that her aunt had guarded her reputation last time. The stooped servant peered left and right along the street, muttering that a shop girl would know better about calling on a bachelor even if he were a man of the cloth. Anna had insisted in getting down from the carriage so at least people could see her mistress wasn't completely alone. Joan knew that her maid hadn't approved of her coming here either. But Anna kept her own counsel and was loyal to a fault.

Briefly Joan had considered asking Maude to accompany her, but her stepmother was already upset over her husband's health and Joan didn't want to add to her woes. Maude would have expected an explanation for the necessity of the visit at such a crucial time. Joan could hardly tell the truth…yet neither did she want to lie.

'Of course, I'm at your service and will do whatever I can to help.' Having conquered his surprise, Vincent ushered Joan towards the parlour. 'Would you like some tea? Shall Mrs Pickles take your maid to the kitchen to wait while we talk?' The moment Vincent had heard the knock on the door he had dropped his pen and jumped up from his desk. Parishioners turned up at all hours with their problems and he did what he could to provide succour. But he'd certainly not expected this young woman to interrupt him composing a sermon.

'Thank you, but, no.' Joan didn't want him summoning back his grumpy housekeeper. 'Anna will wait outside and I cannot tarry as I'm sure you appreciate—' Joan broke off as a loud knock was heard before they had set foot inside the parlour.

Mumbling beneath her breath, Mrs Pickles again attended the door, allowing a youth to hurtle into the hallway. Vincent strode to meet the lad, recognising him as Constance Cook's brother.

'Can you come quick, Reverend? Me sister's sent me to tell you that Old Blackie's got the rattle and he's asking for you. He's gabbling on about getting sent to Old Nick 'less you're there with him when he croaks.'

'Benny Cook's come to say that an elderly parishioner begs my presence at his deathbed, fearing he'll go to hell without my blessing,' Vincent explained as Joan frowned incomprehension.

'Oh, of course, you must hurry then,' Joan said immediately.

'But you have come to ask for my help on an urgent matter,' Vincent reminded her. 'Will it wait till I return? I'm not sure how long I might be gone.'

'Oh…never mind that now.' Joan knew her selfless decision to be the right one. Nevertheless, a twinge of guilt pricked her insides; just for a moment she'd been tempted to delay the vicar to make him hear her out first.

'I feel I should spare you ten minutes at least.' Vincent felt awkward turning out of his house the daughter of an aristocrat known to support Christian causes.

'Please go and give the poor fellow what comfort you can,' Joan urged, aware of the housekeeper and the shabby youth listening.

'I'll return your call tomorrow, Lady Joan, and we'll have that talk.' He began donning his sombre hat and caped cloak, fetched by Mrs Pickles.

'There's really no need, sir…' Joan scoured her mind for another meeting place. She didn't want a clergyman attending the house when her papa was so ill in case the servants jumped to conclusions about last rites being nigh.

'Then forgive me...I must dash...every minute counts at a time like this.' Vincent picked up a small bible from the hall table and put it in his pocket.

After Vincent had sped away Joan gave the housekeeper a firm nod, indicating she was ready to leave. When outside she noticed that Anna was again seated inside the carriage, seeking shelter from the stirring breeze while peeping beneath the blind. Joan closed her eyes in exasperation; after all her agonising over it, the trip had been a squandered effort. But Vincent had the unhappy task of sitting with a frightened man as he breathed his last. The favour she'd been about to ask him now seemed irrelevant and tawdry by comparison.

Her fingers closed about the folded parchment in her pocket that she'd wanted Vincent to deliver for her. She couldn't wander the slums herself seeking the Squire and the only other person cognizant with his whereabouts was Thadeus Pryke. She could hardly approach that man to help!

''Ere...you can have them back, lady.'

Startled, Joan pivoted on a heel to see Benny

Cook tendering a couple of pennies on a grimy palm. She identified the youth then as the dirty-faced young ruffian who'd threatened to steal her aunt's brooch. Today his features appeared less mucky and his expression less defiant. In fact, he looked sheepish.

'You remember hounding me for money, do you? Has your conscience got the better of you, Benny?'

He shook his head. 'Me sister's conscience gets the better of me,' he admitted with a grin. 'She tells me *I'll* end up with Old Nick if I don't go straight and get honest work.'

'Your sister sounds like a sensible young woman.'

'She weren't till she got mixed up with the Squire. Now Constance thinks she's a lady like you.'

'The Squire?' Joan echoed hoarsely.

'He's the fellow what threw all of us off your coach that day you got lost. He forfeit his purse when he saved your bacon, and he had the other cove on the run, too.' Benny gave a proud smile. 'Me sister Constance is the Squire's girl.'

Joan glanced at the lad's thatch of matted fair

hair. She recalled Stokes taunting her over the Squire's Cockney Blonde so could believe the family connection. Benny looked about thirteen and had a solid physique and regular features that held a promise of the handsome man he'd become.

On impulse Joan said, 'Would you like to keep those pennies by earning them honestly, Benny?'

The youth nodded eagerly, his fingers already closing over the coppers.

Joan pulled the letter from her pocket. 'Would you give this to the Squire for me?'

'He'll be supping in the Cock and Hen, I expect. I'll take it to him direct, if you like.'

'Thank you...' Joan handed over the sealed parchment. As she watched the boy sprint away doubts set in over what she'd done. If Benny couldn't find the Squire in the tavern he might forget all about the errand...or worse, he might give the letter to Drew's paramour. Suddenly Joan felt very uncharitable. She might have helped Vincent teach slum urchins to read, but she was counting on Benny and his sister not being able to make head or tail of her message, should they open it. There was nothing incriminating in it and she'd not signed her name, but Benny was sure to say a posh lady had handed over the note. Joan didn't want a jealous mistress thrown into an already explosive mix of lust and greed.

Earlier Joan had penned, then crumpled up and lobbed into the glowing embers of her bedroom fireplace, more than half-a-dozen drafts of the note. Finally she'd settled on dashing off a short paragraph, requesting Rockleigh meet her at five o'clock on the following afternoon. The lane she'd nominated was within reasonable distance of her home, yet was remote enough for their conversation to take place unobserved. She hoped Benny would deliver the letter, yet Joan was again acutely conscious of the risks in such a rendezvous. But there was nothing else to be done; she'd never commit something so scandalous and embarrassing to paper, or speak of it in anybody else's company. In Joan's mind there was no option but to meet Drew Rockleigh swiftly and discreetly and tell him why she now believed that Stokes was an even greater devil than either of them had suspected.

She wondered what Rockleigh would read into her summons. He wouldn't expect her to bring up the matter of the fraud again, but his arrogance might lead him to believe that she'd allowed her passion for him to conquer her pride.

Immediately after their hostile parting on that stormy night Joan had believed that every nuance of his mood would remain lodged in her memory. Now she found it hard to recall if anger had dominated his frustrated lust when he brought her home. The journey done, he had pulled her from his mount quite brusquely as though keen to be rid of her.

Weeks ago he'd warned her to keep a safe distance from him, but she had found staying away impossible, just as she had found resisting his kisses and caresses impossible…

With a sigh Joan increased her pace towards the carriage stationed at the kerb and allowed Pip to help her inside. She pushed thoughts of Rockleigh to the back of her mind and concentrated on her father, eager now to get home and see how he was.

Chapter Twelve

The next morning Joan was awake shortly after a coral-coloured sunrise patterned her bedchamber ceiling.

On her return from the vicarage she had been thankful to find her short absence had gone unnoticed, but her relief had been brief. Her father had been delirious and no amount of gentle coaxing from Joan could make Maude, seated at his bedside, relinquish her husband's hands and go to her chamber to get some rest. Mrs Lewis and Tobias Bartlett had also been keeping a vigil and had looked drawn from the effort of trying to reassure their mistress while concealing their own anxiety over his Grace's deterioration.

Realising she could be of little help, Joan had withdrawn from the room and its fraught atmosphere, charging Mrs Lewis to summon her back should the Duke's condition worsen.

The night had seemed interminable; she had hardly slept for fretting over her father and her coming meeting with Rockleigh. When the night sky had seemed to be at its blackest, so had her mood. Unable to endure the turbulence in her mind she'd pattered barefoot to the window and gazed into the dark, feeling frightened and very alone; if Rockleigh ignored her summons, she'd be forced to fend for herself against Stokes. Joan knew for all her bravado she was no match for a man practised in corruption.

Although feeling unrefreshed, Joan threw off the bedcovers with a groan and shrugged on her velvet wrap. She set her shoulders and inhaled deeply, determined to prepare herself for the challenges that awaited her on this particular day.

A tap on the door heralded Anna's arrival. The maid entered quietly, bearing a copper pitcher of washing water. Her mistress had never been one to idle in bed, nevertheless Anna looked surprised to see her up so early. Lady Joan was always full of vigour and spontaneity. Anna suspected that her exuberance had again landed her in a scrape.

Her mistress's brief meeting with the vicar yesterday had seemed to go badly. For the duration of the journey home Joan had frowned morosely into space, but Anna had suspected that more than an untimely visit and her ailing father had been preying on the young woman's mind. Pip had told her he'd seen Lady Joan creeping into the house on the night of the storm. Much as Anna had wanted to scold her mistress for going abroad without her, she had held her tongue for two reasons: she didn't want to get Pip into trouble for breaking a confidence and neither did she wish to be thought insubordinate.

'Is my stepmother abed?' Joan asked.

'She is, my lady. Tobias told me that the Duchess didn't retire until the early hours when his Grace was finally sleeping soundly.' Anna sorrowfully shook her head. 'Your stepmother will tire herself out.' She continued pouring the steaming water into the washing bowl, then added a few drops of scented oil. 'Take care, my lady, it's very hot…I didn't expect you to be up yet or I'd have fetched it lukewarm.'

'It is good news that the Duke eventually settled down for the night.'

'Indeed, it is,' Anna agreed.

'I can manage, thank you…' Joan slipped free as her maid began to help her remove her night things. 'I might go back to bed and try to snooze for a while longer.' She'd felt a weight lift from her on learning that her father had managed to get some sleep.

'Shall I arrange for a breakfast tray if you'd rather not go down, my lady?'

'I've no appetite, but thank you, anyway.'

Anna's smile was sympathetic. The whole household seemed subdued at present. Below stairs people weren't simply worried over their livelihoods should his Grace take a turn for the worse. Their employer was a good man made better by the woman he'd married a few years ago. The Duke's second wife took a sincere interest in the servants' welfare. In fact, her Grace had made an effort to come to know them all, from scullion to stable hand, greeting them by name. In return, the staff had great respect and affection for the couple.

When Anna left Joan decided against curling up under the eiderdown, knowing that however tightly she squeezed shut her eyes she'd be unable to fall asleep. Placing her warm forehead against the window glass, she watched a vivid blush spreading on the horizon. It was a splendid sight, but her gaze was soon drawn to the spot where she'd last seen Stokes loitcring. At present only a delivery boy occupied the opposite pavement, swinging to a precarious height a basket of eggs as he bowled along.

Joan turned back into the room, regretting having made her meeting with Rockleigh so late in the afternoon. An interminable day seemed to stretch out in front of her and nothing to fill it but her active imagination. She'd as soon grasp the nettle now than anticipate its sting for so many hours.

Bucking herself up, Joan dipped a muslin square into rose-scented water, then briskly washed her face until her cheeks stung and she stopped yawning. Her *toilette* over, she opened her wardrobe, choosing a silk day dress that she'd not worn for some time as the plain style had gone out of fashion. She'd not had the heart to discard the garment after her papa had complimented her on it, declaring that its *marron* colour reminded him of her pretty locks, inherited from her dear mama.

Hoping to please him, Joan put on the dress, then vigorously brushed her hair, tying back the abundant glossy waves in a length of silver ribbon secured at her nape. She doubted her father would be awake, but nevertheless set off towards his chamber. She would be happy to simply sit with him, taking comfort from knowing that a deep sleep helped him heal.

The Duke's even complexion and rhythmic snores reassured Joan that his fever had broken. The rumbling sound had the added bonus of being soporific. She noticed that Tobias had stayed the night with his master; the butler had slumped low in the wingchair opposite, his chin propped on his chest. Following the faithful fellow's lead, Joan settled further into her armchair, closing her eyes.

'There is a gentleman waiting to see you in the small library, my lady.'

Joan came awake with a start, but it took only a few seconds for her daze to clear. The ragged youth she'd met at the vicarage had just figured in a disturbing dream. Now her thoughts jumped to the other person she'd spoken to yesterday evening and the likelihood of Vincent having returned her call despite her asking him not to. She quickly stood up, moving away from her father's side in case the sound of voices woke him.

'What is the time, Anna?' Joan had no idea how long she'd been dozing.

'It is not quite ten o'clock, my lady.'

Only a visitor lacking in manners would arrive at such an hour. And the vicar was well versed in etiquette; either he had been unable to contain his curiosity until the afternoon or... Joan's mind suddenly veered to a fellow who certainly was no stranger to vulgar behaviour. Saul Stokes had threatened an early visit on her father.

'Is it the man who called before?' Joan demanded in an undertone.

'I don't know, my lady. A junior footman attended the door in Tobias's absence and he omitted to press for the gentleman's name.' Anna looked apologetic. 'We're all at sixes and sevens below stairs since his Grace has been poorly.'

Joan was convinced then that Stokes, acting bumptious and aware the Duke was unwell, had returned to turn the screws on her, anticipating that she'd do her utmost to protect her father.

With an anxious glance at the patient she moved

swiftly and softly on slippered feet to the door. Darting down the stairs, she arrived at the small library with slashes of angry colour on her cheekbones, ready to do battle.

Joan stood motionless on the threshold, staring in disbelief into a pair of narrowed amber eyes that had turned her way. He suddenly put to the floor the polished Hessian that had been idly propped on the fender. The movement broke Joan's trance; she remembered to breathe and stepped inside the room. Tugging the door to behind her, she pressed her spine against the panels, gaining support for her wobbly legs. A challenge had sprung immediately to mind, but Joan couldn't force it from her dry mouth; neither could she remove her fingers from where they had clenched on the cool brass handle.

'What…what on earth do you want?' she finally stuttered.

'I was about to ask you the same thing.' With slow deliberation Drew placed Joan's letter on the mantelshelf. 'You desire to see me urgently, I gather. So here I am.'

His cool irony piqued. Her heart was racing from the shock of his presence, yet he seemed quite at ease. No hint of embarrassment caused his eyes to swerve away, as hers did when their gazes collided. Their intimacy on that tempestuous night wasn't memorable for him, Joan guessed... whereas for her the havoc of how close her wantonness had brought her to utter ruin never quit her consciousness.

She forced herself to take two rapid steps towards him. 'I do need to speak to you about something...but not here!' She pointed a quivering finger at the letter lying idle on the timber shelf. 'Did you not read it properly? I made it clear where and when we should rendezvous...'

'I read it.'

'Well, in that case, why come here?' Joan demanded in a despairing voice. 'Poacher's Lane at five o'clock, I wrote.' She would have snatched up the note to check that she'd not sealed the wrong draft, but dark fingers were curled about her wrist, preventing her having it.

'Poacher's Lane at five o'clock...' Drew mimicked softly. 'Very mysterious...but I'm done with playing games, my lady. You're the Duke of Thornley's daughter and if you want to speak to me, you'll have to do so in a seemly fashion in future.'

Joan felt her hackles rise at his implication that she'd needlessly caused a drama to savour the intrigue of it. 'I think once you know the nature of the business, sir, you may deem a secluded spot not only appropriate, but essential. I've no liking for risking my reputation in such a way, but neither do I relish disclosing the matter in my own home, with my family close by!' She tried to twist free of his restraint, but he released her in his own time, his dark fingers slipping leisurely from her skin.

Wondering if she'd imagined the caress in his touch, she glanced up, noticing for the first time the emerald core in his eyes, but long black lashes soon shuttered their expression.

And then, close as she was to him, she noticed something else. She'd sent her note to the Squire… the boxer who had rescued her from a baying mob, hoping he would again be her protector. But here in front of her today was Drew Rockleigh, sophisticate. Aside from the faint trail of a scar on his left cheek and some scabbing on his knuckles there was nothing to hint at his alter ego as a prize fighter.

So startled by this sudden discovery did Joan feel that she unwittingly took a step back to better appreciate the sight of him. At one time Rockleigh had been one of the most impressive gentlemen in all of Mayfair. And like a phoenix arisen from the ashes, he was that noble Corinthian once more.

Joan blinked in confusion; he looked elegance personified: his peat brown tailcoat was of finest wool, cut expertly to mould across broad shoulders. An intricately folded cravat was embellished with a tiger's eye stone and trim hips and muscled thighs were encased in buff breeches.

'Do I measure up?' Drew asked ironically, having watched her inspection terminate on his highly polished Hessians.

'No…I fear you may not, sir,' Joan said with a bitter laugh. From the first moment she had met the Squire, half-nude and bloodied from fighting, Joan had yearned to see him return to the person he'd once been. Now she wasn't so sure about that.

The Drew Rockleigh of old, who'd been welcomed at society parties and had been her brother-in-law's friend and equal, might find it distasteful to get embroiled in a blackmail plot even if he were partly to blame for its creation.

'You'd sooner have me as your inferior?'

'I'd sooner have you as a fellow villains are chary of crossing.'

'I can oblige you on that. So tell me what worries you.' His voice, though smooth as silk, held an undercurrent of command and interest had sharpened his gaze.

Joan shook her head, her face heating at the idea of alluding, beneath her father's roof, to the erotic game they'd played. 'I can't tell you anything here,' she breathed.

'This is private enough; I imagine your father is still in Devon and your stepmother is not yet up.' Drew strolled to the casement and gazed out at a street slowly coming to life.

Joan realised then that his visit had been purposely made at an extraordinary time to minimise the risk of others asking awkward questions. 'I guessed somebody ill mannered would want an audience at this hour in the morning.' It was the only comment Joan had ready.

'Yet you were not anticipating seeing me, were you,' Drew stated. 'I'll take comfort from it.'

Joan was aware of his subtle amusement; indeed, she had not imagined him to be her visitor, but she recalled being impatient for their meeting when she rose at dawn.

Be careful what you wish for...

The phrase rotated mockingly in her mind. Had she believed he might turn up out of the blue she would have been better prepared for this heart-stopping moment. Turning from the window, he plunged his hands into his pockets, his expression darkly quizzical.

'Indeed, I was not expecting you to come here, sir,' Joan blurted. 'And I am still at a loss to know why you have done so...all things considered.'

'I considered all things before taking the liberty of coming here, just as I considered your reason for summoning me.'

'And to what conclusion did you come?' Joan asked hoarsely.

'My conceit brought me one answer that, alas, I now doubt is correct.' Drew's sardonic smile matched his tone. 'Are you still meddling in my affairs despite me asking you not to?'

'No, I am not!' Joan retorted. 'And I do not

think my attempt to warn you about loathsome Mr Stokes was meddling.'

'I know you meant well, Joan,' Drew said gently. 'But you must stop this. Don't bother with me. You don't know who I really am. Stay away…don't contact me again.' His eyes flowed over her, returned hungrily to her face, then he turned, bracing two tanned fists against the window frame. 'Somewhere in Mayfair there's a nice young blue blood waiting for you; don't ruin your chance of having him by risking an unwise association with me.' The lightness in his tone was at odds with a tension she could see whitening his knuckles and hollowing his cheek.

'Don't patronise me, or think I've fallen under your spell just because we…' Joan couldn't finish what she'd been about to say, but she did march closer to him. 'If I want a suitor of blue blood… or red blood or any sort of blood…I'll make up my own mind on it. I'm not a child.'

'Oh…you're not a child…I know that,' Drew said with sour self-mockery. 'But you lack maturity.' His slanting, sideways gaze devoured her sweet curves beneath the modest dress. A loose curl of chestnut hair had fallen across her shoulder, forming a glossy orbit about a small nub beneath silk. Drew felt the burn in his blood; the desire for her never went away no matter how hard Constance tried to woo him. A frustrated curse broke in his throat and he threw back his head to frown at the ceiling.

Joan realised it was gentlemanly of him to try to make her see sense and avoid him, yet it felt horribly like rejection. She also knew she annoyed him, yet her indignation was tempered by need. She could ring for a footman to show him out and preserve some pride, but the thought of losing his company now she had it was unbearable. A latent strength and dynamism seemed to emanate from him, reassuring Joan that he could easily beat Stokes.

She'd been waiting…hoping for him to make a better guess at the purpose of her letter, allowing her a reprieve. It was excruciating to contemplate hinting at the occasion when she'd lain on the seat of a Hackney cab with her bodice unbuttoned and her skirts in disarray while this man had drawn moans of pleasure from her.

Joan paced to and fro to avoid meeting his gaze. 'So you expected me to be up at this time in the morning, or you would not have come, I suppose,' she rattled off.

'I imagine you've had as little sleep as have I since we last met.' Drew retrieved her letter from the mantelshelf and put it in his pocket.

So he'd been restless and thinking of her, had he? Joan wondered if he did so while lying abed with his Cockney Blonde mistress! 'Benny Cook found you in the tavern...he said he would.'

'You were at the vicarage yesterday evening.' It was a toneless statement. 'I believed the school had closed.'

'It has; I'd gone there in the hope of asking the Reverend Walters to deliver that note to you. Before the matter could be discussed Benny turned up with sad news.'

'The blacksmith passed away peacefully in the early hours, so I heard,' Drew informed.

'I'm glad the old fellow had the vicar's comfort and blessing.'

'Benny told you that he knew me?'

'He did. He also said that his sister aspires to better herself since becoming friendly with you.' A frosty note had crept into Joan's voice, but mentioning his paramour's ambition did no more than tilt a corner of his mouth in a half-smile. 'As the lad knew where to find you it seemed fate was on my side and my message would get to you.'

'Why involve the vicar, or Benny, when Thadeus Pryke knows where I am?'

Joan visibly flinched at the mention of her blackmailer's accomplice. But she had been abruptly presented with her opening and must use it.

Drew had noticed her reaction and approached her, tilting her face to his with firm fingers. 'Has Thadeus Pryke done something?' he demanded.

'Indeed he has, sir,' Joan admitted huskily. She slipped free of him and went to gaze into the unlit fire; she couldn't countenance referring to their intimacy while he touched her.

'On that stormy night in Wapping the cab driver heard more of our...' Joan stumbled over the next word '...conversation...than I, or I hope you, would have wanted, and recounted everything to Mr Pryke. Unfortunately, Mr Pryke then told his cousin who happens to be Mr Stokes.' She noticed an immediate stillness in Drew. 'Perhaps you can now guess at what compelled me to send you that letter.' Instead of feeling hot and bothered, as she'd expected she would when referring to their shared passion Joan felt cold and her complexion lost colour rather than gained it. When the silence continued she snapped her eyes to his and ice trailed her spine. She'd seen him wear that expression once before. It had been years ago when he had prevented her father's hand from reaching her cheek in chastisement.

'Stokes sent you a blackmail letter?' Wrathful disbelief had stolen volume from Drew's voice, making his question clipped and husky.

'No...I've nothing in writing from him. He's been shrewd enough to give me no evidence to use against him. He came here...threatened to tell my father of what we did...' Joan pivoted away from a pair of ruthlessly steady eyes. 'When my maid said I'd a visitor this morning I thought it was him, come back again to torment me.'

'I'm sorry,' Drew said softly. 'I'd not have given you that extra hurt, had I known. I withheld my name because I thought you might refuse to see me, preferring to wait for our Poacher's Lane meeting.'

'I *would* have preferred it!' Joan cried in a muted tone. 'And now you can see why, can't you?'

Drew gave a single slow nod as he closed the

space between them. His palm moved as though to cup her face, but it made no more than chest height before being clenched into a fist that was plunged into his pocket.

Joan's lashes fell over her misty eyes; she felt forlorn. Heaven only knew she would have liked the comfort of his strong embrace now the deed was done and she'd unburdened herself. The weight had gone from her shoulders, yet she'd been left feeling oddly weaker.

'I take it your father is still in the West Country and, knowing of his absence, Stokes has taken advantage of it.' Drew's long pace ate up the distance between casement and fender. He ceased prowling and moved towards her to hurry her answer.

Joan had been about to correct his assumption of her father's whereabouts when the door of the small library opened and her stepmother burst in.

'Oh…there you are, Joan. Your papa is feeling better and wants to see you.'

Joan had been startled by Maude's arrival, but managed a smile for the woman, quickly regaining composure.

'I don't know if you remember Mr—' Joan had

been on the point of blurting out an introduction, but Maude interrupted her.

'Indeed I do know you, sir. Well, how odd a co-incidence!' The Duchess approached the handsome gentleman who appeared to be standing rather too close to her stepdaughter, but she allowed it to pass. 'My husband was speaking of you, sir, just last night.'

Maude omitted to add that Alfred had been delirious at the time. Not much of the Duke's rambling had made sense, but Maude had caught the words *Rockleigh* and *capital fellow* being uttered by her husband in almost the same breath. So taking her lead from that, she felt she should make welcome her son-in-law's old friend even if she had heard some scandalous tales about him recently.

Maude had turned up in the sickroom not long after her stepdaughter quit it. Anna had informed her that Joan had a visitor and the news, though softly spoken, seemed to bring the Duke awake. He'd agitatedly demanded to see his daughter and to know who she was with, insisting his wife fetch her immediately.

'I expect you have come to see how the Duke

does, have you not, Mr Rockleigh?' Maude said. 'It is good of you, sir, and I'm pleased to tell you that he is improving. The news of his malady has travelled and I have many notes from his friends praying for his speedy recovery.' Maude drew from a pocket a folded parchment, flapping it. 'The post has been. Luke and Fiona are naturally concerned. But now Alfred seems to be on the mend I would sooner my daughter rest at home rather than make the journey to London. It would be a trial for her in her condition…' Maude's monologue tailed off and she smiled expectantly.

'I'm very glad to know that your husband is better, your Grace.' There was a purposeful spark in the gold of Drew's eyes as they briefly met Joan's. She understood very well that signal: it would be best for people to think he'd turned up unexpectedly to condole about the Duke's health than let them probe for an alternative explanation.

'You had best hurry to your papa, Joan, he will fret else.' Maude stepped towards the bell pull. 'You will take some tea before leaving, Mr Rockleigh?'

'Thank you, but I cannot tarry, ma'am. I've got

the news I wanted. I have an appointment later that I must not miss…'

As their eyes collided Joan read his message: he would be at Poacher's Lane at five o'clock so they could discuss what to do about Stokes. She'd seen, too, that he was sorry for trivialising her need for a private talk; and there had been something else in the depths of his intensely thoughtful gaze that excited and disturbed her.

He would sooner they didn't sneak about, and heaven only knew so would she…yet… Joan was certain that Drew was also tempted by the prospect of the two of them being alone at a secluded spot. The yearning to feel his strong arms about her and his mouth caressing hers never went away and Joan had just seen the fire in his eyes, convincing her that he, too, was being tormented by that burning mutual attraction between them.

'Thank you for calling, sir,' Joan said breathily. 'If you will excuse me, I shall go and see how my father is.' In a few light steps she was gone from the room.

Despite knowing her father was impatient to see her, Joan hesitated at the turn in the stairs, hoping to see Drew enter the hallway. Within seconds he did so and as though he knew she might be watching twin tigerish eyes swung upwards, tangling with her soulful grey stare. A moment later Joan had disappeared in a whisper of silk.

Chapter Thirteen

'Oh, I have missed you!'

As usual, Cecilia had risen late and had been on her way to have breakfast when she'd spotted their maid opening the door to her Uncle Drew. Food forgotten, she had hurtled down the few remaining stairs with a delighted whoop and launched herself at him.

Drew disentangled himself from his niece's clutch, fondly ruffling her fair hair. 'You're still acting like a dreadful hoyden, I see.'

Cecilia nodded, unabashed. 'Where have you been all this while? They wouldn't tell me anything other than you had got into a bad mess and gone away.' Cecilia hugged Drew about the waist again.

'Well, now I am back to keep an eye on you, so you'd best behave yourself.'

'I must start to act like a lady.' Cecilia sighed. 'I want somebody special to think well of me because...' Cecilia glanced about to ensure the maid had gone. 'I have fallen in love properly this time, Uncle Drew,' she hissed in a whisper. 'But Mama can't know or she'll tell *him* and they'll spoil it for me.'

Inwardly Drew cursed; he could have done without Cecilia presenting him with further complications. 'You've received a proposal from Henry Laurenson?' he asked.

Cecilia pouted. 'Not yet...but I'm expecting one... Henry says I'm the most beguiling—how did you know about Henry?' she suddenly interrupted herself to blurt out her question.

'I've not been so far away that I've missed the rumours flying about,' Drew admitted wryly.

'Is it as bad as that?' Cecilia chewed her lip. 'I hoped I hadn't set my cap at Henry quite so obviously. My friend Joan Morland told me the cats might get their claws out if I wasn't careful.'

'Did she?' Drew said softly. 'Well, listen to her; she's a fine young woman.'

'You know Lady Joan?' Cecilia blinked in surprise.

'So the bad penny has turned up.' Bertha had quietly approached, having risen from the dining table to investigate the hum of conversation in the hallway. Raising the napkin scrunched in her hand, she dabbed toast crumbs from her mouth. 'Well, dear Brother,' she continued in the same acid tone, 'you may take yourself off again. Saul won't be long; he has an early appointment at his lawyer's office, but will return soon.'

'I know where he's gone; my attorney set up the meeting to get him from the house and give you and me a chance to talk privately. I am about to offer you some leniency, my dear, so best be nice and take advantage of it.'

Bertha's lips thinned in suspicion. The last time she had seen her half-brother he'd been unshaven, wearing soiled garments and looking in want of two pennies to rub together. Now that sorry individual was nowhere in sight, but any fellow could beg or borrow a decent suit of clothes to make an impression. Bertha wasn't falling for a clever ruse. Still, she felt uneasy that something had happened that she knew nothing about.

She bucked herself up by impressing on herself that her brother and her lover might be very different characters, but nevertheless were evenly matched.

Drew possessed a fine intelligence, but he also had a conscience. Saul was untroubled by morals and what he lacked in education he made up for in craftiness. He'd managed to trick her brother and grab the inheritance she'd long wanted. Bertha was determined to hold on to her ill-gotten gains, no matter what Drew threatened he'd do to try to claw back his property.

Grudgingly Bertha admitted to herself that Drew had provided adequately for her after their stepfather died, but he would never indulge her need for excitement. Extravagant finery and high-stake gaming had to be met from her allowance and her debts—that he'd on all but one occasion refused to pay off—had soared. On her marriage her husband had been keeper of the purse strings, but Bertha had continued to brood on snatching the Rockleigh riches. Robert Denby had been fifteen years her senior, boring in bed and out of it, but a decent enough fellow. With only a modest income, he'd been no more tolerant of her love of luxury than her brother. Had she not been pregnant at the time, Bertha knew she would never have agreed to become Robert's wife.

A succession of lovers during her marriage had kept her satisfied in one respect, but after Denby had died a few years ago, leaving her to scrape by on a paltry pension, netting a protector had become a necessity for Bertha. Saul Stokes wasn't her usual type of prey; he wasn't wealthy or well connected, but he was handsome and a kindred spirit, living on his wits. Bertha knew that not all of the enterprises he was involved in were legal, but she asked no questions and turned a blind eye, glad to simply enjoy the spending cash he gave her. They'd debated how they might feather their nest even more and steal from Drew. Before her brother could stop her Bertha had taken steps to make Saul her daughter's guardian. That had been another reason she'd wanted Drew brought low: he had threatened to have the ruling overturned to free his niece from Stokes's influence. At times Bertha also thought Saul a mite too harsh and uncaring where her daughter was concerned.

Aware of his sister's brooding, Drew remarked scornfully, 'You're a fool, Bertha. After Denby died you could have twined a dozen or more fellows about your finger, yet you settled for a dolt like Stokes.'

'He ruined you,' Bertha shrilled, incautiously, considering her daughter was listening avidly to the hostile exchange. 'If he's a dolt, what are you?'

'I'm the man about to bring him to justice.' Drew approached his sister, feeling quite sorry for her.

'Go to your room, Cecilia,' Bertha ordered, suddenly becoming aware of her daughter close by.

'I'm hungry and would like some breakfast,' Cecilia began, darting a glance between her relatives' grim expressions. She was keen to know more about the reason behind their argument.

'You may do as you are told, miss!' Bertha's snarl showed her breeding, as did the shove she gave her daughter's shoulder.

'You will not go without saying goodbye?' Cecilia turned to Drew.

'I won't. And I'll only keep you from your breakfast for a short while.' Drew glanced at his sister's sullen countenance. 'We will soon be done with our talk.' He nodded at the stairs, wordlessly sanctioning Bertha's dictate that Cecilia go to her room.

'It would be as well to go in there unless you'd like your servant as well as your daughter to know our business.' Drew steered his sister impatiently to a room along the corridor when she remained stubbornly still and silent.

'You should have treated me fairly, then I wouldn't have brought you down,' Bertha hissed the moment the parlour door was closed. She pointed a quivering finger close to her brother's concave cheek. 'You kept me living like a pauper, eating offal while you dined like a king.' The napkin she'd held in her fist was hurled to the floor in temper.

Drew sighed in boredom, walking further into the room. 'If you ate scraps, my dear, it no doubt had something to do with you choosing to put a month's allowance on the turn of a card at Almack's rather than pay the butcher. I recall that I settled for you on that occasion to keep you and your daughter from the Fleet.' He pivoted on an expensively shod heel, surveying her stylish attire. 'Had you entered that place you'd have thought yourself lucky to get a dish of liver.'

Bertha had the grace to blush at that reminder. Indeed, she had lost a vast amount one evening;

deep in her cups, she had wagered a stack of guineas on turning up a King of Hearts, only for the Knave to appear instead.

'You allowed me no pleasure, did you?' she spat.

'There are at least five men of my acquaintance who would dispute that,' Drew murmured sourly. 'But the fellow I would speak about is your daughter's father.'

Bertha looked startled. 'What has Denby to do with any of it?'

'Nothing… I was referring to the man who sired Cecilia. If you think that he or his wife is a fool to be trifled with, you are much mistaken. Lord Regan might desire a pretty daughter to fuss over, and his wife might tolerate his whim, but push him too far and Cecilia's future will be ruined.'

'Nobody knows about their true connection…'

'It would be better if they did than think you're pimping her.'

'You believe a rich man's bastard might be viewed more kindly than his pet fancy?' Bertha sounded contemptuous.

'Even you and Stokes must baulk at Regan's daughter being thought his mistress.' Drew's disgust was obvious. 'Would you really stoop so low for money, Bertha? How much have you taken from him?'

'It's none of your business what a gentleman might pay me to pamper his own flesh and blood. He has contributed nothing to her upbringing until now.'

'An omission that is hardly surprising considering he believed your late husband had fathered Cecilia…and the cuckold knew no better. Neither does Cecilia,' Drew added mockingly, 'and neither do you; you're not certain Regan's the right one, are you? You've settled on him because he's the richest and oldest.' Drew's smile was intensely sardonic. 'If a list were written of the men you were sleeping with then, Lord Regan's name would be top in terms of an inheritance for Cecilia following an early demise.'

Bertha blushed scarlet, hating him for knowing so exactly how she and Saul had worked things out. 'I was Lord Regan's mistress at the right time. He gladly accepts her as his. How dare you moralise when you live with a slut in a slum.'

'We both lived with a slut in a slum for many years,' Drew reminded his sister of their upbringing. 'And, by God, your breeding shows no matter how hard you try to hide it.'

'And so does yours!' Bertha stormed.

'I'm not ashamed of who I am…that's why I went back there. I'd choose to spend time with those people over you and your cicisbeo any day.'

'Go! I'll not listen to insults from such as you.' Bertha pointed a quivering finger at the door.

'You've not answered my question.' Drew ignored her command to leave. 'I'll take it then that Regan's handed over a considerable sum.' Drew nodded at a brooch glittering on Bertha's silk bodice. 'I'll warrant no lavish new gowns and trinkets have been purchased for Cecilia. When his lordship gets wise to your game, I suppose you and Stokes will up and run before he questions the claims you've made on him.'

Bertha swung about, a hand gripping her pulsing throat. 'I hate you,' she spat.

'The feeling is mutual,' Drew returned with something akin to sadness in his tone. 'But your daughter, I have a soft spot for. That's why I'm prepared to be lenient to you and you'd do well to listen to what I have to say…'

* * *

'I'm glad you're feeling up to a shopping trip.' Joan gave her friend a little hug.

'And I'm glad to hear that your papa is on the mend,' Louise replied. 'You must have been dreadfully worried over him.'

'We were all quite frantic at first. The doctor came this morning and said he is still weak and must not get overexcited…which he is wont to do.' Joan linked arms with her friend as they strolled along Regent Street.

When she had spoken to her father earlier she had told him that Mr Rockleigh had called and had wished him a speedy recovery. The news had pleased the Duke and rather than allow him time to find more questions Joan had used the doctor's arrival as an excuse to keep her visit to the sickroom short and sweet. In case her father summoned her after the physician left Joan had decided to go out. Soon she would not be able to fend off his interrogation and was sure to let slip something that would set back his recovery. But she also felt in need of some fresh air and a friend to talk to.

'I wasn't expecting to see my cousin on Regent Street.' Louise gave a cheery wave.

Joan was also surprised to see Vincent Walters striding along.

'I was going to pay a call on you later today, Lady Joan,' Vincent puffed out, having trotted across the road to join them. 'I've just found out from my aunt that your father has been very unwell. Had I known yesterday about it I would have included the Duke in my prayers. I'm so sorry that I had to rush off like that.'

'I would have told you about Papa, of course,' Joan said. 'Happily the worst is over and he is recovering.'

'That is a blessing.' Vincent nodded solemnly.

'It seems that everybody is about in Regent's Street today.' The unexpected sighting of the dapper young buck she'd recently danced with, sauntering along with his friend, made Louise forget to question her cousin over where he had been rushing to, or why Joan had been with him at the time.

The gentlemen stopped to have a chat and, after some pleasantries Joan stepped slightly aside. The Reverend Walters seemed to be itching to resume talking about her visit yesterday and Joan would sooner keep the matter quiet.

'Benny Cook turned up at the blacksmith's house and told his sister that you'd asked him to deliver a letter,' Vincent rattled off in an undertone. 'My guess is that you wanted me to do that for you. You have advised Mr Rockleigh of your father's illness? I recall you said he is a family friend.'

'He is,' Joan murmured, hoping that the vicar wouldn't pry further into why she'd risked a great deal to send the Squire a letter. But something did intrigue her, making her hesitate in joining the others. 'Benny's sister was with you at the old fellow's bedside?'

'Constance is a kind young woman. She felt sorry for Old Blackie, as she calls him, dying alone. She sat with him while her brother fetched me. She stayed with me, doing what she could to make him comfortable right to the end.'

'Indeed, that was good of her,' Joan said huskily. The picture she'd built in her mind's eye of a brash blonde with coarse manners and morals no longer fitted. But then she might have known that Drew Rockleigh would never associate with a person of mean character. He was well bred and no amount of boxing bouts or slum living would eradicate that innate gentility. Often, she'd felt heartened that his manners had not been blunted by his ordeal. Joan was glad that his mistress was nice even if she did feel a stab of jealousy over it.

'I have heard that your mama is holding an anniversary ball, Mr Woodley.' Joan moved towards the others so Vincent would know their tête-à-tête was at an end. 'I shall hope to soon receive an invitation.'

'The cards are being scribbled out, Lady Joan; never fear but your name will be on one.' Ralph grinned.

Joan glanced at Henry Laurenson; he'd been unusually quiet and seemed keen to get going. Then she spotted Cecilia Denby accompanied by a maid, promenading in their direction.

Having glimpsed the group of friends, Cecilia angled her parasol to shield her face and quickly approached a shop window.

'How strange… Miss Denby is out without her mother or that guardian of hers keeping an eye on her.' Louise ducked her head to and fro, attempting to attract Cecilia's attention.

'Must dash…due at my tailor…' Henry executed a quick bow and strode off, Ralph glumly trailing in his wake.

'I must get about my business, too.' Vincent said. 'I promised Miss Cook that I would write a few words for the deceased's funeral.' Vincent gave a rather soppy smile. 'She wants things done properly for Old Blackie, pauper's burial or no.'

'Shall we chase after Cecilia and say hello?' Joan suggested the moment Vincent had gone.

'How odd to see Miss Denby and Henry avoid one another,' Louise remarked archly.

Joan smiled wryly; she had also suspected that the pair had planned to bump into one another on Regent's Street, but had been thwarted by others getting in the way. Joan's thoughts returned to her own tryst later that afternoon with Drew Rockleigh. A ripple of excitement warmed her skin quickly followed by an unpleasant prickle of apprehension.

Following Drew's departure earlier, Joan had sought her own chamber and her own company as soon as her papa had gone back to sleep. She'd sat on the edge of her bed, mulling over how close they had come to disaster when Maude burst in on them. Joan felt quite giddy with relief that they had not been saying anything incriminating at the moment her stepmother had entered. Had Maude overheard a single snippet of *that* discussion… heaven only knew what chaos might have ensued, or whether her father's slow recovery would have suffered as a consequence.

A clandestine meeting later was hazardous, but Drew's attempt to do things more decorously, with her family close by, had also proved to be risky! Discussing how to proceed against vile Stokes would be best done in private.

Joan knew that if she were completely honest there was more to her need to meet him later: deep within her remained a primal urge to be completely alone with the man she loved in a place where they were freed from the restraint of etiquette and could talk…act…freely. Joan felt fire ignite in her veins as his beautifully rugged features filled her head and she wondered if he would kiss her later… Quickly she put Poacher's Lane to the back of her mind and concentrated on the unexpected opportunity to probe Cecilia about her uncle.

From Rockleigh's impeccable appearance earlier Joan guessed he had managed to improve his lot. She had her own ideas on how he'd restored his position, but Cecilia might corroborate them. Drew Rockleigh had once had powerful and influential friends. Joan's own brother-in-law was one such ally. She hoped that in some small part she might have influenced Drew's decision to swallow his pride and accept help.

Linking arms with her friend, Joan steered Louise towards the drapery into which Cecilia had disappeared. Before they could enter the establishment Ralph came bowling up behind, having decided against accompanying Henry to the tailor. 'Might I have a word with you, Miss Finch?' He coughed and inserted two fingers between his neck and cravat. 'Now that my instructor has made some progress with me, there is a favour I would ask about securing you as a dancing partner at the ball. I won't monopolise your company... you'll be inundated with requests, I understand that. But if you didn't find dancing with me too much of an ordeal...'

Louise blushed. 'Well...of course you may ask such a favour, sir. I enjoyed dancing with you; I promise it wasn't an ordeal at all.'

'I'm going to step inside and say hello to Miss Denby.' Joan knew she'd have no better chance to speak to Cecilia alone.

'Oh, I'm well enough, I suppose...' Cecilia shrugged and sighed on being asked how she did. In fact, she felt dejected. She had craved a conversation with Henry, needing his comfort and advice. They had been meeting in secret whenever they could and, like the true friend he was, Ralph had been keeping an eye out for snoopers. With her guardian and mother constantly watching her, slipping away hadn't been easy. But following her uncle's visit the couple had been too wrapped up in themselves to even notice her existence.

As soon as Stokes had arrived home Bertha had rushed to meet him to garble out that her brother had called and something bad must be afoot. Within minutes of them closing the parlour door an explosive argument had started. Cecilia didn't bother to eavesdrop; she had long ago realised the couple were jealous of Rockleigh's popularity and success and had done something spiteful to discredit him. Cecilia had digested that the couple were seriously worried about her uncle's reappearance. From that she'd deduced that everything familiar to her might disintegrate, but she didn't care…in fact, she welcomed it.

Finally, she saw a way to escape and marry Henry…if he would have her. But she'd just missed her chance to tell him so. Cecilia recalled that her uncle had praised Lady Joan and said she should heed her advice. Cecilia always listened to him. Besides, as the two of them were acquainted, it was possible that Joan might already be aware of her Uncle Drew being back in town looking as handsome and important as ever. What she might not know was that her mother and guardian hated him. But Joan seemed a stoic-enough sort not to swoon in shock at her family's feuding and scheming.

'Might I confide in you, please, Lady Joan?' Cecilia burst out.

Chapter Fourteen

'Do sit down, sir. I think I know what your business is about.' Thadeus Pryke had jumped up from behind his desk to blurt out his nervous greeting.

'I'm pleased to hear it; that's saved us both a long and unpleasant conversation.' Drew strolled further into the investigator's office and, having taken a cursory glance about at the dusty interior, propped himself against the wall rather than make use of a battered chair.

'I had no hand in the blackmail, sir, I swear.' Thadeus's defence emerged in a shrill hiss. 'I begged Mr Stokes to remain silent the moment he let slip his foul intention to turn your meeting with Miss Morley to his advantage. I felt like cutting out my own tongue for having mentioned it to him,' Thadeus concluded dramatically.

'You might not need to do that…' Drew returned

with lethal softness and left the rest unsaid. 'The fact that you told Stokes my private business in the first place begs an explanation and an apology.'

'Indeed...I deeply regret it, sir, and apologise profusely. He came to see me about some business and we had a bottle of port to drink.' Remorsefully Thadeus shook his head. 'It oiled my tongue overmuch.'

'What sort of business did he come to speak about?' Drew pounced immediately, wondering if Thadeus Pryke was mired in some of Stokes's other evil schemes.

Thadeus coughed and fidgeted. It wasn't the first time, but he prayed it would be the last, that his cousin badgered him to betray his clients. Being the corrupt bully he was, Stokes had threatened to tell Thadeus's upright brother that he was receiving stolen goods unless he disclosed details of clients' peccadilloes. Thadeus had always been aware of the opportunity in the nature of his work, but had been too chary of a plot backfiring on him, leading to his arrest, to go it alone. Nevertheless, he'd been happy to accept the commission that his cousin slipped his way after the deed was done.

Customarily, the victim was middle class and would pay up rather than have their dirty linen aired in public. Thadeus had been utterly truthful in telling Mr Rockleigh that he'd entreated Stokes not to tangle with such a personage as a duke's daughter. Or a man such as the Squire... prize fighter extraordinaire...

'There's a way for you to put matters right should you choose to accept it.'

'And if I do not?' Thadeus wheezed. It wasn't simply the prospect of taking a beating that kept him quivering; he'd never before seen the Squire so well groomed and wasn't sure who the fellow was now. Though fearful, Thadeus was still sharp enough to know that he was about to be presented with a solution he'd not like and cursed his cousin to hell. Thadeus had always envied Saul's success and his boasts about mingling with the cream of society; but he'd allowed the man to have too much hold over him and now it had led to bad trouble.

'And if I do not?' Thadeus repeated agitatedly, hoping to hurry an answer to what fate awaited him.

'And if you do not,' Drew finally said, idly removing a cheroot from his pocket, 'you will feel the full force of my displeasure for betraying a fine young woman who imagined you to be trustworthy when she engaged your services.' Drew cupped a palm about a flaring match, then glanced across to the office opposite where a fellow who resembled an older version of Thadeus was watching them through the glass partition while feigning interest in a ledger. 'He is the proprietor?'

Thadeus mumbled an affirmative. He'd started sweating the moment he'd noticed Rockleigh staring at his elder brother. His boss was a stickler for propriety and, kin or no, would have him in gaol if he ever learned that he'd been risking the reputation of the agency. 'My brother must not know,' Thadeus said shakily. 'He would skin me alive...'

'In that case, what I'm about to say should prove to be no hardship for you in comparison,' Drew said through a haze of tobacco smoke.

Having quit the investigator's office, the first person Drew passed on the street was his erstwhile employer. Barnaby Smith was on the point of scuttling on when he did a double take and his jaw dropped open. Turning about, he scampered after the urbane gentleman who'd given him a cursory nod.

'Constance Cook is looking for you. She asked me if I knew where you were to be found.'

Drew nodded thanks for the message.

'You've struck lucky then, have you?' Barnaby said, squinting resentfully at Drew's excellent suit of clothes, but he got no response other than an enigmatic smile.

Barnaby Smith watched his best boxer stroll on, knowing that he'd lost the man's services for good and with it a tidy amount of his income until he discovered another pugilist to equal the Squire's skill. He ambled on over cobbles, brooding, then entered a tavern feeling in need of a tot of rum to drown his sorrows.

Slumping into a chair by the mullioned window Smith stared idly through it. His vision focused on a trio of men having a private meeting in the shadow of the stables. Two of the fellows Barnaby knew as crooked itinerants. He had arranged boxing bouts for them both in the past, rigging the matches in their favour for a consideration. Pleased with the outcome, they'd paid his commission and handed over sacks of flour and potatoes as a bribe against future contests. Barnaby had had his own idea on whence those provisions came, but he'd gladly accepted the goods and sold them on to Charlie Clarke at the Cock and Hen for a tidy sum.

The other, smartly dressed fellow Barnaby didn't recognise, but he knew that if the two gypsies were taking orders from him—and it seemed that they were—then the cove must be influential. Fearing a rival boxing promoter was attempting to move in on his territory, Barnaby knocked back his rum and slipped quickly outside.

Quietly he moved into position at the side of an empty stall and strained to hear their conversation. After a few moments he grinned and made his presence known. When the bruisers snarled at him for eavesdropping and shifted threateningly from toe to toe, he concentrated on their paymaster. 'So, you want these two to find Mr Rockleigh...or *the Squire* as I know him, and give him a battering, do you.'

'What's it to you?' Stokes growled and indicated with a nod that his henchmen should prepare to strike the intruder.

'I'm not here to hinder but to help, sir, for I've no

liking for the fellow either.' Barnaby had slickly adopted an obsequious tone. Cautiously he approached to offer a hand to shake. 'Barnaby Smith at your service, sir. I know the man you're after because I used to arrange his matches. Now he's turned his back on me without a by your leave.' Barnaby swung his head and spat on the ground to emphasise his hatred for the Squire.

Saul glanced at his associates and one grunted an endorsement.

'You see, these two fine fellows know that I've spoken the truth. I've done good business with them before, they won't deny it.'

Stokes bent his ear towards the itinerant hissing in it. Obviously satisfied by what he'd heard, he gave Barnaby a brusque nod.

'Say your piece then and be gone,' he growled, looking right and left to spot if anybody else was spying on them.

'If you want to beat the Squire, you'd best be prepared for a hard fight, even three against one.' Smith stuck out a grimy palm. 'That advice you can have for free. The rest of my knowledge comes at a price.'

Stokes bared his teeth, but slapped a few coins

into Smith's outstretched hand, keen to get rid of him.

'If you're after the Squire you'll find him with Constance Cook in the Cock and Hen.'

'Do you take us for fools?' One of the thugs lunged forward, fist shaking beneath Barnaby's bristly chin. 'We know about his doxy and have been around his usual haunts already.'

'Ah…you've not found him there because he's deserted Ratcliffe Highway and his jade. But he'll go back this evening to see her 'cos I've just let him know she's on his tail. He'll pay her off before leaving her for good.'

'You've seen him?' Stokes barked.

'Minutes ago, on Cheapside.' Barnaby had already turned to run, the coins gripped in his palm in case the fellow tried to have them back now he'd got what he wanted.

Stokes cursed inwardly; he knew why his nemesis had been spotted on Cheapside. Rockleigh had paid Thadeus a visit and his cowardly cousin would have admitted everything about the blackmail rather than risk a thrashing. Saul knew he'd plenty of time to deal with Thadeus; first he had to quickly catch up with Rockleigh and beat out of

him how his fortunes had been turned around—
if indeed they had.

Bertha had told him that her brother looked to
be back on his feet and flying high; she'd also said
she thought Drew must be putting on a show as
a last-ditch effort to get even with them. Stokes
trusted nobody but himself. He had fancied he'd
detected something odd about Bertha this afternoon, but she'd burst into tears when he'd interro-
gated her, just as she always did when she wanted
to avoid an unpleasant matter.

One thing was certain though: Bertha's brother
could ruin him and Saul reckoned he'd no choice
but to silence Drew Rockleigh once and for all.

Joan knew that she had arrived early for her appointment with Drew. Nevertheless she had expected him to be waiting for her. But it seemed
he was not. She glanced right and left, jumping as
a magpie took flight overhead. A shiver of mis-
giving rippled through her. Pulling up the hood
on her cloak, she began to trot back the way she'd
come, her skirts held away from her feet. As a
ragged breath scratched her throat she inwardly

castigated herself for having again allowed her impulsive heart to overrule her head.

This thrilling tryst had monopolised her mind for hours; but previously she'd been contemplating it at a safe distance. Now the consequences of wandering alone on a woodland path were a dangerous reality. Most of all Joan felt furiously indignant at the idea that the man she'd risked her reputation for had decided not to come, or worse, had simply forgotten about their meeting.

It was obvious that Drew had important matters of his own to attend to: much must have recently happened to bring about his transformation from boxer to gentleman.

The plain carriage, with Pip at the reins and her maid seated inside, was stationary at the deserted mouth of the lane. Anna had begged to accompany her on the woodland walk, but Joan had adamantly refused to allow it. Anna and Pip were faithful and trustworthy, but if her father ever called them to give an account of this afternoon's escapade the young couple would be torn by divided loyalties. The less they knew, in Joan's opinion, the more she protected them.

Another stirring in the shrubbery brought Joan

to an abrupt halt. She backed away from the sway-ing bush just as a hare sprang out and bounded on its way. Joan clasped her shaking hands in front of her, allowing her speeding heart to steady.

It was a sunny spring afternoon, but Poacher's Lane was cool, dappled in shade. Her surround-ings of gentle pastoral beauty worked their magic and slowly she felt herself calming down. She im-pressed on herself that if she could make a foray into the East End stews after dark then a leafy glade should hold no fears. When in Devon she would walk for miles through meadows—albeit sometimes without her father's knowledge. The Duke had always been conscious of the felons carrying kegs off the nearby beaches and would not have approved of his daughter's lone consti-tutionals.

Tilting up her chin to a proud angle, Joan started to walk with determined step back towards the road. If Drew Rockleigh were not prepared to fight alongside her, then she'd battle Stokes on her own!

The sound of hooves hitting peaty ground shat-tered Joan's intrepid mood. Unsure if it was Drew approaching at such speed she decided to be safe rather than sorry and spontaneously sprinted to conceal herself behind a tree, tripping on roots poking from the ground like cadaverous fingers.

'Why did you not wait close to the road by your servants?' Drew demanded, suppressed anger in his voice as he leapt from the stallion's back to drag her from behind the oak.

Aware of the rebuke in his tone, Joan flung him off, backing away. 'I believed you had gone into the woods to wait for me out of sight.' Her eyes widened in indignation. 'How was I to know you would be late?'

'I'm not late…I sent you an urgent note to tell you not to come here.'

'I didn't get a note!' Joan cried.

'I know; my servant returned from Upper Brook Street with the message that you were out shopping with friends. I guessed then that you might journey on here without returning home first and reading it.'

'You didn't want to see me? You chose, after all, *not* to help find a way to thwart Stokes?' Joan sounded both hurt and affronted.

'No!' Drew groaned. 'But my brain managed to curb that other delinquent part of me that seems to take control whenever an opportunity to be alone with you comes up. You shouldn't be here, Joan and I'm very sorry that I gave way to temptation. Forgive me.'

'There's nothing to forgive… I'm not scared,' Joan said stoutly, conveniently forgetting how uneasy she'd felt moments before.

'I know…you're a very courageous young woman,' Drew said gently. '*I'm* scared…of the risk I've let you face, encouraging you to come here, and of the damage that could be done to your family's good name. It's not your fault, it's mine…I knew it to be madness from the start.'

'I wanted you to agree and was glad when you did,' Joan argued stiltedly. 'I hoped we could discuss how to outwit Stokes. But if you don't want to…'

'I can deal with him…' Drew thrust his long fingers through his hair. 'You should not have strayed this far along the path on your own.' He swung about and came close enough to tower over her. 'This lane is used by disreputable characters—hence its name. You've chanced running into men with far less regard for your safety than I have.'

'It is broad daylight.' Joan gestured with out-stretched hands held palm up. 'Only a foolish felon would sally forth at this time of the day. Besides, a fellow stealing a brace of hare doesn't bother me. I've been in the midst of rogues who kill Revenue men to hawk valuable contraband.'

The magpie suddenly returned to roost in the dense canopy overhead, startling Joan and belying her bravado. She had not overstated the calibre of the West Country criminals, but there she knew her territory. Her only knowledge of this isolated place had come from an overheard conversation between Pip and another stable lad. They had not realised that she was in earshot when discussing an acquaintance who fed his family very well by frequenting Poacher's Lane.

'A hunter might desire better sport than was got from the game he carried if he stumbled upon you wandering about.' Drew sent her a frown. 'A place such as this always attracts a certain class of woman touting for business.'

Joan cast a wary look to and fro. That the lane was also a haunt for the petticoat set plying their trade, she had *not* known!

'I must bow to your superior knowledge on

such things, Mr Rockleigh,' she said tartly. 'As for those other miscreants…I've seen nobody about who might want to ravish me.'

His subtle smile made her blush. They both knew that he was the man who presented the greatest threat to her virtue.

Joan could already sense tension building, bridging the space that separated them. Despite the shadows she had become increasingly aware of his virile attractiveness and the heat of his body seemed to envelop her like an extra cloak. 'Not all folk of low stock are corrupt, you know,' Joan blurted to break the pulsating silence and rouse herself from an odd trance-like state sapping her energy.

'Indeed, I do know.' Drew said quietly. 'Some of the nicest people of my acquaintance have no pedigree or wealth.'

'You mean Constance…' Joan immediately regretted her slip. Since finding out about the goodness in the young woman's character her jealousy had heightened, but so too had her curiosity about Drew's paramour. She especially wanted to know if he had fallen in love with her. 'Benny was rude and intimidating when he begged for pennies on the day we were ambushed. He was friendlier when I saw him at the vicarage.' Joan aimlessly paced to and fro. 'He even seemed quite sorry for what he'd done. He told me his sister does her best to keep him in check.'

'Constance is naturally honest…her brother is not. They might be kin, but they have different natures, like most siblings.'

The sourness in his tone made Joan cease perambulating. He might have spoken about his mistress's family, but she realised he'd been thinking of his own. 'You are like your sister in looks, if nothing else.' Joan noticed that his profile hardened at the mention of Bertha. 'I, on the other hand, am nothing like my brother,' she chattered on. 'His hair is quite fair and his eyes bright blue,' Joan hoped to lighten the atmosphere by talking about George. 'I would like to see him more often, but he is away at school in Rugby. When the holidays come George likes to go and stay with his best friend in Scotland rather than return home.' Her fond smile brought matching dimples to the hollows beneath her cheeks. 'He finds us boring whether we are at home in Mayfair or in Devon. Hamish lives in a castle, you see. The boys enjoy having mock battles amongst the turrets, then there are the lochs and mountains to explore. He is much younger than I…just ten…and I'm lucky if I receive a letter once in a while.' Drew had been attending closely to her rambling tale about her younger brother and Joan's expression turned bashful beneath the golden warmth twinkling in his eyes.

'Luke and I would spend our school holidays together at Rockleigh Hall in Kent, getting up to mischief. He was estranged from his father, but he liked mine.'

'Fiona told me that he was quite unhappy as a child because of family rifts. But you enjoyed idyllic early years, it seems, Mr Rockleigh.'

Drew's laugh—if it could be called such—was chillingly bitter and caused Joan's smile to fade.

'Were you not happy, then?' she asked falteringly.

'My stepfather was well liked by everybody… including me. He was a good man.'

His reply had taken a long time to arrive and did not satisfy her. 'And your mother?' The raw emotion in his eyes made a sharp breath abrade Joan's throat. Just for a moment pity and disgust seemed to vie for dominance, then the look was gone… replaced by his customary sardonic expression.

'Let's not talk of families…let's concentrate on us.' Drew strolled slowly closer. 'You just said you wanted to discuss Stokes's mischief.'

'Stokes will expose me as your paramour unless I pay him.' Joan's cheeks tingled in embarrassment as she loosely paraphrased the villain's threats. From beneath her lowered lashes she studied Drew's strong athletic physique. He was dressed as he had been that morning, although a leather riding coat partially covered his fine tailoring. They had been talking for some minutes and he seemed to have conquered his annoyance at finding her so deep in the woods, now he was here to protect her. She knew he had genuinely been concerned for her safety and welfare and her heart warmed to him further because of it. But she was surprised that he'd not immediately wanted to discuss Stokes's villainy.

A suspicion pricked at her mind. 'Have you already done something to stop Stokes blackmailing me?' His slight nod caused exasperation and great relief to wash over her. 'I didn't go out for some hours after you left my house, yet you knew your intentions straight away, didn't you? You should have sent your note sooner; it would have saved you the bother of coming here at all. Why did you not?' She gazed up into eyes the colour of molten molasses.

Drew raised a finger to tenderly trace the curve of her profile. 'If you don't know the answer to that, my lady...'

'I can guess, but I want you to tell me,' Joan breathed.

'If you want me to admit that it took me a long, long time after we parted to conquer my desire to be alone with you like this...' he smoothed a stray curl back from her forehead with a tender finger '...very well...I am weak...I made a grave mistake in not sending that note sooner. But the craving for you never leaves me.'

Joan felt a surge of joyous relief that he also felt the compulsion for them to be together despite the risks. 'There must be more between us than that, you know. I don't just want kisses from you...'

'I'm glad to hear it,' Drew murmured ironically as the finger fondling her skin became more erotic. 'There's certainly more I want to do than kiss you.'

Joan was acutely aware that he was now so close their bodies were touching. A hint of sandalwood on his freshly shaven jaw teased her nostrils, tempting her to sway against him. She knew she had only to angle her face up in wordless appeal and his mouth would take hers, transporting her back to that world of feverish delight that had been locked for too long in her memory. But she'd meant what she'd said about needing more from him. And she must understand herself better, too.

On their first encounter the Squire had been unkempt in appearance and churlish in manner. Joan could clearly recall how brusquely he'd addressed her and that an essence of sweat and leather had remained long after he'd sprung from their coach.

At one time it would have been inconceivable that she'd find a street fighter appealing. Yet the unashamed ruffian had held an irresistible fascination from the start. The Squire was the character who'd awoken her to sensuality, not the suave gentleman with her now. Whoever he was, she knew she'd fallen in love with him. But she wasn't sure she had his trust, or trusted him, and without something so fundamental to happiness there could be no future for them, even should he offer her one.

'I met your niece by chance when out shopping,' Joan rattled off. 'We had a long talk and that's why I didn't have time to return home before travelling here.' She paused. 'Cecilia confided in me about your feud with your sister and Stokes. I didn't let on that I already knew.' Joan noticed his eyes narrow in immediate interest. 'Cecilia said you'd paid her mother a visit recently.'

'Yes…I did…'

'Have you let Luke assist you financially so you might fight back against her swindle?' Joan asked eagerly. 'You appear quite the eminent gentleman again.' Her admiring gaze flowed over his elegant attire.

'I'm glad you approve.' Drew's gracious dip of the head was vaguely ironic and made her blush. 'As for Luke, I've no need of his help.'

'Somebody else has helped you?'

'In a way…' Drew replied softly, nuzzling her cheek.

'In what way?' Joan persisted, although the sensation of a warm mouth tracing her skin was making it hard for her to concentrate and keep her

296 Compromising the Duke's Daughter

eyes open. She was determined to have her answers before his kisses drugged her into a state of mindless bliss. On the last occasion his hands and lips had worked their addictive magic on her body she had felt as though she'd lost her reason. She took two firm steps back. 'Please answer me or I will think you do not like or trust me enough to tell me.'

'There's no benefit in you knowing about it and I'd sooner you did not until the time is right,' Drew said mildly.

'The time is right!' Joan countered. 'You owe it to me to be open about things. I'd never have become embroiled with odious Mr Pryke or risked life and limb being out in dreadful weather had I not wanted to help you get back on your feet. And, it seems you have.'

'I'm humbled and grateful for what you have done for me. But there was no need for it, as I told you at the time. You've nothing to worry about where Pryke's concerned. He won't bother you or your father again. He's left town.'

'Has he?' Joan gasped. 'What have you done to him? You've not...' She bit her lip, unable to voice a suspicion that he might have fought with the investigator to make him flee.

'I've not harmed him, but he deserves punishment. He's escorting my sister and Cecilia to my hunting lodge in Devon and will stay there with them until I summon him. Punishment, indeed it will be, when you consider my shrew of a sister's nature and that he's getting no fee for putting up with her.'

Joan's lips parted in surprise. 'Your sister has agreed to leave Stokes and go into exile?'

'She wasn't keen on the idea, but she'll fall in line rather than join her lover in gaol. Bertha's first consideration when under fire is herself.' Drew paused. 'She is a survivor…it is perhaps the only trait we share.'

'Has Cecilia agreed to go?' Joan burst out. 'She'd elope with Mr Laurenson if she could, she told me so earlier. I know she ran away once before and you had trouble bringing her home.'

A corner of Drew's mouth quirked on hearing that understatement. 'My niece knows that I have her best interests at heart. But you're right…the little minx proved to be a handful to control when I brought her home after she absconded with Robbie.' He consulted a gold hunter taken from his coat pocket. 'The rig I hired for them will have just started out for the West Country.'

'You sound as though you were quite tolerant of the elopement.' Joan said in surprise.

'I was angry at the time...but I understood why she was desperate to get away.'

'She must have loved Robbie very much to risk doing that.'

'It was infatuation on her part and he offered her a way out of an intolerable situation.'

'What sort of situation?' Joan knew her blunt questioning was impertinent. 'I'm sorry; I don't mean to pry, but it seems we are now talking candidly and you know all of my secrets.'

'And they are safe with me, I swear,' Drew said throatily. 'Come...it's time to go. You shouldn't be loitering in such a place as this.'

Joan pressed her lips together in exasperation as he started to approach his horse. So he had chosen to simply walk away from a difficult question. And he obviously *didn't* trust her. And that, she thought to herself, was rich, considering she had always been open and he had been the one holding back.

'How do you plan to get Stokes committed to gaol? Are you more adept than he at deceit?' she jibed.

'Being duplicitous is a necessary evil at times,' Drew returned drily.

Joan skipped to catch up with him. 'At one time I pitied Drew Rockleigh for his kin. But the Squire and Bertha Denby are similar people, aren't they? I wonder that your niece likes you as much as she does. Has she also been confused as to your true character?' Joan fell abruptly silent as Drew turned and came towards her so fast that she took two clumsy steps backwards to escape him.

'My niece likes me because I'm the one who cares about her and she knows it. After you spoke to Cecilia in town she would have gone home and read the note I left for her. She trusts me to put things right and that is why I know she has gone away without a fuss. Do you trust me to put things right for you, Joan?'

'I don't know!' Joan cried in frustration. 'I'm not sure I really know you.'

Drew threw back his head and barked a harsh laugh, the taut planes of his face and his flaxen hair lit by filtering sunbeams. 'You're quite right;

you don't really know me at all and you should be thankful of that.'

'Tell me something then and let me make up my own mind!'

'It's time to go.' Brusquely, Drew beckoned her, intending to help her mount his horse.

Stubbornly Joan backed away from his outstretched hand; she was exasperated, but decided to try another tack. If they continued to bicker she'd never have answers, so offered an olive branch instead.

'It was good of you to bring Cecilia back when she eloped, considering Stokes is her guardian.'

'It was Stokes who caused her to bolt in the first place.'

'You told Cecilia to heed my advice, so you must think me sensible.' Joan smiled winningly, then recalled something else that had cropped up in her conversation with his niece. She was in two minds about mentioning it, but decided to do so, believing that Drew sincerely had the girl's best interests at heart. 'Cecilia wants me to contact Henry and arrange a meeting between them in the hope he'll propose.'

'I wouldn't want you to get involved in that,' Drew smoothly interrupted.

Joan's hackles stirred at his authoritarian tone, but she said lightly, 'I'm flattered that Cecilia likes me enough to enlist my help. It is a shame you do not feel the same way.'

Drew slanted a mordant look at her indignant face while tightening his mount's saddle. 'You know I like you…'

'But…' Joan prompted. She realised he was in the throes of a dilemma over whether to say something crucial. 'Can you not at least satisfy my curiosity over Stokes causing his ward to run away?'

'He tried to marry her off to a rich widower and she got wind of it.'

'Oh, how awful.' Joan frowned; the poor girl seemed to attract the attention of old lechers. 'Are you aware that Lord Regan has shown a very… odd…interest in your niece?' Joan grimaced. 'Gossip has started about it.'

'Yes… I know.' Drew turned away from the stallion, massaging the nape of his neck with long fingers. If he divulged one aspect of his sister's venal character one thing would lead to another. Joan would keep probing until the root of the matter was exposed. And he didn't want her to know all of it. He couldn't bear to see the shock and disgust in her eyes when she finally understood who he really was and where he'd sprung from.

'You *know*?' Joan sounded disbelieving. 'If you care for Cecilia, you surely won't allow that old roué to pursue her? At least the other one was a widower; Lord Regan's wife is still alive.'

'He's not interested in her in that way,' Drew said hoarsely.

'You obviously have not seen the way his lordship favours her,' Joan returned pithily.

'Lord Regan is her father.' A mirthless laugh scratched at Drew's throat. 'Leastways that is what he has been told. Whether it is true or not…' He shrugged.

Joan gasped in astonishment. 'I see…' she finally murmured, then fell into a thoughtful silence for some moments. 'It makes better sense of why his wife appears tolerant of Cecilia.'

'With no official heirs I imagine the woman has accepted her husband wants to believe Cecilia is his and ignores him fawning over her.'

'Cecilia obviously doesn't know and you are not sure you believe it, are you?' Joan cocked her head to gaze into a pair of narrowed eyes. 'You think it to be another plot, a money-spinner dreamt up by your sister?'

Drew smiled wryly as he watched her pearly teeth nibble at her lower lip and her brow furrow with the ferocity of her concentration. 'Should the detective agency need a new recruit in Mr Pryke's absence, I imagine you would fit the bill.' He approached her, placed a finger against her mouth as it immediately formed another question. 'Come... it is time to go. Your family will have missed you by now.' The digit brushed softly to and fro on warm skin, parting her lips.

Instinctively Joan let her tongue tip meet the tantalising forefinger, recalling how she had done something similar to encourage his caresses in the coach on that stormy night.

The magpie squawking overheard jolted some sense into Joan, but when she would have pulled back Drew slid his hand to her nape, caressing the smooth skin and lowering his dark head close to satiny curls peeping from beneath her bonnet's brim.

'God, I've missed you. Do you know how often I've thought about what we did that night, sweetheart? There's unfinished business between us, Joan, and I can't let go of the memory of it.' He loosened her hat, pushing it back so it hung on its ribbons against her shoulders. His mouth plunged to cover hers, hot and demanding, before swooping to her throat to feast on warm pearly flesh. Then he was again hungrily plundering her lips, tasting her cheeks and eyelids as though he would devour all of her.

Joan swayed towards him as his hands slipped between the edges of her cloak to grasp her narrow waist, drawing her against his solid frame. They travelled upwards, the calloused palms seductively circling her small warm breasts. Overwhelmed by heady emotion, Joan wound her arms about his neck. 'I've missed you too, Drew, so very much because…I love you,' she blurted, having tossed caution to the wind.

Drew became still as the sweet-breathed words were gasped against his cheek. Gripping her shoulders, he gave her a little wakening shake, making her drooping eyelids fly open. Then he strode away from her, five fingers forking his fair hair off his forehead as he cursed at the branches above.

'What's the matter?' Joan asked quietly, coming up behind him. 'I want you to kiss and touch me…I love you…you must know that,' she said shyly, her racing heart trembling her bodice. She prayed that he would say he loved her, too. But he didn't and she took an unsteady pace back, feeling humiliated.

'You're thinking of Constance,' Joan whispered. 'I know she's your mistress. I should be sorry for wanting to steal you from her, but I'm not. I want you to love me, not her,'

Drew swung about to pull Joan close, his mouth descending to capture hers in a forceful kiss that drove her scalp against his forearm.

'It's not thoughts of Constance that torment me,' he murmured, soothing her bruised lips with a stroke of his thumb. 'It's thoughts of you…wanting you and knowing I'm not worthy to touch the hem of your skirt.'

'But you are! I know you are.' Joan's slender fingers shaved his abrasive cheek. 'You have recently lived amongst vagabonds, but I understand the circumstances that forced you to it. If anything, knowing you've suffered degradation yet stayed so gentleman-like makes me love you more.' She angled her face to watch his expression as she said, 'I do not despise the poor, please believe me when I say so. I have always cared about improving the plight of people with so little and will happily get my hands dirty in the doing of it. I met you on just such a mission when returning from teaching children at the vicarage.'

'You looked wholesome enough to me,' Drew said, but there was a throb of amusement in his words.

'I was covered in chalk dust,' Joan protested, but was soon again serious. She clasped her fingers over his lean jaw so he could not avoid her eyes. 'You must explain to my papa how you have been swindled; he will not judge you badly. He will see for himself that you have stopped street fighting. I will endorse every word. Papa is a fair man and will accept the truth—'

'If your father knows the truth, he'll ban me from your life and I wouldn't blame him,' Drew interrupted bleakly. 'There is no future for us, Joan,' he added hoarsely, striding away from her. 'Once I have dealt with Stokes I plan to leave town. Forget about me. I'm not the person you think I am. If you really knew me, you'd not have come here today.'

'I would have! I know that I am perfectly safe here with you.' Joan had followed him, frowning. 'What else is there to know? I am not a snob, so don't think that of me. I'd still be teaching your neighbours' children to read if my father hadn't interfered. I think he pulled strings and had the school closed.' Joan sighed. 'I am cross with him about that and when he is well enough I'll tell him so, and that I intend to take up teaching again.'

'It wasn't your father's doing; it was mine. The man you saw me with in the park was the bishop's clerk. I arranged to have the school closed.'

'Why? How?' Joan demanded, veering between astonishment and annoyance.

'I wanted to keep you safe…and I wanted to keep you from coming back there and finding out things about me that I didn't want you to know.'

'But by then I'd already discovered that you were a street fighter,' Joan argued. 'And Pip knew the route then so we would not have got lost again. There was little risk involved.'

'You're always at risk when you're close to me, don't you understand…' There was a frustrated

groan in his throat as he swung away. 'Come...
I'll take you back to the road.'

Joan slapped away the hand that had reached
for her. She was not satisfied yet. 'You have the
bishop's ear?' She sounded dubious. Important
clergy were not likely to take orders from street
fighters.

'I still have friends from my army days...high-
ranking people who have influence over such
matters.' He smiled ruefully when Joan continued staring at him, wordlessly demanding more
information. 'The Duke of Wellington was once
my commanding officer. We have kept in touch.'

He was right, Joan realised despairingly; there
was no future for them while he cherished that
dark and secret side to his nature. And, noble motive or not, she was furious that he had arranged
to have the school closed, depriving children of
an opportunity to better themselves. 'There is a
lot I do not know about you, isn't there?' Joan said
in a fatalistic tone.

'Indeed, there is.' His toneless statement
emerged as he grasped her by the hand, leading
her and the stallion back towards the road.

'You just want to be rid of me now you've had

your kisses, don't you?' she choked out, attempting to wrench herself free. He allowed her to do so, shaking his head in mock despair.

Joan moved away a distance, but continued walking beside him and a short while later the carriage came into view. 'Forget what I said about love,' she uttered in a stilted tone, rushing ahead. 'I'm sorry to have embarrassed you. It won't happen again.' She took his silence as proof that he had indeed nothing more to say on the subject of her heartfelt declaration.

'Would you wait out of sight until I have got aboard, please?'

Anna had spotted her mistress approaching and was already hurrying to accompany Joan to the protection of the carriage.

Joan didn't once turn to look at him as he walked behind her. The soft clop of the horse's hooves stopped and she knew he had granted her request to let her set off before he came into view.

Almost before Joan had settled against the squabs the coach pulled away as though Pip was conscious of the need to put distance between his mistress and the man in the woods who could ruin her. Joan was aware of Anna's concerned look fixed on her face, but the young woman dutifully kept her thoughts to herself. Turning to the window, Joan gazed out, the tears that she'd dammed behind pride no longer containable. Warm salty water bathed her cheeks as the vehicle hurtled on towards Upper Brook Street.

Chapter Fifteen

'Is it true?'

'It's none of your concern, Connie.' Drew pulled from his pocket a wad of banknotes and put them down on the dirty tabletop.

'Nothing's ever been my concern, has it?' Constance cried, but she pocketed her generous pension money. 'Now you've done with me and this place you're ready to turn your back on us all… even if you are no better than we are.' She flung that last at him with a toss of her flaxen curls.

'Find lodgings somewhere decent for yourself and Benny. You're a good girl and will get a shop position if that's what you want.'

'I want you!' Connie cried. 'I deserve you, too!' she said more forcefully. 'I've been warming your bed and tending your cuts—'

'And I'm grateful to you,' Drew interrupted. 'But it's over now.'

'Why must it be over? Old Blackie was right, wasn't he? We're cut from the same cloth.'

'You said he was delirious and talking rot.' Drew approached her and gave her shoulder a comforting squeeze. 'At the start you accepted that it would be a fleeting affair and we'd simply enjoy one another's company for a short while.'

'That was then.' Constance sniffed, rubbing her watery eyes. She couldn't deny that Drew had told her not to expect anything from him because he would up and go when the time was right. She couldn't deny either that she'd readily accepted his terms when he'd set them out. But men like Drew Rockleigh, with his handsome face and thrilling virility, were few and far between for the likes of Constance and she wanted to hold on to him for as long as possible.

When she'd sat soothing Old Blackie he'd croaked out that she and the Squire were a good match. The dying man had said he'd recognised him as being a lad who'd lived in the neighbourhood decades ago. Constance had barely paid attention, thinking the old fellow raving with the effort of drawing his last breaths. In the days that had followed she'd mulled things over. From the start Drew had seemed to know the area like the back of his hand and there was a dark and dangerous side to his character that was at odds with his cultured voice and sharp intelligence. It was obvious he was Quality, but he fought dirty and had the cunning and strength of a demon. His fighting prowess came courtesy of his time spent in the military, he'd explained. Genteel folk brought low usually floundered in the Ratcliffe Highway. Drew had inhabited the slum like a natural. So Constance had asked him outright about where he'd spent his early life…and he'd avoided answering her…as he always did.

Something else troubled Connie and pricked at her pride. She'd thought she'd beguiled Drew when he chose her as his mistress. But lately she'd wondered if he'd picked her over those others who'd tried to catch him because she worked at the Cock and Hen tavern. Drew spent a lot of time there with her, even though he wasn't a big drinker. Because Connie's attention rarely left him she'd noticed who he watched…and it wasn't her or the fellows who flirted with her. The coves who sneaked Charlie Clarke his cut-price provisions drew the Squire's eyes, carefully concealed beneath his lashes.

'Don't brood on it, Connie,' Drew said kindly. 'Whatever the truth about my past, there's no benefit in you knowing it. I wish you well, but I'm going away for good and I won't be back—'

'Not very gallant, Rockleigh, when you've been tumbling the wench for months.' Stokes had burst into the cottage with his entourage. He gave Constance a lustful look. 'And comely she is, too. Far better suited to such as you than that high-bred harlot you favour. Your sister told me you were an ambitious guttersnipe, but she didn't know that you were bedding the Duke of Thornley's daughter as well as this slut.'

Drew backed away, dragging Constance behind him to protect her. 'I hope Bertha has told you more besides, Stokes. I imagine you're aware I paid her a visit as you've come out of your way to say hello.'

'I'm here to say goodbye, not hello.' Stokes's bloodless lips parted to expose a set of gritting teeth. 'You'll not best me when I've already relished victory. And now I shall watch you die.'

Constance squealed in fright, digging her rigid fingers into Drew's bicep as the gypsies lunged forward.

'I'll do a deal with you, Stokes. But only if you let Miss Cook go.' Drew whipped up a rickety chair by its back and held it out as a barrier while bargaining for his mistress's safety. 'She's no need to be here and you'll not want witnesses to a murder.'

'Sentimental about her after all, are you?' Stokes mocked. 'Very well…' He beckoned to Constance and she hesitantly approached. 'Perhaps you'd like a final kiss from him, would you?' he taunted. 'You won't get one.' Tugging the terrified blonde against him, he plunged his mouth spitefully on hers. 'I'll come and find you when I'm done with him, sweet.' He shoved Constance out of the door with a threat. 'Keep your mouth shut about this or you'll suffer when I do catch up with you.'

Despite his bluster Stokes wasn't certain he had Rockleigh beaten. But he took heart from catching his foe by surprise and from knowing the odds were stacked greatly in his favour.

He'd not expected the Duke's daughter to tell anybody she was being blackmailed. With her father gravely ill Saul had been confident the little hussy would pay up rather than risk her poor papa finding out about her liaison with a street fighter. But instead of banishing the Squire, Lady Joan had summoned him.

A message had been waiting for Saul at his attorney's office. On breaking the seal he'd learned that Rockleigh wanted to meet him to discuss the matter of a lady's reputation. Saul had recognised it as a threat and, sensing something else was wrong, too, had pelted home to speak to Bertha. She had confirmed his suspicions, telling him agitatedly that Drew had called, looking in suspiciously fine fettle.

'Before I let loose these two brutes, tell me how you've managed to turn your fortunes around. Bertha maintained you'd too much pride to go cap in hand to any fellow...but it seems you have,' he sneered.

'I haven't needed to beg; my fortunes have always been well guarded and safe from your scheming.'

The uneasiness that had been building within Stokes ignited into rage. Bertha had told him all along not to underestimate her brother because nobody ever had got the better of him. Stokes had been arrogantly certain he could change that. But there was something about Rockleigh's cool confidence that troubled him more than any of the man's bragging would have done. Saul feared he'd not duped Bertha's brother well enough and had somehow been outwitted. But he still held the upper hand…

'You spoke of a deal?' he barked, gesturing brusquely that he'd hear more about it.

'Oh…that was a lie. I don't deal with the likes of you, Stokes.'

Saul snarled an order at his two henchmen to attack, then held up a hand to stop them before they could strike.

'I've an inkling that you still hold the original documents,' Saul said. 'Where are they? Tell me and I'll have them despatch you quickly rather than draw out their sport.' Stokes craftily stroked his chin, peering sideway at his quarry.

'Documents?'

'Don't act the dolt, Rockleigh. You know very well that I refer to the original bills of lading and the estate deeds that I copied; and copied so well, I might add, that I hoodwinked the lot of you.'

'Hoodwinked me?' Drew tutted. 'Why do you think I took so long bringing Cecilia back from her jaunt to Gretna Green?' He smiled mockingly. 'It was to give you and Bertha time to do your dirty work while digging yourself a hole to fall into.'

'You're lying!' Stokes spluttered. 'I counterfeited them and I could again, but I'd sooner be rid of you than go to the bother of it.'

'If you do it again, take care not to leave a clause out next time. Careless…' Drew deliberately provoked him.

'There was no mistake! I'm a master forger.' Stokes's lips frothed in rage. 'Where are the originals? I'll check them and make you eat your words, and the parchments, too.'

'Those parchments? Oh, they're safe and sound in Mayfair.'

'And pray where exactly might that be in Mayfair?' Stokes prowled to and fro. He knew Rockleigh was purposely aggravating him, but found it impossible to ignore the bait.

Drew shrugged. 'I'd be a fool to tell you.'

'You'd be a fool not to in the circumstances,' Stokes snarled and signalled to the bruisers.

Drew blocked the first punch aimed at his face with the chair, but the blow had been hard enough to split the seat in two. The other thug hit low at his belly and Drew countered the worst of it with a savage kick to his assailant's kneecap. The man stumbled back with a howl, giving Drew time to smash the stool against the wall and break free a length of jagged timber to use as a makeshift dagger.

'You're a good fighter, Rockleigh, but you're outnumbered. You might just as well give me what I want and save yourself unnecessary pain.' Stokes was panting in frustration. He felt in his pocket for the comforting weight of the blade he'd brought with him. If his two henchmen failed to overcome Rockleigh, he'd pitch in as well although he'd sooner keep clear of the Squire's granite fists.

Drew had seen his enemy's sly movement and knew he'd no option but to quickly end it now before Stokes had a chance to use his weapon. 'You're right, Stokes; against these odds I've little chance of winning.' Drew let the timber fall to his side. 'Do you swear to leave my women alone and give me time to leave London in return for the original documents?'

'Well, naturally...' Stokes purred nastily. 'What do you take me for, a mean devil, such as yourself?'

Drew could tell that Stokes wasn't convinced he'd got so easy a victory but his henchmen were distracted, waiting for instructions. Drew plunged a hand into a pocket and in a fluid movement jerked the stubby duck's-foot pistol up, shooting through wool. He'd aimed at the legs of the two itinerants and they fell together like cut corn, roaring in agony.

Drew sprang forward and one-handedly grabbed Stokes by the throat, dragging him upright. Despite his military background the coward had crouched, cowering, the moment he'd recognised gunshot.

'Regrettably ungentlemanly tactics, I know,' Drew said between his teeth. He removed his hand from the spent pistol in his smouldering pocket and it joined the other one about Stokes's throat. 'But in the circumstances...fair play be damned, don't you think?' Drew narrowed his eyes on his captive's florid physiognomy. 'There is some information I need from you, actually, and you'd do well to let me have it.' Drew tightened his fingers.

'What?' Stokes croaked, confused.

'I want the names of your army cohorts.'

'I don't know what you're talking about,' Stokes coughed out, renewing his efforts to break free.

Drew jerked his head at the injured henchmen. 'They'll sing like birds and implicate you as soon as the dragoons get here. The game's up, Stokes. Tell what you know about the embezzlement and thefts and perhaps the courts will take that into consideration when sentencing you.'

'Never forget I have that niece of yours within my power,' Stokes wheezed through his crushed windpipe. 'Let me go and I'll not harm her. I know you're fond of the pretty chit.'

'I am…that's why I've removed her, and my sister, from your clutches. Not that Bertha merits consideration, but she's blood, I suppose.'

Stokes's eyes bulged up at his captor. 'You've done *what*?' he spluttered.

'They'll be well into their journey by now. I've persuaded your old business partner, Pryke, to accompany them to ensure their safety.' Drew shoved Stokes away from him and paced to and fro. 'You jeopardised your cousin's livelihood and his liberty with your pathetic blackmail plot.'

Stokes was enraged to hear that he'd lost his mistress and his meal ticket. He'd had expectations of extorting more cash from Lord Regan. 'A pathetic plot, was it?' He began massaging his bruised neck. 'It hit you where it hurt, didn't it. Lady Joan Morland is the ruthless Squire's Achilles' heel,' he scoffed. 'When her father finds out you've bedded her, you'll wish I'd finished you off here instead.'

Drew swung a fist at Stokes's mouth. 'Keep quiet,' he growled. 'You're not fit to mention her name.' Forcing him towards the door, Drew added calmly, 'The magistrate is expecting us. I'm obliged that you sought me out and saved me the bother of hunting you down.'

'Get up and fight!' Stokes bawled through ragged lips at the men bleeding on the floor, struggling to escape from Rockleigh's brutal imprisonment.

But he got no response from his mercenaries other than a groan from one and a foul curse from the other.

'Your papa said he will get up for an hour or two now he is feeling so much better.'

'Is that wise?' Joan had been curled up on her bedspread, reflecting sadly on her meeting with Drew earlier on Poacher's Lane, when her stepmother entered her chamber.

'Well, you know your papa, Joan…what is wise is not always what he wants to do.' The Duchess sighed. 'I have told him another whole day in bed would benefit him. But he says he'd sooner starve than take another spoon of gruel; he is getting up to dine with us.' Maude's wry smile faded. 'Have you been crying, my dear?' She wiped smudges from Joan's face with her fingertips.

'Oh, I've just had a fit of the doldrums, that's all.' Joan slid her feet to the floor. 'It is good news that Papa feels well enough to come downstairs. Perhaps a little stroll in the conservatory after supper might do him good.'

'Is it just your papa's health worrying you?' Maude took Joan's hands. 'It has been a trying time for us all these past weeks. Your father has been harried by something he's been reluctant to discuss with me. Thankfully he seems to have forgotten about it now, though.'

Joan knew Rockleigh's trustworthiness had been on her father's mind. But there was nothing to worry about on that score and Joan would tell her father so. Drew was leaving town, and even if he were not, Joan knew that he'd keep her secrets as firmly hidden as he kept his own. 'I'll freshen up and join you downstairs.' Joan brushed crumples from her skirts.

Maude had been gone from the room just a few minutes when Anna slipped in as Joan was untangling her thick locks with a brush.

'I shall wear something quite simple this evening,' she told Anna, assuming the maid had quickly arrived to help her dress.

'I have a message for you, my lady,' Anna whispered, eyes wide in apprehensiveness.

Joan swivelled on her stool. 'Message? From whom?' Her heart soared as her mind pounced on the possibility of Drew having sent her a note.

Anna quickly approached. 'A young woman came to the back door, asking for the Duke of Thornley's daughter. By lucky chance Pip and I were chatting in the courtyard and managed to intercept her before anybody else knew her business.'

Joan got to her feet, her stomach lurching. 'And who is she? What did she say?'

Anna glanced at the closed door, fearful of somebody overhearing. 'She gave her name as Miss Constance Cook; she said she had urgent news of Mr Rockleigh.' Anna moved her head in consternation. 'She would give no more details. I was for sending her away; she is polite enough but of obviously low class. Pip said you must have her message because of the friendship between you and Mr Rockleigh.'

'Pip was right to tell me of it,' Joan said hoarsely. 'Where is Miss Cook now?'

'She is waiting by the side gate.'

Joan was already pulling on her cloak with nervous fingers. 'I must speak to her directly.' She rushed to the door, then spun about. 'Oh…please tell them that I have a migraine or some such. My stepmother knows that I have been feeling low, so it is plausible. Say I shall join them later in the drawing room, after supper.'

Anna nodded. 'I must accompany you, my lady if you are going out to see her.'

'There's no need; I know of her through the Reverend Walters. I shall stay out of sight.' Joan was soon darting into the corridor. As she flew down the stairs she wondered what on earth the young woman had to say that was so vital it had brought her from Wapping to Mayfair. And how did Constance Cook know her name and address?

A cloudy sky had brought dusk down early, but Joan immediately spotted Constance's buxom figure pressed against the brick wall. As she rapidly approached, the young woman tipped back her cloak's hood, exposing a bright blonde fringe of curls. For what seemed an interminable moment the two of them simply exchanged a stare.

Drew's mistress was uncommonly pretty, Joan obliquely realised, but a combatant glint in Constance's eyes begged a question. Joan was certain that Drew would not have mentioned their affair to his paramour, so how *had* she found out? 'You wanted to speak to me urgently, I believe,' Joan said briskly, moving further into the shadows cast by the shrubbery.

'I know that you are fond of Mr Rockleigh and beg you will help him, my lady,' Constance rattled off.

'What's happened to him?' Joan's alarm increased on noticing that the young woman's eyes were glistening. This was no meeting planned by a jealous woman set on confronting her rival; if

Constance Cook wasn't genuinely worried and frightened, she was a consummate actress.

'Drew has been set upon by three fellows. The ringleader of the gang spoke of you and Mr Rockleigh in the same breath, so I've come to beg you to do what you can to stop them killing him. The bruisers will likely turncoat for anybody offering a better payment. I've nothing to give but myself. A duke's daughter such as you has riches to tempt them to spare him and I reckon it's money they're after, not tumbling a tavern wench.'

Joan felt in equal part terrified and astonished by what she'd heard, but retained sense enough to grip the hysterical young woman's shoulders and shake her into silence so she might have more facts. 'Who spoke my name? Where is the gang?'

'Drew called him Stokes. Drew made the fiend let me go and I ran to Mr Pryke's office in Cheapside to find out where to find the Duke of Thornley's residence.' Constance frowned. 'I'd guessed that the detective had delivered your message, you see. I hoped Mr Pryke would oblige with your direction.'

'Did Mr Pryke not go back with you to fight off those brutes?' Joan sounded infuriated.

'He wasn't there. An older fellow was alone in the office.' Constance despairingly shook her head. 'Nobody wants to help if you live around Ratcliffe Highway. Mr Pryke's brother told me where you lived just to be rid of me.' Constance lifted misty eyes to Joan, in wordless appeal.

'I'll help,' Joan said forcefully. 'We must go immediately.'

Constance choked back a sob. 'Drew might already be dead…beaten to a pulp in my lodgings.' She turned a blameful gaze on Joan. 'Is it your fault? Are they fighting over you?'

'I don't know,' Joan murmured, tense with anxiety. She didn't know if the plot to blackmail her had brought matters to a head between the two men, or whether Stokes was out for Drew's blood because his fraud had been thwarted.

'Wait here while I fetch a carriage,' Joan said shakily. She turned and sprinted towards the stables, finding Pip easily as he had been standing at a distance observing them.

It took Pip less than five minutes to prepare the small rig, yet Joan paced to and fro impatiently as though she had waited an hour for the journey to begin. When aboard the two young women travelled in silence, both lost in their own frantic thoughts, although Joan had sensed Constance darting glances at her profile.

'Have you some money to give them?' Constance blurted.

Joan had also been concentrating hard on how she must barter for Drew's life. Not wanting to waste precious time, or risk being stopped by her stepmother, she had not returned to the house. She had little ready cash, in any case, and would need to visit the bank to obtain a ransom. She raised a finger to her ear, flicking the gold-and-amethyst drop dangling there. 'Stokes can have these. They are valuable.' Inwardly she prayed that it was an exchange the evil villain would accept. Joan glanced at the woman sitting opposite. She looked young…perhaps not yet twenty and her large glossy eyes and sweet snub nose gave her an air of innocence and vulnerability. 'Would you really have let those beasts ravish you to save Mr Rockleigh?'

Constance nodded. 'I'd do that for him.' A challenge was back in her eyes and voice. 'He'd not think badly of me for it either. He knows I love him.'

'And does he love you?' Joan asked before she could stop herself. She noted the proud tilt to Constance's chin and anticipated having her worst fears confirmed.

But the blonde smiled sourly. 'He's leaving me.'

'I'm sorry,' Joan said and felt a fraud.

'You're not!' Constance snapped. 'You're the one that's stolen him off me. Fine lady like you could have any man you wanted. Why take mine? He's suited to me...gutter born and bred. Why d'you want him when your papa could buy you an earl?'

'What do you mean...gutter born and bred?' Joan echoed, ignoring the rest of Constance's argument. 'Mr Rockleigh has had bad luck, but is from good family.'

'That's what he's told you, is it?' Constance snorted. 'I believed him a nob, too, then Old Blackie told me the Squire had been reared in the neighbourhood. That beast Stokes said something that proved the old fellow hadn't been gibbering as he shuffled off.' Constance pressed together her lips. She knew she'd said far too much and regretted doing so. Drew would never forgive her for betraying him to his lady love. And Constance knew in her heart that he did love the Duke's daughter.

'What did Stokes say to make you believe it true?' Joan's voice was trembling. 'Tell me!' she demanded when the young woman turned away, pulling her hood forward to conceal her guilty expression.

'He said I was far better suited to Rockleigh than the high-bred harlot he favoured.' Constance peeked at Joan to see how she'd taken that insult. 'Stokes had learned from Drew's sister that he was an ambitious guttersnipe,' she continued. 'Stokes said, too, that Bertha didn't know her brother was bedding the Duke of Thornley's daughter.' Constance's chin drooped towards her chest. A glance sideways told her that Lady Joan had been shocked to the core by what she'd heard. But Constance wasn't feeling triumphant; even if the woman he loved shunned him, she knew there was no hope of Drew coming back to her. She wished now she'd kept her mouth shut.

Joan sat very still, coldness seeping slowly through her as she went over and over in her mind what she'd heard. The names she'd been called didn't bother her. But she wondered why she had not realised sooner about the rest. The secret that she'd believed Rockleigh kept so closely concealed, he had in fact disclosed to her earlier that day, on Poacher's Lane:

'It's not thoughts of Constance that torment me…it's thoughts of you…wanting you and knowing I'm not worthy to touch the hem of your skirt.'

'You'll still help him, won't you?' Constance begged quietly. 'He's a good man, wherever he sprung from.'

'I know he is,' Joan replied in a ragged whisper. 'I won't desert him…I swear.' She leapt up and rapped loudly on the roof for Pip to increase pace. Her driver immediately cracked the whip, jolting her back against the squabs.

Joan gripped the leather seat either side of her, her heart drumming crazily, but she refused to think about the astonishing revelation of Rockleigh's early life. She concentrated on the fact that he was in danger and she must help him…whoever he might be and however large the chasm between them. Just as in the past he had helped her without hesitation.

Chapter Sixteen

'Which dwelling is yours?' Joan demanded as soon as Miss Cook called out that they had arrived in her neighbourhood. Her companion had travelled with her head poked out of the open coach window for the last few minutes, shouting directions to Pip to guide him through the quickest route to her home.

Constance pointed to a cottage with a crumbling entrance that nevertheless appeared sturdier than those set either side. 'That's it, there! My room is the first on the left,' she breathlessly informed.

Having shouted at Pip to pull up, Joan alighted nimbly, her skirts held away from clogged gutters, and dashed towards the house. The door whined open and she sped through a grimy corridor, tripping over debris while trying to block out a permeating odour of decay. Plunging into

Constance's lodgings, she sensed the room was empty even though it was too dark for her vision to penetrate the inky shadows.

Constance had soon entered behind and found a match to put to the oil lamp on the table. The young woman lifted it immediately, allowing its weak beam to play on every wall.

Joan blinked at the strangeness of her surroundings. Unsavoury, indeed they were, and the wavering flame daubing giants on the ceiling did nothing but add to an eerie atmosphere. Yet oddly Joan was not disgusted; rather she felt an overwhelming and shameful sense of her own privilege to inhabit a property whose cupboards were larger and finer than this dingy sitting room.

'They've taken him.' Constance swung about and deposited the light on the table.

Joan immediately took it up and marched to and fro with it, examining the dilapidated nooks and crannies. Suddenly the lamplight passed over something that dragged her eyes back for a second look. She hurried to a corner and crouched down. 'There's a lot of blood on the floor.' She gingerly touched a finger to a viscous dark pool on bare boards, then used her skirt to wipe the digit clean.

Constance sagged against the table, clapping a hand to her mouth. 'They've killed him then,' she wailed.

'No! No, they have not.' Joan was determined to believe Drew still alive. 'Stokes would have left his victim here and bolted had he committed a murder. Mr Rockleigh might be injured but he still lives, I know it...I know it!' she exclaimed, dropping her forehead to her palms. 'I'd know if he were dead...I *would* know...' she keened quietly to herself.

Slowly her fingers slid from her eyes and she turned on a heel, aware of another person's presence. Or perhaps it was the familiar smoky aroma overlaid with a hint of sandalwood that had filled her nostrils, blocking out the damp.

Slowly, she rose to her feet, her eyes entangled with a dark brooding gaze that came and went as the lamp flickered.

'Are you hurt?' she eventually croaked out.

He shook his head just once.

'Are you?' he asked sardonically.

Joan swallowed. They both knew to what he referred—was she hurt by the knowing the truth about him.

'No…did you imagine I would be?' Joan glanced at Constance; the young woman was standing, watching the tense interaction between her lover and the interloper who could have any man she wanted.

But Joan knew that wasn't true. If it had been, she might have succumbed a year or more ago to one of the fellows who besieged her at balls and parties, imploring to be allowed to call on her father. Yes, at times, she'd danced and flirted with them…but she'd sent them all away. Because in a recess of her mind remained the precious memory of a tall, fair-haired stranger who had brought her home safely one dark Devon night and had stopped her father from chastising her with a slap…though she'd deserved it.

And he was the only man she wanted.

'As you are unhurt I shall go home,' Joan said with admirable composure.

'I'm very sorry I bothered you, my lady,' Constance said in a small voice. 'I should have known he'd get away. He's got the devil's own luck…' She shot a wary glance at Drew, expecting his rebuke for interfering in his affairs. Constance sighed in resignation; he'd forgotten her and was watching the Duke's daughter as if they were alone.

'I'm glad you did come and get me, Miss Cook; better to be safe than sorry.' Joan tore her eyes away from the bewitching intensity of Drew's stare. 'As all is well with Mr Rockleigh, I must return home immediately, or all will not be well for me.'

'All is not well for either of us, as you know,' Drew corrected quietly. 'So for the moment you stay.' He glanced at Constance. 'Go to work now, Connie, you're late for your shift. Tomorrow you should pack your things and find yourself and your brother a better place.'

For a fleeting moment it seemed that Constance might object, but her pout softened as her fingers tightened about the banknotes in her pocket. She cheered herself up, accepting it was all she could do when the fellow she wanted desired someone who just happened to be a beauty and an aristocrat's daughter. Constance knew the Squire wasn't a fortune hunter; he was a man who was in turmoil because he'd fallen in love unwisely. And as she was fond of him Constance found herself feeling sorry for the ill-starred lovers.

'All is not well for either of us...' he'd just said to Lady Joan. Constance could only agree and sympathise; there was no consolation in knowing they had a rocky road in front of them.

Being a pragmatic character Constance realised she could chase a daydream and end up bitterly disappointed, or she could take good advice and keep herself and Benny out of trouble on the Squire's generosity. With the cash he'd given her she could get a respectable address, then obtain a position working in a swanky shop. She'd always fancied being an apprentice seamstress, learning to fashion beautiful clothes from silks and satins. And she'd always wanted to properly learn her letters so she could read and write. When she'd sat with the vicar at Old Blackie's bedside, they'd talked to while away the time and the Reverend Walters had said he'd gladly educate her. The vicar was a nice fellow in Constance's opinion.

'Don't take any notice of anything I said earlier, my lady.' Constance had turned to go and the comment drifted over her shoulder. 'It was just me talking daft 'cos I got frightened witless over what went on. But I'm all right now.'

Once they were alone Joan attempted to slip past

Drew, feeling awkward for having believed he'd need her help. Obviously he did not. He blocked her path, making her skitter back as his rock-like body collided with hers.

'Your friend is a fine young woman,' Joan blurted the first thing that came into her head. 'She was brave and loyal in trying to help you.'

'And so were you...' Drew's eyes were relentlessly steady, watching every nuance of emotion shaping her delicate features.

'I hope the future is kind to Miss Cook wherever she may go,' Joan said simply.

'As do I...despite the fact that she was unforgivably stupid to have drawn you into such danger.'

'If she were prepared to face those perils, then so was I!' Joan returned.

'Your strength of character isn't in question... in fact, considering your pampered upbringing you're quite a marvel, Lady Joan Morland.'

'And now you're mocking me.'

'No...I wouldn't do that.'

The note of husky sincerity in his voice made Joan's heart skip a beat. She had grown used to him teasing and provoking her, but not this time, it seemed.

'Where does Miss Cook work?' she asked, curious about Drew's paramour.

'At the Cock and Hen tavern, although I imagine she'll quit tonight.'

'Will she be able to afford a nicer place to live if she does that?' Joan feared she sounded too inquisitive.

'I've provided her with the means to better herself. It's up to her whether she chooses to do so.'

Joan was itching to ask him whether he had just cut ties with his mistress, or whether he would follow her and resume their liaison. She swallowed the urge, attending instead to practicalities niggling at the back of her mind. 'I have to get home; my papa is feeling much better and is coming down to dine with us this evening. I don't want to miss seeing him.'

'You risked not seeing him…for me. You risked a dangerous encounter with Stokes and his men… for me. Though I'm furious that you acted so foolhardy, I want you to at least give me a chance to thank you and to explain myself.'

'I would have tried to help any person in such awful danger. Miss Cook said it was an unfair fight: three against one.' Joan sighed. 'I had no idea how I might intervene other than to buy the thugs off with these.' She touched her eardrops. 'Miss Cook thought they might be avaricious enough to accept a bribe and turn on Stokes.'

'Possibly she is right, but it's more likely that they would have stolen the jewellery and assaulted you while remaining in Stokes's pay. You should not have come here under any circumstances, Joan,' Drew said, his tone harshening.

'I acted on instinct. There was no time to consider finer points!' Joan retorted.

'I know…and I'm grateful to you.'

'Miss Cook must love you very much,' Joan blurted. 'She was prepared to suffer their lechery to save you.'

Drew traced a thumb softly on her mouth. 'Hush…I would have not wanted her to do that and there was no need in any case.'

'But she does love you.'

'She likes the idea of being in love with a good man.' His lips twitched in self-deprecation. 'Compared to some of her previous gentlemen friends I *am* a good man, in her opinion. Whereas in your eyes I'm—'

'An excellent man,' Joan interrupted quietly,

becoming bashful beneath his answering smile. She turned away and her eyes skimmed over the blood on the floor. 'What have you done to those three villains?' she whispered. 'Have you killed them all?'

'I haven't killed any of them as far as I know. I imagine Stokes might swing for his crimes, but that's for a court to decide. As for the two itinerants, they'll probably recover from the bullets I put in them and join Stokes in gaol.'

Joan's teeth anxiously nipped her lower lip. 'Where are they all now?'

'The bruisers had disappeared by the time I got back from delivering Stokes to the magistrate. They've doubtless dragged themselves off to find a sawbones to patch them up, but they won't get far. The dragoons are already hunting them down.' Drew plunged his hands in his pockets. 'Stokes was my primary concern; I wanted him safely under lock and key without delay.' He paused. 'The magistrate has a full report of what went on here and that I shot two men.'

'You were only defending yourself!' Joan cried hotly. 'I hope they all rot! Especially Stokes. He attempted to vilely blackmail me. I'll gladly testify on your behalf against that wretch and risk the consequences of a scandal.'

Her passionate speech prompted Drew to chuckle and the warmth in his eyes caused a self-conscious blush to stain Joan's cheeks.

'Thank you for the offer and for everything else you've done for me tonight. But there's no need for you to get dragged in any further. I've influential friends who will speak for me.' Drew shrugged. 'I've done nothing I regret and pulled a gun on them as a last resort.'

He brushed a scarred knuckle over her sharp little chin. 'Somebody as sweet and innocent as you doesn't deserve to be tainted by this or to be tattled over.'

'I wish you wouldn't talk to me as though I'm a child. I'm older than your mistress, I'll warrant,' Joan returned waspishly.

'In years, maybe…'

'What do you mean by that?' Joan demanded, bristling.

'You've had little experience of life's dark side, Joan. And I'm not criticising, but paying you a wonderful compliment when I say so…' About to add something, he gestured in frustration instead. 'Come, it is time you went home now. If your father grows anxious over your whereabouts he'll suffer a relapse.'

'It's good of you to think of him, and, yes…indeed, I must go.' Joan sighed. The idea that her father might fret over her absence was already spurring her to head towards the exit.

She turned at the kerb and gazed up at him; there was so much more she wanted to discover about his past. Equally she wanted to know what the future might hold for them; she wasn't ready to relinquish her dreams of them spending their lives together, happily married with a brood of children. In her mind played a sweet domestic scene of a loving husband and a doting papa showing his heirs how to ride ponies and fish the lakes and streams, as her own father had kindly taken time to teach her. But Joan knew there were obstacles to overcome…the greatest of which was that she couldn't be certain that the man she had fallen in love with and wanted to marry returned her feelings. Oh, he wanted her still…desire was smouldering at the backs of his eyes and every touch he gave her, however small, held a caress. And she believed his gallant need to protect her person and her family's reputation was also genuine.

'Would you come with me to Mayfair?' The plea had tripped off her tongue before she could stop it. The longer they were together the likelier it was that she'd learn more about it all.

'Of course I'll take you home.' Drew glanced over her head, his mouth slanting in sultry amusement. 'If you want my company in that coach I'm happy to oblige.'

The tempestuous passion they had shared the last time they had travelled alone was already building into tangible force between them. On that stormy night Joan had wanted to be rid of Drew's presence. This time she would beg if necessary for him to stay with her. Her breathing had slowed and her bosom felt heavy and tender in anticipation of him touching her as he had before. Quickly she turned away, feeling unbearably restless, and allowed Drew to help her alight.

Having settled into the seat with a soft sigh, Joan realised that, wanton or not, there was nothing she craved more than his wooing casting out of her mind a depressing fact: people would be shocked at the idea of a duke's daughter seeking a match with a street fighter.

Chapter Seventeen

Pip grinned as his new passenger gave an order to make good speed to Mayfair, then sprang lithely aboard. Pip had always liked Mr Rockleigh and if Lady Joan Morland had fallen for the gentleman boxer then in Pip's eyes she was a finer person because of it. He realised that others wouldn't hold that view...her kith and kin, for example. Pip had high hopes that the Duke and Duchess would put Lady Joan's happiness above all else, but her snooty Aunt Dorothea was likely to swoon at the idea of the bare-chested ruffian who'd rescued them from a mob joining the family.

Pip knew what it was to be the underdog: there were plenty of folk who thought Anna a cut above him and that a lady's maid deserved better than a stablehand. Whistling, he took up the reins, impatient to get out of the narrow lanes and to the open road. He'd get a warm welcome from his sweetheart when he arrived back in Upper Brook Street with his mistress safe and sound.

The moment the coach lurched forward Joan quickly resumed their conversation. She was still hungry for information about Drew's background and wanted to encourage him to speak about Stokes's association with his family. The more they talked, the more trust would build between them. Physically they seemed made for one another, but Joan craved a strong emotional bond, too, for without it desire would eventually wither and die.

'Were you referring to Wellington when you said you had an ally to call on should Stokes try to blacken your name?' They were sitting face to face and she inclined closer, eager for his answer.

Drew nodded. 'Wellington is aware that Stokes is corrupt.'

'Did you tell him that Stokes schemed against you?'

'Wellington knew of Stokes's villainy long before I had personal experience of it. Stokes used to be a quartermaster in the army.' Drew pressed his broad shoulders back against the hide upholstery, staring into the night. 'His rank gave him access to the stores and their valuable contents. He began counterfeiting bills for provisions and taking payment for himself. He got away with it for quite some time, but eventually was suspected of theft. As soon as he got wind of an investigation he deserted before he could be formally charged.'

'The treacherous villain!' Joan gasped.

'Indeed, and considering an army marches on its belly, and we were at war with France at the time, he wasn't just a thief but a traitor, depriving troops of essential rations.'

Joan shook her head in utter disgust, but her deep-grey eyes clung to his, appealing for him to continue the story.

'He'd feathered his nest, but still wasn't satisfied. After he absconded he coerced serving soldiers to steal victuals so he could continue making a profit. He avoided respectable areas of London, concentrating on selling to innkeepers on the rougher side of town. He made sure to cover his tracks well, keeping himself out of sight by hiring a gang of itinerants to distribute the goods.'

Joan frowned in concentration, while weighing

up facts. 'Miss Cook worked at an inn. Did the landlord of the Cock and Hen buy from Stokes's men?'

'I saw Charlie Clarke paying for sacks of flour and barley on several occasions. It's possible he didn't know they belonged to the Crown, but he's no angel. He would have realised they'd been stolen.'

'It was quite a lucky coincidence that you and Miss Cook became friends; you might not have been at the tavern to witness the crime otherwise.'

'A lucky coincidence, indeed,' Drew echoed, a touch of wry amusement in his voice.

'Why do you say it like that?' Joan asked.

'The Cock and Hen is a haunt for thirsty boxers after a tournament. Stokes's men are street fighters and regulars in Charlie's place...I made sure I had an excuse to be there to observe them.'

'You sounds as though you *chose* to become the Squire rather than were forced to it,' Joan said slowly. 'And it seems that Miss Cook's employment was also of benefit to you.'

'Yes...I chose to inhabit Ratcliffe Highway.' He paused. 'And I needed a reason to frequent the Cock and Hen so often. Constance's presence there proved useful.' He met Joan's eyes squarely. 'Constance is a sweet girl and I grew quite fond of her…but for me our relationship was as much business as pleasure.' Drew's gaze remained steady, a spark of defiance at the backs of his eyes. 'I know I sound callous, but Constance was aware from the start that it would be a brief liaison, not a love affair.'

'You found her useful, you mean,' Joan said coolly.

'I treated her well and promised her nothing. I was honest with her up to a point. She never knew about my ulterior motive for being in the locality,' Drew admitted tonelessly.

'And you had an ulterior motive for that as well! Had she known you were acting a part, she would have thrown you out of her bed, I expect,' Joan said tartly. 'I know I would have done so, in her place.'

Joan caught her lower lip between her small teeth, becoming warm beneath his sultry, quizzical look. He was confident enough of his powers of seduction to make light of her comment. She wondered if she would also have accepted his terms and the crumbs of his affection as Constance had, rather than do without him.

'So, you have been masquerading as a man down on his luck, street fighting to earn his living. In fact, you have been working undercover for the Duke of Wellington.'

'That's about the size of it,' Drew confirmed, sounding unapologetic. 'Wellington did me a great service, protecting my family's good name. It was the least I could do to help him break up the gang stealing from the military while at the same time thwarting my sister's avarice.'

'You lied to me about having been defrauded?'

'I've never lied to you,' Drew replied and, leaning towards her, he caught her small hands in his. 'But I have allowed you to believe that I'd been swindled, just as I've let my sister and Stokes believe it.'

Drew let go of her fingers as they stiffened in his.

'I want to tell you everything so I'll start at the beginning.' He sat back in the seat. 'After Stokes deserted, Wellington sent out investigators to hunt him down. They managed to find him after a few months; it then came to light that he'd met my sister and they'd become lovers.' His mouth twitched ruefully. 'This all happened at about the same time as I first made your acquaintance, when I was spending a lot of time in Devon. The Iron Duke is a good friend despite the differences in our stations in life. He got a message to me, offering me the chance to get my sister and niece away from Stokes before the dragoons closed in. It was good of him to allow me time to protect my niece's reputation and what remained of my sister's good name.' He paused. 'Within a short time of returning to London to try to sort things out I realised that Bertha and Stokes were plotting to swindle me.'

'If you knew, why did you not nip it in the bud?' Joan frowned.

'I could have stopped them, but I knew Bertha would never let the matter drop. She'd always been determined to snatch some of our stepfather's legacy.' Drew paused. 'In Stokes she had somebody who would back her to the hilt; but had he been taken by Wellington's dragoons, she wouldn't have given up her scheming. She'd have seduced another poor fool into assisting her and would have continued plotting to rob me. I thought the simplest way to stop her might be to allow her to try, then thwart her.'

'Are you *sure* she was so determined to steal from you?' Joan was shocked to hear that Drew thought his sibling so perfidious.

'I had caught Bertha going through my private papers. On that occasion she explained away her impertinence by saying she'd been looking for jewellery, hoping to show it to Cecilia.' Drew chuckled softly. 'She knew very well that the ruby parure was kept in a bank vault because she'd pleaded to be given it on several occasions. I knew she wanted the gems to sell, so refused; besides, our stepfather's will stated that the parure be presented as a wedding gift to the first of any granddaughters he might have as long as the prospective bridegroom had my blessing. Peter Rockleigh had passed away before Cecilia was born.'

'You think that your sister was interested in finding documents rather than the jewellery?'

'She was searching for property deeds to take and would have got away with the originals that day had I not caught her red-handed.'

'You moved them somewhere safe after that?' Joan guessed.

'Yes…I did…but I left good copies in their place. When Cecilia eloped with her groom I set off to catch up with her, knowing that in my absence Bertha would rifle my desk. She was a regular visitor to my house, always turning up petitioning for loans. My servants had been instructed to let her in if she called. And she did, with the excuse that she'd left her gloves in my study. She behaved exactly as I expected her to: she suspected nothing and took fakes, then returned a day or two later, leaving counterfeits in their place. The originals have been lodged in a bank vault for quite a while now.'

'Did they *sell* your property?' Joan sounded both angry and sorrowful.

'No…they wouldn't risk that in case the lawyers looked too carefully at the documents and uncovered the fraud. But they had no trouble in using them as collateral against loans from usurers. My apparent fall from grace gave their tale a ring of authenticity: Stokes maintained that I had sold out to him to pay off foreign creditors and had afterwards slipped out of sight rather than be incarcerated in the Fleet.'

Joan sat quietly digesting all she'd heard. 'It's a

truly evil thing to have done. You hate your sister, don't you? I can't blame you,' she stated sadly, reflecting on the great affection she felt for her stepsister Fiona.

'It is a mutual feeling. Bertha has long resented the fact that my stepfather favoured me. Understanding her profligate nature, Peter Rockleigh left her little in his will other than some small pieces of our mother's jewellery.'

'What will become of her?'

Drew shrugged. 'She deserves to be punished for her part in the crime, but any scandal would attach to Cecilia and my sister knows it. In time she'll find another besotted fool to link up with.'

'You won't allow Cecilia to be in such another's orbit, surely?' Joan said, astonished.

'I have a feeling that Cecilia might soon be another man's responsibility and I'll gladly relinquish the chit to him and the ruby parure.'

'May I take that as a hint she is about to receive a proposal from somebody of whom you approve?' Joan sounded optimistic.

Drew smiled slowly. 'You may...and that's why I didn't want you approaching the fellow. There was no need for my niece to have asked you to intervene on her behalf; I had already done so.'

Joan slid forward on the seat, for the first time that evening smiling with real happiness. 'You have spoken to Mr Laurenson and know of his intentions?'

Drew pulled a face that was as good as a confirmation, but he teased, 'I couldn't possibly say... just yet. I'll let the poor chump approach her first. He is intending to journey to the West Country next week.' Drew frowned. 'As for the other poor chump... Lord Regan was not so happy to hear what I had to say. He's no fool and knew there was a chance he might not be Cecilia's father. He genuinely thought that the money he handed over would be used for her benefit rather than Bertha's. Finding a girl an eligible husband is a costly business and he wanted to finance her Season in town and see her settled in case she was his offspring.'

'It was good of him.' Joan felt rather guilty for having thought the old fellow a lecher. 'Will Lord Regan cause a rumpus over it and want back his money?'

'No...he knows he's been a gullible fool, but he doesn't want the whole *ton* to be aware of it. Besides, he was pleased to hear that Henry Laurenson is on the point of proposing.'

'Cecilia will be delighted that Henry has followed her to Devon. She might not want to wait to formalise it all. I hope she doesn't persuade him to elope.' Joan giggled, quite tempted to hug Drew for being so kind to his niece. 'If they do make for Gretna, you must still allow her to have her rubies!' However casually he spoke of the lovebirds, Joan knew that he had taken time and trouble to broker the match to please Cecilia. And he had set everything else to rights, even to the extent of making a difficult explanation to Lord Regan.

'You indeed do know how to survive and succeed, don't you, Mr Rockleigh?' Joan said rather soberly.

'It's in my nature,' he said, 'as you know.'

Their eyes held and the lightness in the atmosphere was dispersed by renewed tension.

'Is there a chance that you and your sister might be reconciled?'

'I don't think so; we share blood, but nothing else. She whores to get what she wants; she got that from our mother…I fight to get ahead. Perhaps I got that from my father, but I couldn't say for sure,' he ended with grim humour.

'Who was she?'

Drew's eyes swerved from the coach window to narrow on her.

'Your mother...who was she?' Joan asked.

'Rosemary Wilding. She lived off the docks as did most people round Ratcliffe Highway.' He stared through the window as the carriage turned a corner.

'And your father?'

Drew shrugged. 'I never knew him. She said he was a soldier, although I can't be certain of it, or that she ever married him.'

The lack of feeling in his voice mirrored the bleakness in his profile and made Joan feel like weeping for the sorrow he must have endured as the child of such feckless parents. Of course he knew how to look after himself...for who else had he ever had to rely on? Joan suddenly felt a fierce longing to comfort and protect that lost boy she sensed was still imprisoned in his soul.

'Your stepfather... Peter Rockleigh...he knew about your mother's background, didn't he, and loved her despite her faults.' Joan's voice was soft, persuading him to trust her…tell her more of his childhood.

'He did, the fool, and God knows he strove to have her…all of us…accepted, using his money and his influence to blot out our pasts and build our futures.'

'And it worked; he did a fine job for all of you. I've never heard a whisper of scandal about your family. My father holds your stepfather in high esteem and he's never spoken ill of your mother, or any of you. Even when Papa knew you were a street fighter he didn't change his mind. He was saddened by your misfortune but his greatest concern was that you knew too much about my misdemeanours.'

Drew swung a mordant look at her. 'You mean he feared me a blackmailer no better than Pryke and Stokes.'

Joan bit her lip, then said carefully, 'He said he understood how an empty belly might make a sinner of a saint.'

'I'm no saint.' Drew's mouth twisted in a half-smile. 'And I've not gone hungry since I was nine years old…so no way of knowing whether your father's theory that I'm easily corrupted is right.'

'You wouldn't betray me.' Joan's flat statement was followed by a small contented sigh.

'Why would I not?'

'Because a gentleman does not seek to turn a lady's peccadilloes to his own advantage.'

Drew's sardonic smile was back, twisting his mouth. 'And now that you know I am not a gentleman will you reconsider what you've said?'

'The fact that you had an unfortunate start in life does not mean you are a base character. A true gentleman is made, not born.'

Drew threw back his head and barked a mirthless laugh. 'That's a nice way of putting it.'

'When I arrive home, will you come in and speak to my father and tell him all that you've told me?'

'Why? The man is recovering from illness; I doubt he wants to be regaled with a sordid tale of my past.'

'He would want to know. *I* want him to know. I have said that he likes you…he always has…even when you snubbed him and refused to marry me.'

Drew jerked his head around to again brood at the night sky. 'I imagine your father will soon be counting his blessings on that score, and so should you. His Grace would reach for his pistols if I had the temerity to ask you for a dance now.' His mouth pursed in ironic humour. 'Yet once I could have taken his assets and his daughter, and he'd have thanked me for it.'

'Why did you not?' Joan whispered.

'Because you didn't want me to,' he replied through his teeth as though every word was an effort to expel.

'But I did,' Joan quietly confessed. As he swung his face her way she averted her bashful expression. 'Oh, I know I said I would not have you… but only after Papa told me you'd refused to countenance the match even should he pay you handsomely.' She moved her head, recalling her despair. 'I was so humiliated when I found out he'd done that.' She glanced up, meeting a forceful stare that seemed to pin her down. 'Why are you looking at me like that?' she whispered.

'You'd have accepted a simple proposal?'

'Yes…' Joan croaked, her eyes stinging with unshed tears.

'There's no need to be upset now, sweetheart.' Drew gave a hollow laugh. 'I had pride, too, and decided not to risk my high-born wife despising me when she learned of my lowly roots. I was too cowardly to do it so kept quiet.'

Joan grabbed at his strong dark fingers and gave them a punishing shake. 'I *have* discovered your roots and I do *not* despise you! Do you think my father, or me, to be people who disregard our emotions and instincts about a person to worship pedigree instead?' Joan flung his hands from her and gestured angrily. 'Papa had experienced knowing you in society and thought you a fine fellow. I... I intuitively recognised that you were kind and decent when you escorted me home.' Joan tutted in exasperation. 'I think *you* must despise *me,* if you believe me so shallow—'

'What are you implying?' Drew interrupted. He leant forward, his hands shooting out to recapture her fidgeting fingers.

'I'm saying that the person you are now is what is important to me and it makes no difference where you started,' Joan answered hotly. 'I know that it should; I know it is expected that I will make a match with a rich nobleman's heir... blue bloods, you called them. But why should I be shaped by my birth any more than you should be by yours? Why must I follow custom when I don't care for lineage or a loveless marriage any more than your stepfather did, or Henry Laurenson does, or, for that matter, my maid does?' She sighed. 'Oh, Anna's beau is also my father's servant, but expectations exist below stairs just as they do above. Anna is content with who Pip is and what he does, and ignores her colleagues' mutterings.' Joan freed one of her hands, hesitating slightly before cupping his lean, shady jaw. She knew there was no going back now. The uncertainty and wonderment in his eyes made him look young and vulnerable. 'Your father saw in your mother something that you did not…something worth fighting…perhaps even dying for.' She blinked away the tears forming on her lashes. 'I felt that way about you today. I would have tried to rescue you, you know, with my puny fists, if necessary. But of course you did not need my help. You never need my help. It is always me who needs your assistance.'

'It's the right way of things…a man should protect the woman he loves.'

Barely had Joan absorbed his husky declaration when two strong arms whipped her from her seat. Drew deposited her next to him, then braced an arm across her. Lowering his head, he took her lips in a wooing salute. 'You mean it, don't you?' he said. 'It makes no difference to you that I'm the bastard son of a whore and can't be sure who my father is. You still love me.'

'I do mean every word and you should not speak of your mother like that,' Joan gently chided. 'We must cherish our memories of our mamas, for it seems both were taken from us too soon.' Joan rested her forehead against his rough chin. 'I miss my mother and think about her every day although Maude is the sweetest, kindest of women. And she makes my father happy for which I am very thankful. But blood is blood and the bond at birth is surely strongly forged.' Joan sighed. 'I know you must have harrowing memories of your childhood, but never forget that your mother brought you into Peter Rockleigh's world. She is the one who made a fine gentleman love her enough to raise her children as his own after she had passed on. Your stepfather did not do it for you, Drew... he did it for her, to honour her memory. And you should not think the worse of him for it.'

Drew tenderly raised her face with a long finger, touching together their lips. 'My mother seemed cold to my stepfather at times and I have often questioned if she really loved him at all. She certainly did not adore him as he did her. I have wondered if she sacrificed her passion for riotous living for the sakes of her children's futures.'

'Let us believe that indeed she did do that and that she also loved Mr Rockleigh in her own way.' Joan smiled winsomely, then she raised her face, tempting him to kiss her again.

Coiling her arms about his neck, Joan eagerly responded when his tongue slid to caress the silky contours of her mouth. As their lips unsealed, Joan whispered, not wholly joking, 'But understand this, Drew Rockleigh, I'll accept you being a guttersnipe, but I will never share you with any woman…even one as nice as Constance Cook.'

Drew buried his face against her neck, concealing his smile at her jealousy. 'I swear that I had finished with Constance even before you told me how you felt about me this afternoon.'

'Good…' Joan murmured. 'But there is something else I must scold you about: you should not have had the vicarage school closed and made the children suffer.'

'I know and I regret doing it, but my main concern was for your safety,' he answered huskily. 'I was scared that you'd come back at a time when I wasn't there to protect you. The idea that you might have been robbed or assaulted by the likes of Stokes's itinerants was something that has tortured me.'

'I understand that, Drew,' Joan said quietly. 'But it is not fair to deprive the children for my sake. I now feel as guilty as you over it.'

'You've no need to feel guilty and neither shall I when my plans come to fruition.'

'Plans? For what?' Joan immediately asked, a smile emerging.

'I know how important schooling is for slum children…it is their passage to a different existence. I, of all people, know that.' Drew paused. 'My stepfather bestowed on us his respectable life; equally important to me as good food and clothes was self-respect and an education.' He frowned. 'Bertha saw things differently and would escape her governess at every opportunity. Perhaps if she had stayed in the classroom and read something of value instead of hiding in cupboards, browsing the fashion journals, she might have set her sights higher than a future of harlotry and swindle.'

'I loved learning, too,' Joan enthused. 'Foreign lands and the weird and wonderful folk that live there…I have long wished to travel and learn more about those magical things that I have read about in books.'

'I'd like to travel with you and I know that you will love learning about things that are magical on that particular trip.'

Drew's smile was tinged with a wickedness that made Joan blush. 'What plans did you speak of?' Quickly she returned to her original line of questioning. 'Are you hinting at helping to start a ragged school to replace the one you had closed?'

'I have purchased a freehold on a small disused warehouse by the docks. At present it is dilapidated, but workmen have started on the repairs. When it is close to being finished I shall offer the building to the Reverend Walters to turn it into a school for local children.'

'Oh, that's so kind, Drew! I'm sure Vincent will be delighted to accept. Thank you…' Joan flung her arms about him, hugging him and rewarding him with a spontaneous kiss. 'I will dedicate every possible free moment to assisting the vicar when it opens.'

'Perhaps you will…on those days that I accompany you there,' Drew said smoothly. Before she could protest he added, 'I should act the gentleman now and insist you speak to your father before offering yourself to an unworthy rogue such as me.' He gazed at her, his frown deepening. 'But I don't want to be brave in case he denies me what I want most in the world.'

'I need no advice; I know my own mind and I have gained my majority. I believe in myself and in you. If Papa were to object it would surprise me…and sadden me. But I would follow my heart and go with you…if you'll take me.'

'You know I've been aching to do that for a very long time.' He groaned against the soft cushion of ringlets draping her shoulder.

'You really love me, Drew?' she asked softly and as he raised his silver head she watched his eyes.

'I didn't think I would ever fall in love or get married,' he admitted huskily. 'What I had seen of the relationships between men and women made me think matrimony was for fools. I didn't like being a cynic, but it seemed to suit me.'

'And now?'

'Now…if wanting you always with me, wanting you as my wife and the mother of my children, means that I'm in love…then I love you with heart, body and soul.' He smiled wolfishly. 'If wanting to sleep with you within minutes of meeting you counts, then I went head over heels the moment you entered my hunting lodge and demanded an audience with my friend.'

'I expect you thought I was the veriest hussy that night.'

'I thought I'd struck lucky, sweetheart.' Drew chuckled. 'I imagined you'd come from a local hostelry to offer me your services.'

'Did you, indeed!' Joan gasped a scandalised laugh. 'That's the second time this evening I've been confused with a harlot. Miss Cook said that Stokes called me names.'

'And he deserves to meet his maker just for that,' Drew growled.

'Are we to marry, then?' Joan said, soothing his anger by softly brushing her lips on his cheek.

'Is that a proposal, my lady?' Drew asked solemnly.

'I suppose it is as it seems you're too shy to ask

me; but I refuse to go down on one knee. There are some things that only the gentleman should do.'

Drew slipped humbly on to his knees on the floor of the coach. Gently taking both her hands in his, he raised them to kiss the soft white knuckles with utmost reverence. 'Please will you do this undeserving wretch the great honour of becoming his wife and allow him to take you on a magical honeymoon across the seas?'

'I will, with the utmost pleasure, sir,' Joan replied quietly, her hand slipping over the crown of his head, relishing the stroke of the silver strands against her fingers.

'I'll do all in my power to prove to you you've not mistaken my character. I have a good income and a substantial property in both London and the countryside. I'll work hard to improve on what I've got and give you everything you deserve.'

'Oh, you don't need to, Drew,' Joan soothed him. 'I have everything I need because I know you will love and cherish me and our children every day of our lives,' she said with simple sincerity. 'And in return I will always believe in you and love you no matter what spiteful people say to try to spoil it for us,' Joan concluded through the wedge of emotion blocking her throat.

'There will be some, too, who will rejoice in the chance of that.' Drew's statement was devoid of self-pity.

Joan accepted his warning with a sorrowful nod, thinking of her Aunt Dorothea and her cronies. 'We must speak to my father straight away. We will be home quite soon,' Joan whispered in a way that made him smile.

'Not much time, then.' He glanced up, an ardent gleam in his tawny eyes. 'What would you like to do, my lady, while we ride those few miles?'

Joan sank back against the squabs and in a fluid movement Drew had risen to settle beside her.

Joan's fingers went to her cloak fastenings and she opened them slowly, quivering in delight as his hands immediately slipped inside to shape her body with caresses.

'We're suited, you and I,' Drew murmured against her pulsating lips. 'In every possible way and especially in this wonderful way.'

Joan nodded, her tongue unconsciously wetting her lips in anticipation of a kiss.

Drew watched the movement, then his eyes

closed and he gave a strangled laugh. Tenderly he brushed his lips on hers, pulling together the edges of her cloak. 'Don't tempt me, Joan, I beg, because I might not be able to stop this time. Your first proper loving should be slow and luxurious and savoured to the full on a feather bed.'

'I…I don't mind now,' she said, blushing to the roots of her chestnut locks.

'But I do, sweetheart,' Drew said softly. 'A savage I may be…but not with you…never with you.'

He put his arm around her and pulled her close so her head rested on his chest and he could cuddle her to him.

'Besides…a honeymoon baby we might get away with, any sooner than that and the Duke *will* call for seconds.'

Joan slanted a look up at him, her grey eyes aglow with adoration. 'You had better bring the Squire along on our wedding night, sir, or I shall think I've greatly mistaken you and demand an annulment.'

Drew threw back his head to choke a guffaw. 'If it's a ruffian you want…I'll gladly oblige,' he teased in a sultry tone, then bruised her lips with a kiss. 'But in return, my lady, I shall want you to wear your tiara to bed…but nothing else…'

With a kittenish sigh Joan murmured agreement, then Drew's mouth again covered his future wife's, making her playfully wrestle him for her freedom.

As the coach swayed and a few muffled squeals and giggles met his ears, Pip, atop his perch, smiled in satisfaction and reined in the horses to a slower pace so my lady and her boxer might revel in one another's company for what was left of the journey to Upper Brook Street.

Chapter Eighteen

'Why…I had no idea you had gone out, Lady Joan! The Duke and Duchess thought you were resting in your room.'

Tobias Bartlett's startled exclamation was accompanied by a bleary-eyed stare at the handsome gentleman with the master's daughter. Had Tobias known what surprise awaited him prior to locking up he'd not have succumbed to snoozing in the winged armchair. The young people had entered quietly, but Tobias, used to the nocturnal outings of frisky footmen, was alert to the sound of a key turning gently in a lock. He had come awake with a start and staggered to his feet in the alcove, straightening his uniform.

Tobias was acquainted with all the family's kith and kin. Mr Rockleigh had been a welcome, if infrequent, visitor to the Duke's address. In common with others, Tobias had heard that the fellow had sunk very low, but he had bounced back judging by the look of him. From Lady Joan's doe eyes Tobias took it that Rockleigh remained very much an intimate friend of the family.

'The Duke and Duchess have finished dining,' Tobias rattled off. 'Your father ate quite heartily, but he is still frail and it would be best not to worry him in any way, my lady…' A respectful caution had crept into the butler's voice.

'There is nothing for Papa to fret over,' Joan calmly reassured, trying to ignore the rueful expression spreading on the rugged features of the man at her side. 'I'm quite sure my father will be happy to see Mr Rockleigh.' She sent Drew a twinkling smile, inwardly praying her optimism was not misplaced.

'Your parents are partaking of their usual nightcap in the rose salon,' Tobias informed. 'When the Duchess got up from the table she mentioned popping in on you before retiring for the night.'

Joan realised that Maude had thankfully not yet gone upstairs as all was calm and peaceful. 'We shall join them, Tobias; I expect Mr Rockleigh might like a tot of something.'

'For Dutch courage?' Drew suggested ironically as Joan slipped her hand on to his arm, urging him on.

As they walked to meet their fate a surge of mingling excitement and apprehensiveness made Joan feel light-headed and she tightened her fingers on the arm supporting her. 'I think I can guess how those poor French people must have felt when approaching the guillotine.' She gave her unofficial fiancé a wan smile.

'Are you sure you're ready for this?' Drew asked, seriousness beneath his light question as he drew them both to a halt.

'Are you?' Joan turned towards him, searching his hawkish eyes for regrets.

'I'm ready...I've always been ready and willing to do battle on your behalf, my love, even on the first night that I met you. But there's time for you to change your mind about throwing your lot in with mine,' Drew concluded softly. 'Your stepmother believed I'd come earlier today to see how her husband did. I can explain away my presence in a convincing way again and find a reason for your absence, too, if need be.'

'Don't you dare!' Joan exclaimed, covering the

long fingers cupping her face with her own small digits. 'Are you frightened of my papa?' she demanded.

'Terrified,' Drew admitted with a half-smile. 'If he banishes me from your life I don't know whether I'm capable of retreating gracefully...yet do it, I must.'

'He will not send you away!' Joan hugged Drew fiercely about the waist, her cheek pressed to his broad shoulder. 'But if he should do so, then he loses me, too, for I'll not let you go.'

'You know I can't allow you to do that, Joan.' Drew's face lowered so his lips could rush over a silky crown of chestnut hair. 'I must tell your father everything about myself. He has a right to know. If my suit is then rejected, I have only one choice because I'll never let you face scandal or be estranged from your family for my sake.'

'Well...that's a blessing...' a croaky voice said. 'But would you stick to it, I wonder, if put to the test?'

Joan gasped and sprang away from Drew as her father shuffled slowly towards them along the corridor.

'I…we…we thought you were inside the room, Papa,' Joan stuttered.

'I imagined that was the case,' the Duke said in the same dry tone. 'And indeed I was sitting in there a few minutes earlier.' Alfred indicated the scrap of silk in his hands. 'The Duchess felt chilly and wanted her shawl. I've been cooped up for so long on that wretched sickbed that I'll take any excuse to stretch my legs, so offered to fetch it.'

Joan was still in shock from her father having caught her locked in an embrace with a gentleman. 'You look to be recovering well, Papa,' she blurted, clasping her hands in confusion.

'And long may I do so for it seems there are pressing matters afoot to be dealt with…' Alfred cast a long and deliberate look on his daughter's companion. 'I take it you and I have a serious conversation in front of us, sir.'

Drew took Joan's hand, drawing her possessively closer to him.

'Indeed…I have come here to beg a private audience with you, your Grace.' Drew gave the older man a polite nod.

The Duke had slowly come to a stop and swung a glance between the couple; his daughter's wide dewy eyes were vivid with pleading, but Alfred noticed the defiance there, too, and it made him inwardly smile. Joan was her mother's daughter and once she had her heart set on something she'd see it through to the bitter end. But she'd no need to fret.

Alfred's brush with death had made him more determined than ever to see his daughter protected by a husband's strength and love before he curled up his toes. Never before had he seen his little Joan look so happy and comfortable as he had a moment ago on rounding the corner and catching her in Drew Rockleigh's embrace. But there was more to say, so he'd not let on about his inner peacefulness just yet.

'I recall my daughter slipped out once before to see you on the sly and when you returned her I was angry enough to raise my hand to her.'

'I haven't forgotten it.' Drew took a step forward, placing himself between father and daughter.

'If you had both listened to me then, you'd have been wed these past two years or more and I'd not have needlessly worried over likely betrayals.'

Joan's eyes darted to Drew, joy and optimism in

their shining depths. But he seemed less pleased by what the Duke had said.

'In what way might I have betrayed you, your Grace?' Drew asked. 'If you believe me capable of hurting Joan, or any of those people she holds dear, then I suspect I already have the answer to my question.'

'Oh, fiddlesticks!' The Duke flicked some fingers. 'How was I to know you still loved her? A lot of fellows higher up the pecking order than a boxer would have turned what they knew to their advantage, y'know.'

'I'm not one of those fellows.'

'No…you're not…' Alfred said in a tone of humble admiration.

'Might I take that as a sign that you will grant me an audience?'

'Oh, there's no need for all that now.' The Duke almost smiled. 'I know the procedure; you want to bore me to death telling me you're unworthy of her, but beg me to listen to your pleas all the same.'

'In my case it would be no false modesty, but the truth.' Drew's voice held a note of sombre irony.

Joan glanced up at the proud profile of the

man she adored. Her eyes swerved to her father, fiercely challenging.

'You have already compromised my daughter the once and got off scot free. I wouldn't allow it to happen a second time, you know. So I think you have my answer on the matter, sir, and that leaves just the details to go over in the morning.'

'There is more you should know about me before giving me your consent,' Drew said hoarsely. 'I'm not worthy of Joan and thus it's hard to make a joke of it.'

'Not on a par with her, eh? Well, in that we have something in common then,' the Duke said. 'My first wife was a tea merchant's daughter. I was already a duke at twenty-nine years old. It is a fallacy that the higher one climbs the nobler becomes the character. Joan's mother's family was in trade, but they were nicer people than us.' The Duke rested his stooped back against the wall, gazing up at a portrait hanging opposite. He inclined his head at the arrogant features of a fellow sporting a wig and doublet. 'He was the first of our black sheep. Plantations in the Indies brought the Morlands untold riches, all got from murder and mayhem. Cedric Morland returned triumphant to these shores to buy his pedigree and sit in Parliament, but at heart he was a bloody marauder.'

'You've never told me that story, Papa!' Joan declared on a shocked laugh. 'You said the first Duke built a dynasty as an intrepid adventurer.'

'A pretty description, my dear…I always planned to explain more to you when the time was right… when you were of an age to know.' He gave Drew a long thorough look. 'The time is right because I can tell you've grown up. You know from experience, as I do, that good and bad exists in every class of people, be they rich or poor.'

Drew gave a small dip of his head, indicating he understood and was grateful for the Duke's attitude.

'Delirium is a curse.' Alfred sighed. 'It brings odd ideas vividly to life, but in the madness lies always a grain of truth.' He shook his old head wearily. 'I dwelled often on the time you had compromised my daughter in Devon and swore if ever you did so again you'd marry her or I'd have to shoot you.' He consulted his pocket watch and clucked his tongue. 'No time at all for a spinster

to be abroad with a fellow she's unrelated to…
especially as they are in love…'

Joan glanced at Drew, her eyes dancing with
joyful amusement. 'Please tell my father you will
do the honourable thing and ask to marry me. I'll
not know who to second otherwise.'

'Gladly will I do that,' Drew vowed throatily.

Alfred put up a freckled hand. 'But not now, Mr
Rockleigh, if you please. Tomorrow morning is
soon enough. I'll expect you by ten of the clock.
Now I'd like to rest my weary bones and take another tot of brandy to help me sleep.' He allowed
his smiling daughter to take his arm, supporting
him to the door of the rose salon. 'In my lucid
moments during that ague I swore I would forgo
all I owned in exchange for my recovery. I would
be content just to see my daughter wed to a man
worthy of her and my son go up to Oxford.' The
Duke looked from his daughter to his future son-
in-law with an expression of pure contentment.
'Come, let us go inside and tell the Duchess that
I have at least one of my dearest wishes granted.'

* * * * *

If you enjoyed this story, you won't want to miss these other great reads from Mary Brendan:

TARNISHED, TEMPTED AND TAMED
THE RAKE'S RUINED LADY
A DATE WITH DISHONOUR
DANGEROUS LORD, SEDUCTIVE MISS
CHIVALROUS RAKE, SCANDALOUS LADY